ARIZONA AMES

Grieve's crow-black eyes set upon Ames. "Do you call yourself Arizona?"

"No I don't," returned Ames. "But I can't help what others call me. An' I'm bound to admit that name is hard to shake."

"Why'd you want to shake it?" asked Grieve, suspiciously.

"I don't like bein' reminded of Arizona—that's all."

"You rode for Raskin once?" asked Grieve.

"Yes."

"How long?"

"Reckon all of two years."

"Up till his death?"

"Yes."

"Did you see him shot?" inquired Grieve, coming closer, his eyes like black coals.

HarperPaperbacks
by Zane Grey

THE DUDE RANGER
THE LOST WAGON TRAIN
THE MAN OF THE FOREST
THE RAINBOW TRAIL
WILDFIRE
THE BORDER LEGION
SUNSET PASS
30,000 ON THE HOOF
WANDERER OF THE WASTELAND
TWIN SOMBREROS
BOULDER DAM
THE MYSTERIOUS RIDER
THE DEER STALKER
THE TRAIL DRIVER
THE DESERT OF WHEAT
THE U.P. TRAIL
THUNDER MOUNTAIN
WESTERN UNION
TO THE LAST MAN
CODE OF THE WEST

ZANE GREY

ARIZONA AMES

HarperPaperbacks
A Division of HarperCollins*Publishers*

HarperPaperbacks *A Division of* HarperCollins*Publishers*
10 East 53rd Street, New York, N.Y. 10022

Copyright 1932 by Zane Grey
Copyright © renewed 1960 by Romer Zane Grey,
Elizabeth Grey Grosso, and Loren Zane Grey.
All rights reserved. No part of this book may be used or reproduced in any manner whatsoever without written permission of the publisher, except in the case of brief quotations embodied in critical articles and reviews. For information address HarperCollins*Publishers*,
10 East 53rd Street, New York, N.Y. 10022.

Cover photo courtesy of the Bettmann Archive

First HarperPaperbacks printing: July 1991

Printed in the United States of America

HarperPaperbacks and colophon are trademarks of HarperCollins*Publishers*

10 9 8 7 6 5 4 3 2 1

*I*T WAS November in the Tonto Basin.

From Mescal Ridge the jagged white teeth of the ranges pierced the blue sky on three horizons—to the west the wild ragged Mazatzals; to the south the lofty symmetrical Four Peaks; and far away to the east the dim blue-white Sierra Ancas. Behind and above Mescal Ridge—forbiddingly close the rarefied atmosphere made it—towered the black-fringed, snow-belted rim of the Mogallan Mesa, blocking the whole north with its three hundred miles of bold promontories and purple canyons.

But though it was winter on the heights, down on the innumerable ridges of the Basin, which slanted like the ribs of a colossal washboard, late fall lingered. In sheltered nooks, deep down where the sun could reach through gaps, sycamores shone with

green-gold leaves, and oaks smoldered in rich
bronze, standing out vividly from the steel-gray
shaggy slopes. Tonto Creek wound down between
them, a shining strip of water, here white in rushing
rapids and there circling in green eddies or long leaf-
spotted pools. The ridge tops waved away from Mescal Ridge, a sea of evergreen, pine and spruce and
cedar and piñon, a thick dark mantle in the distance,
but close at hand showing bare spots, gray rocks and
red cliffs, patches of brown pine needles, scarlet su-
mac and blue juniper.

Mescal Ridge was high and long and winding
and rough, yet its crest curved gracefully, open and
bare, covered by many acres of silver grass, where
flourished abundantly the short, spiked, pale-green
clusters of cactus—mescal, which gave the ridge its
name. The tips of mescal leaves narrowed to hard
black thorns, much dreaded by cattle and horses.
Like the thorns of the cholla cactus, these mescal
points broke off in flesh and worked in. Mescal, both
in its deadly thorns and the liquor distilled from its
heart, typified the hard and acrid nature of the Tonto.

Old Cappy Tanner, trapper, had driven his seven
burros in from the south this year; and this time he
was later than on any other of the many autumns he
had returned to the Tonto. His last two trapping seasons had been prosperous ones, which accounted
partly for his late arrival. He had tarried in Prescott
and Maricopa to buy presents for his good friends,
the Ames family. For Tanner that had been a labor
of love, but nevertheless a most perplexing one.

Three miles west of Tonto Creek the trail to

Mescal Ridge left the road. Cappy turned into it, glad to reach the last leg of his long tramp. Every giant pine seemed to greet him. He knew them all, and the logs, and the checker-barked junipers, and even the manzanita bushes, bare this year of their yellow berries. No cattle or horse tracks showed in the grass-grown trail. That surprised him. There had been no rain along there for weeks, and if any hoofs had stepped on this trail lately the tracks would have shown.

Cappy sat down against a huge pine to rest and to eat a little bread and meat. The sun shone hot and the shade was pleasant. His burros began to graze on the long grass. It occurred to him that he had rested often on the six weeks' walk north. He seemed to realize he was a little slower than last year.

The old familiar sough of the wind in the pines was music to him, and the sweet, dry, pungent odor of the evergreens was medicine. What soothing relief and rest after the desert! Cappy watched the burros, the slow shadows of the pine boughs, the squalling blue jays. He had been six months away from the Tonto, and the preceding night, at the tavern in Shelby, he had listened to disturbing gossip that involved his friends and their neighbors, the Tates.

It had occupied his mind all during the eighteen-mile journey from Shelby; to such significance that he had not stopped at Spring Valley to pay his respects to the Tates, an omission they would be sure to note.

"Reckon thet Pleasant Valley war left bitter feelin' which never will die out," soliloquized Tanner, wagging his head sadly. He had been in the Tonto during the climax of the terrible feud among cattle-men, sheepmen, and rustlers; and he had seen it end in extermination of every faction. But the heritage of bad blood had descended on the few families left in that wild north section of the Tonto Basin.

Having finished his lunch and rested, Tanner re-sumed his journey, growing more at ease as he drew farther from the road, deeper into the forest. When he began to catch glimpses of deer and flocks of wild turkeys, and to see where bears had broken the branches of the junipers to feed off the berries, he knew he was getting near home.

At length the trail led out of the deep shade of the forest into open sunlight, that shone on rough oak ridges, with dense thickets in the gulches be-tween. The trail headed many draws all sloping down in the same direction. Here and there glimpses of the rough canyon country framed themselves in notches of the ridges—wild dark purple canyon, powerfully suggestive of the haunts of bear and panther.

He turned abruptly round an oak-thicketed cor-ner to emerge on the high slope of Tonto Canyon. The scene was magnificent, lonely and wild and rug-ged in the extreme. A melodious murmur of running water made memory active. How would he find the Ameses—Nesta and Rich and the younger twins?

The deep canyon yawned narrow and blue, with rough rock slopes and patches of spruce and oak on the opposite side; and it deepened and constricted to dark bronze walls leading into the gloomy and inaccessible chasm called Hell Gate. When the hounds pursued a bear down that canyon the chase ended. Bears would take to the deep pools and rapids where no dogs could follow.

The whole length of Mescal Ridge stretched away before Tanner's eager gaze. Silver and black and green, a mighty hog-back among all those Tonto ridges, it lay somewhat below Tanner, open to his gaze. Cattle and deer dotted the gray patches of grass. This was the range where the Ames family ran the few cattle they owned, and it struck Tanner that their stock had increased, if all he saw belonged to them.

He strode on down, then, and for some time lost the beautiful panorama. When again he came out upon a jutting point of the trail he was halfway down, and could see the colorful flat nestling under the beetling brow of Mescal Ridge. The log cabin shone brown and tiny beside the three great spruce trees; patches of the garden, like green and gray squares, led to the cornfield, where horses browsed on the stalks; the rail fences, which Tanner had helped Rich Ames to build, were now overgrown with wine-colored vines.

The old trapper showed the same eagerness that animated his burros, and strode swiftly down the remaining zigzag stretches of the trail, out across the sandy, oak-shaded flat to the creek. The water was low and sycamore leaves floated with the swift current. Cappy went above the ford where his burros were drinking, and throwing aside his hat he stretched himself on a flat rock and drank his fill.

"Auggh!" he exclaimed, as he got up, wiping his wet beard. Tonto Creek! Snow water that flowed through granite! It took a desert man, or a trapper long away from the rocky hills, to appreciate fully that pure, cold, clear water.

Beyond the ford the trail led along the bank which sloped up to the flat and around to the three spruce trees and the moss-greened cabin. Dogs heralded Tanner's arrival, not by any means in a welcoming manner. But upon recognizing the trapper they quieted down and the big red leader condescended to wag his tail. Then shrill girlish shrieks attested further to Tanner's arrival. Two young girls came tearing out, their bright hair flying.

"Oh, Uncle Cappy!" they screamed in unison, and made at him, breathless, wild with the delight of lonesome souls at the advent of a beloved friend.

"Wal! Wal!—Mescal an' Manzanita!—I shore am glad to see you. . . . How you have growed!"

"It's been so—so long," panted the one he took for Mescal, as she clung to him.

"We—we was afraid you wasn't never comin'," added Manzanita.

The twins were six years old, if Cappy's memory served him well. It had been one of Cappy's proud boasts that he could distinguish which was Mescal and which was Manzanita, but he did not dare risk it yet. How the warmth of their flashing blue eyes thrilled him, and the rose bloom in the brown cheeks and the parted red lips! Cappy feared his eyes were not so good as they used to be, or maybe they had dimmed for the moment.

"Wal, now, girls, you knowed I'd come back," replied Tanner, reprovingly.

"Mother always said you would," replied one of the twins.

"An' Rich he'd always laugh an' tell as you couldn't stay away from Mescal Ridge," added the other.

"Rich is shore right. Wal, how are you-all?"

"Mother is well. We're all fine. But Nesta is away visitin'. She'll be back today, an' won't she be glad? ...Rich is out huntin' with Sam."

"Sam who?" queried Cappy, remembering that Rich seldom hunted with anyone.

"Sam Playford. He's been here since last spring. Homesteaded up the creek near Doubtful. Rich is with him a lot. We all like him fine, Uncle Cappy. He's terrible sweet on Nesta."

"Ahuh! Small wonder. An' is Nesta sweet on him?"

"Mother says she is an' Rich says she isn't," laughed Mescal.

"Humph! What does Nesta say?" asked Cappy, conscious of misgivings.

"Nesta! You know her. She tosses her head," replied Manzanita.

"But she *did* like Sam," protested Mescal, seriously. "We saw her let Sam kiss her."

"That was ages ago, Manzi." When she spoke this name, Cappy realized he had taken Mescal for Manzanita. "Lee Tate is runnin' her hard now, uncle."

"No!—Lee Tate?" returned the old trapper, incredulously.

"Yes. It was a secret," said Mescal, most seriously. "But Rich found Nesta out....An' say, didn't he lay into her! It didn't do no good. Nesta is as crazy as a young hen-turkey, so mother says."

"Wal, wal, this is news," rejoined Tanner,

thoughtfully, as he kept looking toward the cabin. "Where's Tommy? I reckoned I'd see him first off."

Mescal's blue eyes darkened and dimmed with tears. Manzanita averted her face. And then something struck cold at the old trapper's heart.

"Tommy's dead," whispered Mescal.

"Aw, no!" burst out Cappy, poignantly.

"Yes. It was in June. He fell off the rocks. Hurt himself. Rich an' Nesta weren't home. We couldn't get a doctor. An' he died."

"Lord! I'm sorry!" exclaimed the trapper.

"It hurt us all—an' near broke Rich's heart."

At this juncture the mother of the girls appeared on the cabin porch, wiping flour from her strong brown arms. She was under forty and still handsome, fair-haired, tall and strong, a pioneer woman whom the recent Tonto war had made a widow.

"If it ain't Uncle Cappy!" she ejaculated, warmly. "I wondered what-all the twins was yelling at. Then I seen the burros.... Old timer, you're welcome as mayflowers."

"Thanks, an' you're shore lookin' fine, Mrs. Ames," replied Cappy, shaking her hand. "I'm awful glad to get back to Mescal Ridge. It's about the only home I ever had—of late years, anyhow.... Thet about Tommy digs me deep.... I—I'm shore surprised an' sorry."

"It wouldn't have been so hard for us if he'd been killed outright," she rejoined, sadly. "But the hell of it was he might have been saved if we could have got him out."

"Wal—wal!... I reckon I'd better move along. I've fetched some things for you-all. I'll drop them off here, then go on back to my cabin, an' soon as I unpack I'll come back."

"An' have supper. Rich will be back an' mebbe Nesta."

"You bet I'll have supper," returned Cappy. Then he loosened a pack from one of the burros, and carrying it to the porch he deposited it there. The twins, radiantly expectant, hung mutely upon his movements.

"See hyar, Mescal Ames," declared Cappy, shaking a horny finger at one of the glowing faces, "if you—"

"But I'm Manzi, Uncle Cappy," interrupted the girl, archly.

"Aw—so you are," went on Cappy, discomfited.

"You've forgotten the way to tell us," interposed Mescal, gayly.

"Wal, I reckon so.... But no matter, I'll remember soon.... An' see hyar, Manzi, an' Mescal—don't you dare open this pack."

"But, uncle, you'll be so long!" wailed the twins together.

"No I won't, either. Not an hour. Promise you'll wait. Why, girls, I wouldn't miss seein' your faces when I undo thet pack—not for a whole winter's trappin'."

"We'll promise—if you'll hurry back."

Mrs. Ames vowed she would have to fight temptation herself and besought him to make haste.

"I'll not be long," called Tanner, and slapping the tired burros out of the shade he headed them into the trail.

At the end of the clearing, the level narrowed to

a strip of land, high above the creek, and the trail led under huge pines and cone-shaped spruces and birches to a shady leaf-strewn opening in the rocky bluff, from which a tiny stream flowed in cascades and deep brown pools. This was a gateway to a high-walled canyon, into which the sun shone only part of the day. It opened out above the break in the bluff into a miniature valley, isolated and lonely, rich in evergreens, and shadowed by stained cliffs and mossy ledges.

Cappy arrived at his little log cabin with a sense of profound gratitude.

"By gum! I'm glad to be home," he said, as if the picturesque little abode had ears. He had built this house three years before, aided now and then by Rich Ames. Before that time he had lived up at the head of Doubtful Canyon, where that "rough Jasper," as Rich called it, yawned black and doubtful under the great wall of the mesa.

Throwing packs, he strapped bells on the burros, and giving them a slap he called cheerily: "Get out an' rustle, you tin-can-label-eatin' flop-ears! You've got a long rest, an' if you've sense you'll stay in the canyon."

The door of the cabin was half ajar. Cappy pushed it all the way open. An odor of bear assailed his nostrils. Had he left a bearskin there, or had Rich Ames, in his absence? No, the cabin walls and floor were uncovered. But his trained eyes quickly detected a round depression in the thick mat of pine needles that covered his bough couch. A good-sized bear must have used it for a bed. In the dust of the floor bear tracks showed distinctly, and the left hind foot was minus a toe. Cappy recognized that track. The bear that had made it had once blundered into one of Cappy's fox traps, had broken the trap and left part of his foot in it.

"Wal, the son-of-a-gun!" ejaculated the old trapper. "Addin' insult to injury. I'll jest bet he knowed this was my cabin.... Wonder why Rich didn't shoot him."

Cappy swept out, carried his packs inside, and opening one of them he took out his lantern and fuel, cooking utensils, and camp tools, which he put in their places. Then he unrolled his bed of blankets and spread it on the couch. "Reckon I won't light no fire tonight, but I'll fix one ready, anyhow," he decided, and repairing to his woodpile he discovered very little left of the dry hardwood that he had cut the winter before. Rich Ames, the lonely fire-grazer, had been burning it! Presently Cappy was ready to go back to the Ames' cabin. But he bethought himself of his unkempt appearance. That was because he remembered Nesta Ames. So he tarried to remedy the defect. He shaved, washed, and put on a new flannel shirt of gorgeous hue, which he had purchased solely to dazzle the color-loving Nesta. Then he sallied forth.

A thick amber light hung under the trees, heavy as if it had substance. A strong exhilaration possessed Tanner. He was growing old, but the effect of the Tonto seemed to renew his youth. The solitude of the slopes and valleys, the signs of wild game in the dust of the trail, the babble of the brook, the penetrating fragrance of pine and spruce, the brush, the dead leaves, the fallen cones, the mat of needles, the lichened rocks—these were physical proofs that he had come home to the environment he loved best.

"Reckon I'll not go away no more," he muttered as he trudged through the gap in the cliff, up and down over the gray stones. "Onless, of course, the Ameses go," he added as an afterthought. "Shore was a good idee thet I planned to send my winter's catch out by stage."

The valley of the Tonto was full of golden light. The sun had just set behind the bold brow of Mescal Ridge, and a wonderful flare of gold, thrown up against a dark bank of purple cloud, seemed to be reflected down into the valley. Cappy sat down on a log above the creek, where many a time he had rested before, and watched the magic glow on field and slope and water. Already the air had begun to cool. The gold swept by as if it had been the transparent shadow of a cloud, swift and evanescent, like a dream, or a fleeting happiness. Wild ducks went whirring down the creek, the white bars on their wings twinkling. A big buck, his coat the gray-blue of fall, crossed an opening in the brush. Up high somewhere an old gobbler was calling his flock to roost.

Tanner's watch and reverie were interrupted by the cracking of hoofs on the rocks of the trail up the creek. Soon two riders emerged from the green, and the first was Rich Ames. He waved a glad hand, then came on at a trot. Cappy stood up, conscious of how good it was to see this Tonto lad again. Rich Ames on horse-back was surely pleasant to gaze upon, but when he slid out of his saddle, in one long lithe step, he sent a thrill to the old trapper's heart.

"Wal, lad, hyar I am, an' damn glad to see you,"

said Tanner, as he swung on the extended hand and gripped it hard.

"Same heah, old timer," drawled Rich Ames, his cool, lazy voice in strong contrast to the smile that was like a warm flash.

The second rider trotted up and dismounted. He was as tall as Ames, only heavier, and evidently several years the senior. His features were homely, especially his enormous nose. He had a winning smile and clear gray eyes. He wore the plain jeans of the homesteader, which looked dull and drab beside Rich Ames' gray fringed buckskin.

"Sam, it's shore old Cappy Tanner, my trapper pard," said Rich. "Cap, meet my friend, Sam Playford."

"How do!" greeted Playford, with an honest grin. "What I haven't heard about you ain't worth hearin'."

"Wal, any friend of Rich's is mine," replied Cappy, cordially. "You're new hyarabouts?"

"Yes. I come in last April."

"Homesteadin'?"

"I been tryin' to. But between these two Ames twins I have a plumb job of it."

"Twins?—Which ones?"

The boys laughed uproariously, and Rich jabbed a thumb into Sam's side.

"Cappy, it shore's not Manzi an' Mescal," he drawled.

"Ahuh! Must be Nesta an' you, then? I'm always forgettin' you're twins, too. Though, Lord knows, you look like two peas in a pod."

"Yep, Cap, only I take a back seat to Nesta."

"Where is thet lass? My pore eyes are achin' for a sight of her," returned Tanner.

"You'll have them cured pronto, then," said Rich. "For she's comin' along the trail somewheres behind. Mad as a wet hen!"

"Mad! What's the matter?"

"Nothin'. She's been stayin' at Snells', over at Turkey Flat. She an' Lil Snell have got thick since last winter. I like Lil an' I reckon she's all right. But all the same I don't want Nesta stayin' long over there. So I went after her."

Sam turned down the trail. "She's comin' now, an' I reckon it'll be safer for me to run along till you cheer her up," he said.

"Take my horse with you, Sam, an' turn him loose in the pasture," rejoined Rich.

Cappy strained his eyes up the leafy trail.

"Wal, I see something," he said at last. "But if it's Nesta she's comin' awful slow."

"Cap, she's got an eye like a hawk. She sees me, an' she'll hang back till I go....Old timer, I'd begun to fear you'd died or somethin'. Doggone, but I'm glad you've come!"

In these words and the wistfulness of his glance Rich Ames betrayed not only what he said but the fact that a half year had made him older and graver.

"You've had some trouble, Rich?"

"Shore have."

"Somethin' beside—Tommy's death?"

"Reckon so."

"Wal, what is it?"

"It's aboot Nesta. An' it's got me plumb up a tree.

...But, Cap, I want more time to tell you. So I'll run along home while you meet Nesta."

A bay pony emerged from the wall of green down the trail. Its rider was a bareheaded girl whose bonnet hung over her shoulders. She sat her saddle sideways. But when she neared the pine log where the trapper leaned watching, she partly turned. Then she sat up, startled. The petulant droop of her vanished and her red lips curled in a smile of surprise and delight. She slid off the saddle to confront him.

"Cappy Tanner!...So it was you Rich was talkin' to?" she cried.

"Wal, Nesta, if it's really *you*, I'm sayin' howdy," rejoined the trapper.

"It's me, Cappy....Have I changed so—so much?"

The beatuful blue-flashing eyes, so characteristic of the Ameses, met his only for a moment. It was the change in her and not the constraint that inhibited Tanner. Hardly more than six months ago she had been a slender, pale-faced girl, pretty with all the fairness of the family. And now she seemed a woman, strange to him, grown tall, full-bosomed, beautiful as one of the golden flowers of the valley. Cappy passed a reluctant gaze from her head to her feet, and back again. He had never seen her dressed becomingly like this. Her thick rich hair, so fair that it was almost silver, was parted in the middle above a low forehead just now marred by a little frown. Under level fine brows her eyes, sky-blue, yet full of fire, roved everywhere, refusing to concentrate upon her old friend. Any stranger who had ever seen Rich Ames would have recognized her as his twin sister, yet the softness of her face, its sweetness, its femininity were features singularly her own.

"Changed? Wal, lass, you are," replied the old trapper, slowly, as he took her hands. "Growed into a woman! ... Nesta, you're the purtiest thing in all the Tonto."

"Ah, Cappy, *you* haven't changed," she replied, suddenly gay and glad. And she kissed him, not with the old innocent freedom, but shyly, in a restraint that did not lack warmth. "Oh, I'm so happy you're here! I've thought of you every day for a month. Did you come today? You must have, for Rich didn't know."

"Jest got in, lass, an' I never knowed what home seemed like before."

She slipped an arm under his, and then, with her horse following, she led him toward the cabin.

"Cappy, I'm more in need of a true friend than every before in all my life," she said, soberly.

"Why, lass, you talk as if you hadn't any!" returned Tanner, reprovingly.

"I haven't. Not one single friend—unless it's you."

"Wal, Nesta, I don't savvy thet, but you can depend on me."

"Cappy, I don't mean no one *cares* for me.... Rich, and Sam Playford—and—and others—care for me, far beyond my deserts. But they *boss* and *want* and *force* me.... They don't help. They can't see my side.... Cappy, I'm in the most terrible fix any girl was ever in. I'm caught in a trap. Do you remember the day you took me on a round of your traps? And we came upon a poor little beaver caught by the foot? ... Well, I'm like that."

"Nesta, I'm awful interested, but I reckon not much scared," replied Cappy, with a laugh that did not quite ring true.

They reached the three huge spruces overspreading the cabin, and Nesta turned to unsaddle her pony. Sam Playford, who evidently had been waiting, approached from the porch.

"I'll tend to him, Nesta," he said.

"Thank you, Mr. Playford," she returned, with sarcasm. "I can manage as well here as I had to at Snells'."

Mescal and Manzanita ran out to overwhelm Tanner, shouting gleefully, "Here comes Santa Claus!"

"Wal, mebbe, when Christmas comes, but not *now*," retorted the trapper, resolutely. He had once before encountered a predicament similar to this.

"Uncle, when will you open the pack?" begged Manzi.

"Wal, some time after supper."

"I can't eat till you do open it," declared Mescal, tragically.

"If I do open it before supper, then you won't eat nothin' but candy," declared Tanner.

"*Candy!*" screamed Manzanita. "Who wants to eat deer meat and beans if there's candy?"

"Oooooummm!" cried her sister, ecstatically.

"Wal, let's have a vote on it," said the trapper, as if inspired. "Mescal an' Manzi have declared for openin' the pack before supper.... What do you say, Mrs. Ames?"

"Supper ain't ready yet," she rejoined, significantly.

"How about you, Nesta?"

"Me! How about what?" she returned, as she deposited her saddle on the porch, apparently unaware of Sam Playford's disapproval.

"Why, about openin' my pack. I fetched you-all a lot of presents."

"Cappy!—Open it *now!*" she flashed, suddenly radiant.

"An' what do you say, Mr. Playford?"

"Cappy, if you don't mind," replied that worthy, "if you're includin' me, I'll say if you got anythin' to give anybody, do it quick."

"Hey, Rich, you're in on this," went on the trapper.

"Cap, suppose you leave it to me?" responded Rich, with tantalizing coolness.

"Wal, I'm willin'. You 'pear to be the only level-headed one hyar."

"Open the pack after Nesta an' the twins have gone to bed."

The feminine triangle thus arraigned burst out with a vociferous, incoherent, yet unanimous decision that they never would go to bed.

"Wal, reckon I'll compromise," decided Tanner. "Right after supper, then, I'll open the show."

"Come in, Cap," said Rich. "This November air gets cold once the sun goes down."

The living-room extended the width of the cabin, and perhaps half the length. With a fire burning in the stone fireplace it presented a cheery, comfortable aspect. It also served as dining-room, and two beds, one in each corner, indicated that some of the family slept there. A door near the chimney opened into the kitchen, a small and recent addition. Two other rooms completed the cabin, neither of which opened into this large apartment. Rich Ames, like all the Tontonians, liked open fires, to which the three yellow stone chimneys rising above the cabin gave ample testimony.

"Manzi, you an' Mescal wash up, an' brush your hair," observed Mrs. Ames from the kitchen. Nesta had vanished.

"How's tracks, Rich?" queried Tanner, with interest.

"Cap, I never saw so much game sign since I can remember," replied Ames, with reflective satisfaction. "Dad once told me aboot a fall like this. Reckon ten years ago, long before the Pleasant Valley war."

"Wal, thet's good news. What kind of tracks?"

"All kinds. Beaver, mink, martin, fox—why, old timer, if you catch all of the varmints in Doubtful you can buy out the fur companies. How are prices likely to be?"

"Top notch. An' ain't it lucky to come when fur is plentiful? Reckon it's a late fall, too."

"Shore is. Hardly any snow heah at all. An' only lately on top. Bear, deer, turkey so thick up Tonto that you can kick them out of the trails. An' lots of lions, too."

"I reckon feed is plentiful, or all this game would be somewhere else?"

"Just wonderful, Cap. Acorns on the ground thick as hops. Berries aplenty, a good few wild grapes, an' the first big crop of piñon nuts for years. The game

is high up yet, an' shore won't work down till the
weather gets bad. We had lots of rain at the right
season, an' the winter snows will be late. I'll bet I
know of a hundred bee trees. We been waitin' for
you, rememberin' your weakness for honey."

"Haw! Haw! As if you didn't have the same?—
How about you, Playford, on Tonto honey?"

"Me? I've as sweet a tooth as one of these Tonto
bears."

"Wal, thet's all fine for me," declared the trapper,
with gratification. "I reckon you boys will throw in
with me, this winter anyway?"

"We shore will, Cap," replied Rich.

"I'm darn glad of the chance," added Playford.
"My place is all tidy for the winter, even to firewood
cut."

"Jest luck thet I fetched a sack of new traps,"
said Tanner.

"Hey, Rich," called his mother from the kitchen,
"come pack in the supper before I throw it out."

Rich responded with alacrity, and every time he
emerged from the kitchen, laden with steaming pans,
he winked mysteriously at Cappy Tanner, subtly im-
plicating Nesta, who had come in dressed in white,
very sweet and aloof, and Sam Playford, who could
not keep his humble worshipful eyes off her.

"Cappy, you set in your old seat," directed Mrs.
Ames, beaming upon him. Then the twins came rushing in like whirlwinds, and they fought over who
should have the place next to Tanner. Nesta was the
last to seat herself, with an air of faint disapproval
at the close proximity to Playford.

This byplay amused the trapper, yet began to

arouse curiosity and concern in him. Nesta had never before had an admirer who had been accepted by her family, if not by her. In the Tonto, girls of sixteen were usually married or about to be; and here was Nesta Ames, past eighteen, still single, and for all Cappy could tell, fancy free. He could be sure of little, except her charm and the change in her, the mystery of which only made her more attractive. Conversation lagged, and the interest of everybody, even the trapper, appeared to center on getting the meal over. The clearing off of the table was accomplished with miraculous brevity, and the kitchen lamp was brought in to add more light. Rich threw a couple of billets on the fire.

"Wal, you all set around the table an' I'll play Santa Claus," directed Tanner, and to the twins' screams of delight he repaired to the porch, leaving the door open.

This was an hour for which he had long planned. In order to make a magnificent impression he decided to carry all the bundles and parcels in at once, and thereby overwhelm the Ameses at one fell swoop. But he had not calculated on the difficulty of handling the mass when it was not snugly bound in a canvas. Not only did he stagger under the load, but he stumbled on the rude threshold and lost his balance.

"*Whoopee!*" roared Rich Ames, in enormous glee.

Cappy went down with his burdens, jarring the cabin.

A FEW moments later Cappy Tanner gazed around the living-room, utterly happy to contemplate the joy he had brought to the Ames family. Not for nothing had he, in the past, made note of what they needed and what they had longed for.

For once Mescal and Manzanita were confounded and mute. Mrs. Ames was not ashamed of her tears, if she were aware of them, and she regarded Tanner as if he were beyond comprehension. Nesta had been most blessed by the trapper's generosity. As she opened parcel after parcel she gasped. The last was a large flat box, somewhat crushed from the many packings on the back of a burro, but the contents were uninjured. The old trapper had engaged the good offices of a clever girl in Prescott to help him make these particular purchases of finery, but he did not betray that. He had the smiling nonchalant air of a man to whom such remarkable knowledge was nothing unusual. At first Nesta seemed rapt and spellbound. Then she hugged him. Cappy felt rewarded beyond his deserts, for the radiance and eloquence of her face had more than repaid him. At last she wept, and fled with her possessions to her room.

Rich Ames sat on a bench, gazing down on the floor, where he had laid side by side, a new .44 Winchester, a Colt of the latest pattern, row after row of boxes of shells, a hunting-knife and a hand ax, a pair of wonderful silver-mounted Mexican spurs, a cartridge-belt of black carved leather with silver buckle and a gun-sheath ornamented by a large letter A in silver.

"You son-of-a-gun!" burst out Rich, gulping. "Spent all last winter's catch on us!"

"No. I bought a new outfit for myself, two more burros, some pack saddles, an' a lot of good grub," replied Tanner, complacently.

"Cap, if you had to do this heah job, why didn't you wait till Christmas?" asked Ames, spreading wide his hands.

Tanner bit his wayward tongue in time to keep secret the second pack which was full of Christmas presents.

"Wal, Rich, if I have anythin' good to tell a fellar or give him, I do it quick."

"You've ruined this Ames outfit. Sam, what do you say aboot it?"

"If I had a million I'd give it to see Nesta look

like she did," replied Playford, fervently.

"So would I. Wasn't she wild?—Poor Nesta!... She's a girl an' she's had so little."

"Wal, folks, I'll mosey back to my cabin," said Tanner. "I'm pretty tired an' now thet I've had my little party I'll say good night."

"You goin' an' we haven't thanked you?" queried Ames, aghast at a fact that seemed irremedial.

"Rich, I'm thanked enough," laughed Tanner. "It's something to knock the pins out of you Arizona twins. I've been layin' to do it."

"Ahuh, I see....All right, Cap. What I'll do aboot it I can't say now."

Tanner bade his friends good night and went out. He thought Nesta might be waiting to waylay him outside, but she was not. No doubt she had been struck even deeper than Rich. How strange that she had burst out crying! She seemed quite beyond his understanding, but this did not mitigate his gladness at having given her things her heart desired. Nesta's lot had not been an easy one, nor had that of any of the Ameses, though for Rich no life could anywhere have been preferable to this wild Tonto. Their father came of fine Southern stock, probably Texan, and once he had been better off. Tanner had always inclined to the conviction that Ames had been involved in some feud in the South and had left to escape it. But he had only prolonged fatality. Though he had not been an active participant in the notorious Pleasant Valley war, he had been a victim to it. The Tonto had linked the name of Tate with the murder of Ames, but like many another of the legends of this wild lonely basin, it had never been verified.

The old trapper wended a thoughtful way along the trail under the bold black slope. The night was now cold. A keen wind made him draw his coat tight. The stars shone white out of a dark-blue sky; the creek ran with low murmur under the rocky banks; a pack of wolves were running prey over the top of Dead Horse Hill.

He had brought happiness to the Ameses and thereby to himself. But was all well with them? One of the things about the Ameses that had so appealed to Tanner was their devotion to one another. Could the loss of little Tommy and the advent of suitors for Nesta account for something the old trapper sensed yet could not define?

The trail through the break in the cliff lay in deep darkness, and Tanner, after half a year's absence, had to go slowly over the boulders. He gained the valley presently and soon reached his cabin, and without making a light he went to bed.

Then he did not at once fall asleep, as was usual with him. The branches of spruce and maple that overgrew the cabin brushed against the roof and the leaves rustled. The wind under the eaves had a wailing note. It brought to Tanner more than the meaning of November.

He awoke late for him, and when he went out to the spring with his pail the gray frost on the grass sparkled in the clear light, and far above, on the west rim of the valley, the fringed line of pine burned gold in the sun. A thin film of ice covered the still pool below where the spring gushed out. He saw fresh deer tracks. While he was retracing his steps to the cabin he heard faint but sharp rifle-shots from the flat below. Rich Ames was out testing the new Winchester. He expected Rich to come stalking along any moment now, but he had cooked and eaten his breakfast, had cleared his utensils away, and was unpacking supplies when a familiar soft footfall thrilled him.

Rich entered the cabin, seeming to fill it with a potential force. He radiated youth, vitality, and that flashing fire characteristic of the Ameses, but this morning he was not gay.

"Howdy, Cap! Look at that," he said, holding up his old sombrero.

Tanner espied three bullet holes through the crown of it. "Pretty good, if you wasn't close."

"Cap, I was close—fifty feet or so."

"Humph!" ejaculated Tanner, and laying the hat on the table he flattened the crown, and put a silver dollar over the three holes. It hid them.

"If thet'd been at a hundred steps, I'd say tip-top."

"Cap, I couldn't hit a barn door with the rifle," replied Rich, grinning. "I shot at rocks an' things all aboot, but either I'm no good or the Winchester shoots high. I reckon it does. I put those holes in my hat with the Colt. First three shots! Just throwed the gun—you know—an' I was thinkin' aboot Lee Tate."

"Rich!—What kind of talk is thet?" rejoined Tanner, with reproof. "Reckon your shootin' was wonderful, but your talk is crazy."

"Shore it is, Cap. But don't mind. I just was in fun. He's been a lot on my mind lately."

"Ahuh! Wal, forget him, an' all the rest of the Tates.... Throw a stick on the fire and set down."

Rich laid aside the rifle and replenished the fire, after which he settled himself in his favorite seat.

"I had a fight with Nesta this mawnin'," he announced.

"Fight! What you talkin' about, boy?"

"Twice I caught her slippin' out. She wanted to get to you first."

"Wal, I reckon I'm between the devil an' the deep sea," returned Tanner, ruefully.

"Meanin' me as the devil, an' Nesta as the deep sea!—it's shore aboot right. I'm gettin' mean an' Nesta is deep. But she wouldn't lie to me. I know that.... My Gawd, Cap—how I love her!—We Ameses are a queer outfit. Reckon it's because so many of us are twins. My father had a twin brother. An' there were twins among his people before. But never brother an' sister. Nesta an' I are the first.... If anythin' bad happened to her it'd be like cuttin' part of me out.... Nature plays some tricks, Cap. An' she shore hasn't any respect for anybody. There was a family over heah named Hines. They had twins—an' they were fastened to each other in a way that if they'd lived would have been shore horrible. We had a cow once that gave birth to two calves fastened together. We had to kill them. I reckon it doesn't make no difference to nature whether it's cattle or people. Anyway, Nesta an' I are awful close together. It scares hell out of me lately. I feel so much the way she feels that it's hard to be myself."

"Ahuh. Wal, Rich, what's on your mind?" returned Tanner, straddling a bench.

"There's shore a lot. But Nesta first an' most. . . .
Cap, it was darn good of you to fetch us all those
presents. Only if you had to give all that pretty stuff
to Nesta I wish you'd waited. Till Christmas, anyway."

"Why so, lad?"

"Nesta's been strange this summer an' fall. Now
she'll be plumb out of her haid."

"Rich, are you afraid the pretty clothes will hurry
her into marryin'?"

"Lord! I wish they would!" ejaculated Ames.
"Cap, the truth'll sound sort of silly, I reckon. But I
cain't help my feelin's. . . . Lil Snell is goin' to be married this month at Shelby. Hall Barnes is the fellow,
I reckon you don't know him. I do—a little, an' I'm
not crazy aboot him. Nesta went to school with him.
You know father sent Nesta back to Texas before an'
through the cattle war heah. Well, she knows Hall
an' says he's not such a bad sort. Maybe it's true. But
he's related to the Tates, an' he's thick with Lee. . . .
Well, Nesta wasn't goin' to this weddin' because she
hadn't no dress. An' I was plumb glad. Now you've
gone an' fetched her one! Cap, last night after you
left she came runnin' in on us, dressed all in white.
My Gawd! You should have seen her! Well, she raved
aboot goin' to the weddin'. An' mother raved with
her."

"Wal, lad, there's nothin' hardly worrisome in
thet," rejoined the trapper. "I think it's fine. An' I'm
goin' to show up in Shelby, jest to see Nesta in thet
white outfit."

"Cap, Nesta has got you the same way she's got
Sam," expostualted Rich.

"Humph! An' how's thet?"

"Plumb out of your haid."

"Haw! Haw! Is thet why she wanted so much to see me before you?"

"Shore, so far as I know. But Nesta has got me guessin'. Now, listen, old timer, an' bear in mind I wouldn't lie to you. . . . When Sam Playford came heah last April he fell in love with Nesta just like that. Head over heels! An' Nesta fell in love with him. She told me. Up till lately she never had any secrets from me. Reckon I sort of took father's place. Well, she told me, an' as I thought a heap of Sam myself, it was all right. Mother, too, was pleased, an' relieved, I reckon. Pretty soon Sam went down in the dumps an' Nesta got her haid in the air. They quarreled. Sam wouldn't tell me what aboot. An' for the first time in her life Nesta kept things from me. She'd been goin' to Shelby to dances—stayin' overnight with Lil Snell, at her home. Sam didn't go to some of these latest dances. He roamed around like a lost dawg. . . . Well, I took up the trail. An', Cap, so help me Heaven, I found out Nesta was carryin' on with Lee Tate."

"No!" repudiated Tanner, passionately, jerking up with fire in his eye.

"Yes!—It's damn hard to believe, Cap, but it's true."

"Aw! . . . Then she'd broke off with Playford?"

"Not a bit of it. They stayed engaged, an' they're still engaged. Now what do you think aboot it?"

"You said Nesta was carryin' on with Tate. Jest how do you mean? Carryin' on?"

Rich Ames shrank from the query. He writhed with his strong brown hands clenched between his knees, and the blue flash of his eyes centered with piteous doubt and entreaty upon the fire.

"If it was any girl but Nesta, I'd say she'd been more'n foolish," he went on, slowly. "Nesta isn't like any other girl. An' I don't mean headstrong an' proud an' moonstruck. Most girls are that way. I don't know just what I mean. But Nesta is different. She might be mad at Sam. She shore hates to be bossed. All the same, lettin' Lee Tate make up to her was daid wrong."

"It was," agreed Tanner, soberly. "Tate is a hand-some fellar."

"Shore. An' he's slick with girls. On an' off he's had most of the girls in the Tonto crazy about him. Nesta may be innocent of goin' that far, but she shore has the name of it. Well, I didn't believe much of the gossip. But when I watched Nesta an' Tate one night at a dance, an' later found out she met him at Snell's, I got pretty sick. Then if I'd gone at Nesta sort of kind an' understandin' it'd been better. But I didn't un-derstand, an' I was shore sore. So I made it worse."

"Ahuh. Natural enough. Looks like a bad mess, Rich. But I'll withhold my judgment till Nesta tells me her side."

"Shore. You cain't do no less. Lord! I'm glad you're heah, Cap. Nesta is fond of you an' she'll listen to you. But, just now, if this goes on it'll get beyond you an' me. An' poor Sam—why, he's the laughin'-stock of Shelby! He knows it, too, an' he doesn't go there. I must say he has been fine. Never a word against Nesta! But it's hurtin' him."

"Wal, I shouldn't wonder. It hurts me deep, Rich. I don't quite savvy. Thet's not like Nesta. What's got into the girl?"

"Cap, there's bad blood in the Ameses. I've got it, an' I'm scared. Maybe it's comin' out in Nesta. Mother now—she took Nesta's part. You'd think she was proud of the girl's conquests. Mother must get somethin' out of it herself. I shore couldn't talk more aboot it."

"Ahuh. I see your side, Rich. You not only feel bad about Sam, but you're worried for Nesta. An' if Lee Tate bragged, you know—"

"Cap, he has already bragged," interrupted Rich, darkly. "That's Lee's way. Girls are easy for him. So far his talk hasn't been—well, any shame to Nesta. But it's most damned irritatin'."

"Wal, Rich, his talk an' Nesta's odd behavior have got to be stopped."

"Right, old timer," returned Ames, quickly. "I reckon if we can fetch Nesta to her senses we won't have to go further."

"Don't say 'if,' Rich. We'll do it. An' is thet all you've been worryin' over?"

"Shore. Everythin' else concernin' us couldn't be better. We've got over two hundred haid of cattle now. In another year Sam an' I will need help. This head is a fine range. In dry seasons the cattle browse up high while those down in the basin starve. No rustlin' to speak of on this side. I can see how in a few years we shore will be rich. We live off the farm. An' Sam is doin' mighty fine. If Nesta will only settle down now we'll all be happy, with the brightest prospects. Next year we'll send the twins to school."

"Wal, wal!—Thet's good news. But it'd be sad if thet big-eyed lass spoiled it all. . . . I don't believe she will, even allowin' for the freaks of life. I know Nesta an' I trust her. I'll bet when her side of the story comes out we'll see the thing different."

"Cap, you cheer me up," replied Ames, rising with a brighter face. "I'll chase myself now. An' if Nesta doesn't come heah, you find her. An' if you cain't talk her out of goin' to Lil Snell's weddin' we'll all go."

"It'll be better to do our talkin' afterward," said Tanner, sagely.

Tanner busied himself in and around his cabin, an expectant eye on the trail for Nesta. Some of the Ameses' hounds came over to make friends with the trapper again. But Nesta did not put in an appearance. Tanner's optimism began to fall and he grew troubled. Whereupon he sallied forth to find the girl.

The noonday sun poured warmly down into the valley. The heights looked clear and cold. There was a tang in the air, and the oak slopes gleamed steely gray. Deer and turkey watched the trapper as he plodded down the trail. He halted in the shady gulch to rest and ponder, then went on, to repeat the performance out in the flat, and he sat a long time on the old log. When he finally arrived at the Ames cabin the afternoon was well advanced.

Cappy found Mescal and Manzanita very much the worse for a prodigious consumption of candy. "Little pigs!" averred Mrs. Ames. "I had to take the candy away from them." Mescal was sick in bed with colic, and Manzanita gave a capital imitation of a torpid lizard motionless in the sun.

"Cappy, you shore gave us a wonderful evenin'," said Mrs. Ames. "But I'm afraid you've spoilt us."

"Aw, what's a little spoilin'?" laughed the trapper. "Once or twice a year won't hurt nobody. Where's Nesta?"

"She was flittin' around like a butterfly all mawnin'," rejoined Mrs. Ames. "Singin' like a lark one minute, then mopin' the next. She's outdoors now. You'll find her somewhere dreamin' under a tree."

"Mrs. Ames, what ails the lass?"

"Ails Nesta!—Nothin' in the world. You men just cain't understand us women."

"Wal, perhaps not. But I'm tryin' hard. An' I reckon Rich an' this Sam Playford are wuss off than me."

"Rich been talkin' to you?" queried the mother, sharply.

"Yes, a little. The lad is worried about Nesta. An' I reckon he has cause."

"I'm not gainsayin' that, Cappy. He an' Sam worship Nesta. An' they haven't sense enough to let the poor girl alone. Nesta is goin' through a bad time. Her first love affairs. She was late startin'. Before I was sixteen I had half a dozen."

"Aw, I see," said Cappy, but he did not see at all. "So it's love *affairs*."

"Shore. She's in love with two young men I know of. There might be another. This heah Sam Playford is a mighty fine boy. He's good an' gentle, an' he's powerful ugly. Now this Lee Tate is a handsome devil. He's not good, an' I'll vouch he has a rough hand with girls. I've been tryin' to make Rich an' Sam see that they must let her alone. Sam is beginnin' to. But Rich is like all the Ameses."

"But, Mrs. Ames," expostulated Cappy, "if they or all of us let Nesta alone, she—she'll get a bit between her teeth an'—an' I don't know what."

"Cappy, she has done that already. An' if we nag her she'll ride off wild. I know girls. I was one once. An' Nesta is an Ames clear through. My advice to you is to let her alone, agree with her, pet her. An' if you have to talk, why, praise Lee Tate to her."

"Good Lord, woman!" ejaculated Tanner, in bewildered disapproval.

"Cappy, take my word for it. If there's any harm done, it's *done*. You cain't help it. Nesta is genuinely fond of Sam Playford. But she's also fascinated by this young Tate. That's natural. Sam will get her, though, if he doesn't make a jackass out of himself He's not worryin' me much. Sam is a reasonable fellow. He rings true. But Rich will give me gray hairs. He's his father over again. An' more—Cappy. He's the livin' likeness of his father's twin brother, Jess Ames. An' if ever there was a fightin' Texan it was Jess Ames. Their father was Caleb Ames, who fought in the Texas invasion in the 'forties. He was a Texas Ranger. Rich is a grandson of that old warrior. You see what kind of blood he has. An' he hasn't any reason to love the Tates, has he?"

"I reckon not," rejoined Tanner, gloomily, yet he thrilled in his gloom.

"It's Rich I'm afraid of, an' not Nesta."

"Wal, it's the other way round with me," returned Tanner, and he went out to look for the girl.

He sought her at the barn and the corral, along the trail, up the gulch at his own cabin, and farther on, without success. Mescal Ridge could easily have hidden a thousand girls. Then returning to the creek valley he went farther, and at last espied Nesta's fair head shining in the sun. She was sitting above the Rock Pool. This was a deep dark eddy at the head of the valley, a lonesome spot, where the slopes met in a V-shaped notch. Only from one place could Tanner have espied the girl, and it had been just accident that he had done so. He descended the bank and clambered over the boulders, and eventually gained the huge flat rock upon which she sat.

Tanner was old in years, yet at close sight of Nesta Ames he grew young again. She personified youth, beauty, love, tragedy. The environment seemed in harmony with all these. It was a wild, romantic spot. The leafless sycamore branches spread out over the rocks and the dark pool. A low roar of falling water came from up the creek. Opposite the yellow cliff bulged out, with its niches of green and its red-leafed vines. Downstream the whole of the gorge opened clear to the sight, to where it turned into the shadowy Hell Gate.

Under Nesta Ames' blue eyes were dark circles. Her fair face showed the stains of recent tears. At sight of Cappy she seemed divided between gladness and resentment, neither of which she could control.

"Howdy, lass!" said Cappy, mildly.

A curved arm of the great sycamore reached out low over the rock. Nesta leaned against it. Manifestly this was a favorite retreat. A layer of pine needles made a comfortable seat. Cappy sat down close to her and leaned against the branch.

"So you tracked me?" she queried, flippantly and aloofly.

"Awful nice hyar," replied Cappy, with a sigh. "Reckon I found you hyar once—long ago, before you growed up. Protected from thet north wind an' open to the sun from the south."

He laid aside his sombrero, and feeling Nesta's gaze he thought it just as well that Mrs. Ames had given him some advice.

"What do you want?" asked Nesta, presently, and the tone was not propitious.

"Wal, seein' you didn't come to me, I reckon I had to come to you."

"What for?"

"Nothin', except the joy of seein' you, lass. Course I'm not forgettin' what you said yesterday about needin' a friend."

"Honest?"

"Cross my heart," replied Cappy, and he suited the act to the words.

"But you saw Rich," she flashed.

"Yes, he was over a little while."

"He talked aboot me?"

"Reckon he did, some."

"Good or bad?"

"Wal, a little of one an' a lot of the other. You can take your choice."

"Bad!" she retorted, with passion.

"Lass, I didn't say so. An' what Rich said ain't botherin' me none. Poor boy! He had to talk to me. I've always listened an' kept my mouth shut."

"It's a pity he cain't keep *his* mouth shut," she returned, hotly. "This mawnin' he called me a spoiled kid. Then when I spoke *my* mind he swore an' boxed my ears."

"No! You don't say!—Wal, wal! I'm afraid Rich doesn't savvy you're growed up."

"Do you?"

"Wal, I reckon. I seen thet yesterday."

"You didn't track me heah to scold and nag? To find fault with me? To worry me into being bossed by Rich?"

"Nesta, where'd you get such an idee as thet?" queried Cappy, as if surprised. Nevertheless, he did not trust himself to meet the wonderful blue eyes. After a moment she slipped a hand under his arm and moved almost imperceptibly closer.

"Forgive me, Cappy," she murmured, contritely. "I guess Rich is right. I'm a cat sometimes."

"Rich is all right, lass. He's only weak where we're all weak."

"And where's that, Cappy?"

"Where a certain Tonto lass is concerned."

Nesta trilled a little gay laugh that yet had a note of sadness.

"Cappy, are you weak there?"

"Yes, lass. In the last stages."

At that she slipped her hand farther under his arm and leaned her head against his shoulder. Cappy could have blessed the girl's mother. He felt more in that moment than he could have explained in an hour of pondering thought. She seemed a wistful, lovable, willful girl merging into womanhood, uncertain and doubtful of herself, passionately sensitive to criticism, intolerant of restraint.

"Cappy, last night I was gloriously happy," she said. "I loved you for your generous gifts—more for the affection that prompted them....But this mawnin' I—I—oh, I'm sad. I'm crazy to wear that white gown—the stockings—the slippers. Oh, how did you ever—ever choose so beautifully? Why, they fit to perfection!...I cain't resist them. I *must* go to Lil Snell's wedding. I ought not to go, but I *shall* go."

"Wal, why not, lass? I'm sure goin'. I wouldn't miss seein' you for a hundred beaver skins."

"Why, Cappy?" she murmured, dreamily.

"Because you'll look lovely an' make them Tonto girls sick."

"*Ah!*...You've hit it, Cappy. That's my weakness. ...There are several girls who have rubbed it into me. Laughed at my old shabby clothes. And there's one girl I—I hate,...Oh yes, I've been jealous of her. I *am* jealous....But neither she nor any other Tonto girl ever saw as beautiful a dress as mine. But for that I could stay home and obey Rich—and—and not hurt Sam anymore."

"Sam?—Aw, a little hurtin' won't hurt him. Let him see you with thet handsome Tate lad. You two will make a team. Sam is an ugly, slow fellar, an'—"

"Cappy, don't say anything against Sam Playford," interrupted Nesta, with surprising spirit.

"Excuse me, Nesta," replied Cappy, guilty in his realization. "I sort of got the idee you didn't give a rap for Sam."

"But—I do," said Nesta, with a catch in her breath. "*I do!*—That's what makes it so hard. I've got to break with Sam and I—I cain't."

Cappy let well enough alone, though he was consumed with curiosity. In all good time Nesta would betray herself. There was deeper trouble here than Rich had guessed, though the lad's misgivings were poignant.

"Cappy, you've pushed me over the fence," went

on Nesta. "I was heah fighting my vanity. And when you said I'd look lovely—and make these Tonto girls sick—I—I just fell over."

"Wal, I'm glad I happened along," lied Cappy. "Because it's true an' I want to see it."

"You old dear! How comforting you are!... Cappy, I'll do it. I'll go—cost what it will."

"Wal, lass, the cost is paid," replied Cappy, with a laugh. "I'd hate to have to tell you what thet outfit cost."

"I didn't mean cost in money," she said, with remorse.

"What then, lass?"

"I don't know, but it might be terrible," she rejoined, gravely. "These Tonto girls say I'm a stuck-up Texan. To outshine them won't make them friendlier. Then that Madge Low hates me already. She has spread the—the talk aboot Lee Tate and me. She will be poison now. She is mad aboot Lee. He—he only trifled with her.... Then Rich will be really angry with me. He has never been yet. And Sam—he'll be more hurt. But he didn't ask me not to go. He's never said an unkind word. That shore makes me ashamed.... But, if I stay away from Shelby *afterward*, maybe it won't be so terrible.... If I stay away from Lee Tate *afterward*—"

Nesta broke off, evidently realizing she was thinking aloud. Cappy needed no more to divine that she would not stay away from Shelby or from Lee Tate, and therein lay the menace to the future. Nesta must have divined it also, for her head dropped lower and heavier upon the trapper. He put a comforting, sympathizing arm around her, and gritted his teeth to keep silent. She was not proof against both, and the seething emotion within. She burst out crying.

"Oh, Cappy, I wish I were daid!" she sobbed. Her grief grew uncontrollable then. She wept with a wild abandon, as if such passion had been long dammed within her. It frightened the old trapper. When had he seen a woman weep? Nesta clung to him with the grip of one who feared she was slipping into an abyss. Little used as he was to feminine moods, he felt that something dreadful lay behind this unabatable grief. He sensed something he could not explain—that he was the only one to whom she could have betrayed herself.

CHAPTER

3

*C*APPY TANNER roamed the woods next day from dawn till dark, studying the game trails, the beaver dams, the piñon ridges, to find the run of fur-bearing animals so that he could plan a line-up for his traps. He found sign so plentiful that he assured himself of a bountiful season.

Next day he tramped up-country, through Doubtful Canyon, an all-day trip for even a hardy mountaineer like himself. So far as Cappy was concerned, Doubtful was going to have an unfelicitous name this winter. It was a certainty. The magnificent gorge had six beaver dams, one of them backing up a long lake acres in extent, and it seemed alive with beaver. A colony of bears had located high up on the east slope, which was covered with oak thickets. Deer and turkey had descended from the rim in numbers exceeding any he remembered. Round the springs were game tracks so thick that only the big bear sign could be distinguished.

But the beaver alone assured Tanner of a rich harvest. Evidently beaver had migrated from all over the country to this deep black gorge. The cuttings of aspen saplings far outnumbered the sum of all those in the years he had trapped there. It was unprecedented, and the opportunity to make him independent for life. He planned to devote himself solely to beaver-trapping, and to direct Rich Ames and Sam Playford in operations on fox, mink, martin, and other valuable fur-bearing species.

Cappy, in his way, was practical and thorough, so far as trapping was concerned. But always he had been a romancer and a dreamer over plans for the future. Unquestionably this winter's catch would net him thousands of dollars, and also be a very profitable venture for Rich and Sam. He decided he would locate in the Tonto, somewhere between Doubtful and Mescal Ridge, and go into the cattle business with the boys. The idea grew on him. It was great. Thus indirectly he could bring prosperity to the Ames family, and possibly happiness to Nesta.

Sunset gilded the Mazatzals when he stalked through the grand outlet of Doubtful. First he looked back, and when he saw the lofty walls, cragged and ledged and turreted, shining in the golden light, and the yawning black gulf of timber with which the canyon was choked, he had a sudden stirring inspiration. He would homestead the gateway leading into Doubtful. No hunter of incipient rancher had yet despoiled Doubtful. It was too rough, too wild, too hard to clear and make into a paying proposition. But Cappy saw how he could do it; and right then and there he built a pyramid of rocks to identify his location. At last he had found a home. Only three miles from Mescal Ridge! And in the event that Nesta married Sam—a consummation to which Tanner pledged himself— he would be only a short walk over the ridge, to their homestead.

He sat there on a rock dreaming while the golden flare in the west grew dusky red and died. He was hungry and tired, and a long walk from his cabin. All at once his supreme loneliness struck him. Except for the Ames family he had no friends in all the world. Relatives were long gone and forgotten. He was dependent upon the Ames couplet of twins for what happiness there might be left. He realized then how and why his wandering life could no longer be sufficient.

In the gathering dusk he trudged down the Tonto trail, fighting his doubts, standing loyally by what he hoped and believed, despite the encroachment of sadness. Darkness overtook him on the trail, but he knew it as well as a horse familiar with the country. When he reached the valley under Mescal Ridge a light shone out of the darkness of the flat, and it was the lamp Mrs. Ames always burned, so long as any of her brood were absent. It cheered Tanner. The hounds scented him and bayed till the welkin rang. He stood a moment listening and watching.

"Wal, it's settled I'll stick hyar my remainin' years," he soliloquized, and there was content in the prospect.

*   *   *

Next morning while Cappy applied himself briskly to his chores Rich Ames appeared, hatless, gunless, with a blue flame in his eyes.

"Mornin', son," said the trapper, innocently, but he was perturbed.

"Mawnin'—hell!" returned Ames, hotly. "Where you been for two weeks?"

"Why, Rich, it's only been two days!" rejoined Tanner, suddenly conscious that even two days could brew disaster. "I've been plannin' some lines for my winter trappin'."

"Yes, you have.... You double-crossed me with Nesta an' then run off an' hid."

"Double-crossed you!" ejaculated Tanner, facing about, red under his beard. "No, lad ... at least not on purpose."

"You backed her up aboot goin' to the weddin'."

"Wal—I saw thet she intended to go an' I jest agreed. I figgered Nesta was in a queer state of mind. She can't be drove anymore, Rich. If you try thet any more, you'll lose her."

"Cap, it's not a question of losin' her anymore. She's lost."

"Aw, Rich, you talk like a boy. What's up?"

"Nesta's gone."

"Where ?"

"Lil Snell rode in heah yesterday. She's rushin' her weddin' an' she said she needed Nesta bad. I wasn't home an' mother let Nesta go. When I got back I lit out on their trail, an' over across the creek a couple of miles I found where they met up with two more horses. Then I was in a hell of a fix. If I'd caught up with them an' Nesta had met Lee Tate again—Lord only knows what I'd have done. So I came home."

"You did right. Nesta is not a child like Mescal or Manzi. She's eighteen years old. If she chooses to meet Lee Tate or any other fellar, what can you do about it?"

"If it's Tate I can do a hell of a lot," declared Rich.

"Wal, mebbe it wasn't. Mebbe it wasn't nothin' at all. A weddin' is sure excuse for girls to be excited. ...When is Lil Snell's weddin' comin' off?"

"Day after tomorrow at her uncle's in Shelby. A weddin', dinner, an' dance! Shelby will shore be roarin'."

"Wal, we can go an' roar a little ourselves, if we want to."

"Cap, I'll be there, but I wouldn't take a drink for anythin'."

"When'd you see Nesta last?"

"Day before yesterday. In the mawnin' she went singin' round the cabin, her cheeks like roses, an' her eyes went right through you. I was sore an' let her alone. Then Sam came down. Poor faithful jack-ass that he is!...I had to get away from them, though secretly I was glad she seemed kind to him again. But she wouldn't let me alone, either. I'm as easy as Sam, only I can hide it. Well, she was full of honey an' lightnin'. My insides just sort of curled up hot an' tight. You cain't help lovin' Nesta. You cain't!"

"Agree with you," replied Tanner, bluntly, "so we'll love her an' let it go at thet. How'd you know she'd made a softy out of me?"

"I guessed that much. All Nesta said was you

tracked her to Rock Pool. She gave me just one mysterious look an' she held her chin up, in the way she has that makes you want to slap her pretty face. She didn't need to tell me any more. *You* were her good friend if *I* wasn't. You would back her against me or anybody. Then I reckoned you had double-crossed me."

"Rich, you don't believe that now?"

"I shore do. I know it. You crawled like a yellow dawg. You're like mother. Just cain't bear Nesta bein' angry with you. Anythin' but losin' her. It's always been that way. I'm the only one who has ever opposed her."

"Wal, wal! I wonder," rejoined Tanner, helplessly. "Rich, you're only a lad. Only eighteen, an' Nesta is heaps older. You may be wrong. Your mother seems wise about girls."

"Mother makes me furious," flashed Rich, heatedly. "She cain't do a damn thing with Nesta. She likes to have the girl spoiled by men. She even gets somethin' out of Lee Tate's case on Nesta. *Lee Tate!* Who comes of the Tates that made away with father! ...In her day mother was a flirt. I've heard father say so—an' he didn't mean to be funny, either."

"But Nesta isn't a flirt," declared Cappy.

"No, I cain't say that. At least not in a raw sense like Lil Snell an' some more of these Tonto females. I reckon I know Nesta better than anyone, even our own mother. Nesta is half me....An' I'm tellin' you, Cap, that if harm hasn't already come to her through this Lee Tate-Lil Snell mixup it will come *now*, shore as Gawd made little apples."

"Ahuh.—This Lil Snell used to be a bold one, didn't she?"

"Ha! Used to be? She is yet, when the chance offers. Lil was one of Lee Tate's girls an' they were thick. I know. Well, she was always jealous of Nesta. Liked her, shore, because nobody can help that. But underneath all this late friendship between Nesta an' Lil is somethin' deeper. I felt it the first time I ever saw Nesta an' Lil together. Lil has been playin' Lee Tate's game. That's all. No one can tell me. An' I've just had hell with Nesta an' mother."

"Son, if you're figgerin' correct, it's too late," replied Tanner, grimly, as he looked straight into the troubled eyes of Ames.

"Then I hope to Gawd I'm wrong," burst out Rich. "But right or wrong, I'm goin' to break up this case between Nesta an' Tate. One way or another! Before he took after Nesta she was the sweetest, gayest, happiest girl in the world. She loved Sam an' was contented at the prospect of helpin' him with his homestead. But Tate flattered her, excited her, upset her—an' I don't know what else. Nesta used to like pretty clothes, but she wasn't crazy over them. She could bake an' sew—why, she was most as good a worker as mother. Lately she's idle. She moons around. She has somethin' on her mind.... Now, Cap, you can look me square in the eye an' declare yourself."

"Wal, son, you're callin' my hand," replied the old trapper, not without dignity. "I'm bound to admit you've got this situation figgered. I didn't have. An' if your mother did, she either ain't carin' much or else she sees it's no use. Mebbe she knows more of life than both of us together. I'm mighty fond of Nesta. I couldn't be more so if she was my own. But now you put it up to me, I'd sacrifice her love for me to do her good. Reckon thet's what you mean an' what you'll have to do. If we lose her we'll still have Mescal an' Manzi....I agree. We've got to break Tate's hold on Nesta. One way or another. I reckon the best way would be to marry her to Playford. Onless she doesn't care for him anymore."

"She does. An' that's shore my first plan."

"How about Playford? Nesta said he was fine. Never nagged her. But will he stand anymore ?"

"Sam is true as steel. Yesterday we talked aboot it. An' he said: 'Rich, if you cain't bust up this moonshine of Tate's, I'll have to. Nesta will never marry me then, even if I came out of it free. But it's got to be done.'...An' I swore I'd do it."

"Wal, let Nesta have her fling for this weddin'. Watch her close, without her knowin'. Then the three of us will go after her, one at a time, or all together, an' persuade her to marry Sam....But, Ames, she told me she just had to break off with Sam, only she couldn't."

"Did she say that?" queried Rich, in consternation. "Lord! but we're up against a tough knot! If she still cares for Sam, an' she swears she does— why must she break it off?"

Tanner shook his grizzled head. He did not have the courage to voice his fears. When had he ever seen agony and terror in the lad's once fearless blue eyes? It struck the old trapper that Rich Ames had been forced into manhood.

"Cap, she's ashamed of somethin'," went on Ames, hoarsely.

"Reckon she is. But if she still loves Sam an' he'll stand for—for anythin'—why, it'll all come out. All's well thet ends well."

"Damn you, Tanner!" bit out Ames, his lips suddenly drawn. "You know more'n you'll tell." Then he covered his face with his hands and sobbed: "Nesta!—Nesta!—Oh, little—sister!"

This was an ordeal for Tanner. He cursed.

"Hyar! What the hell kind of talk an' goin's-on is this?" he demanded, struck to the heart by Rich's grief. "Nesta ain't no little sister. She's a big one. A grown woman, hot-headed an' provokin' the more for thet. Her beauty an' sweetness only make her wuss.... Women hurt men. You can lay to thet. We'll save her an' I reckon she'll turn out good as gold. But for Gawd's sake get over the idee she's still a baby."

Rich Ames uncovered his face, now haggard and wet, and stood unashamed, as if not conscious of his weakness.

"Thanks, Cap. I reckon you hit the nail on the haid," he declared, and with a strange smile and violent wrestle he seemed to recover his equanimity. "Sam an' I are ridin' in to Shelby today. Shall I saddle a horse for you?"

"Might as well. I hate ridin', but I reckon I won't have to keep up with you young bucks."

"Sam will be heah by now. So come along," said Ames, turning on his heel.

"I'll be there pronto," replied Cappy, watching the lithe figure glide away down the trail. Suddenly, he had a queer premonition or a wondering thought that he would never again see Rich Ames like that.

Cappy hurried to change his soiled garb for the best he owned, and sallied forth to meet the boys. They were waiting with the horses under the spruces, talking earnestly. Cappy saw Rich make a gesture of fierce repudiation, as if he were thrusting back the thing that opposed him.

"Mother an' the kids have gone," announced Rich, when Cappy joined them. "They rode up to Lows', who're goin' to town in their wagon."

"Howdy, Cap! You're all spruced up," said Playford.

"Wal, I don't see as you boys are wearin' your wust. . . . Ride along now, an' never mind about me."

It took a few moments for Tanner to adjust the stirrups for his short legs, during which time Ames and Playford rode on ahead. When Cappy mounted they were fording the creek. The day was perfect. Indian summer still lingered in these deep canyons of the Tonto. A smoky haze filled the air. Mescal Ridge shone silver and green under the mounting sun.

Up on top, however, the air was cool, and the wind whipped at the pine thickets. Cappy did not see Rich and Sam again. He let his horse walk and found the miles and hours too short for the problem on his mind. The Tate ranch at Spring Valley appeared to have been vacated by its human inhabitants, of whom there were many. The wide green pastures were dotted with horses and colts. Wild ducks on the way south had descended to sport in the pond. Well-cared-for acres and fences, the numerous corrals and barns, and the big rambling house surrounded by cabins attested to the prosperity of the Tates. The whole range south of Spring Valley was under their dominance, if it did not actually belong to them. Possessions, however, were not the sole attributes that rendered the Tates formidable. Slink Tate, a nephew of the rancher, bore a bad repute and had taken the initiative in several fatal shooting affrays. Veiled Tonto rumor linked his name with the ambush of Rich Ames' father. Most of the younger Tates were hard riders, hard drinkers, and not slow with guns. Lee Tate, however, did not shine with horses, ropes, or guns; but as a damsel-killer he stood supreme in the Tonto.

Cappy Tanner rode by Spring Valley with these reflections gradually rousing rancor in his usually mild breast. He had a lonely ride and ample time for cogitation. Darkness fell before he reached Shelby, and it was something more than an hour later when he rode down the wide dark street, with its dim yellow lights, its high board fronts. Cappy had anticipated that the tavern would be full, so he went to the house of a blacksmith, Henry, by name, a friend who did a little trapping, who welcomed him heartily. The blacksmith's genial wife filled Cappy's ears with the current gossip, and the last of it, anent the supposed jilting of Sam Playford by Nesta Ames, in the interest of a wild infatuation for devil-may-care Lee Tate, augured ill for the hopes and plans of Rich Ames.

Cappy went out, ostensibly to do the same as all visitors, stroll from tavern to store and from store to saloon, to chat or drink with acquaintances, to watch the gambling games; but in reality he was anxious to find Rich Ames. Presently he encountered Sam Playford, who, even in the dim light, appeared pale and gloomy.

"Where's Rich?" queried Tanner, brusquely, without even a greeting.

"Just put him to bed an' locked him in," replied Playford.

"Bed!—Aw, don't say Rich went an' got drunk?"

"We had a couple of drinks," admitted the other, seriously. "But they never phased me. Went to Rich's head or somethin'. You know he drinks very little, an' can't stand much. We heard some talk right off. Must have upset Rich. He sure had a chip on his shoulder. Was goin' to punch some fellow with Jim Tate. But I blocked that. Then this damn sheriff, Stringer, threatened to arrest Rich. His meanness sure came out, an' his friendship for the Tates. . . . My God, but Rich scared me! He said: 'Go ahaid, Stringer, an' try it!'—Stringer laughed it off, but he was scared, too. So I dragged Rich off to bed an' I'll go back to our room pronto. He might climb out of the window."

"What talk did you hear?" queried Tanner, gruffly.

"It's all over town that Nesta has jilted me for Lee Tate. An' worse, they say it won't do her any good. Tate is only playin' with her. They say his father wouldn't hear of him marryin' into the Ames family."

"Ahuh. Is there any ground for this jilt talk?"

"Nesta has never even hinted it to me. Yesterday she was somethin' like her old self. Lately, though, she has been queer an' cold when we met, then little by little she'd grown more natural. Yesterday she even thawed out. I'm afraid I cain't understand it all."

"Wal, I reckon I can," responded Cappy. "You don't need to. But stick to thet girl till hell freezes over."

"You bet," replied Sam, with emotion. "But just now it's Rich who worries me most."

"Huh! Rich ain't worryin' me none," declared Tanner. "I've a hunch lately he's on the right trail to clear up this mess. He's got blood in him, Playford. An' it's workin'. But Rich has sense. Even if he got drunk he'd never lose his head. If he breaks loose you can gamble there's reason. All we want to do is stand by an' back him, if it comes to a fight. Are you packin' a gun?"

"I reckon I am," replied Sam, tersely. "But for Nesta's sake—her good name—I hope we dodge a fight."

"Dodge nothin'. So far as this two-bit of a town is concerned, gossip has already done for Nesta's good name. An' a healthy fight would help more'n hurt her. But let's keep Rich from drinkin'. You go back to your room an' stick with him. I'll mosey around an' listen. See you early in the mornin'."

They parted. Tanner went the rounds of all the places in town where men congregated, and while pretending to be a little loquacious from liquor, he had a keen ear for all the talk. Late at night he returned to his lodgings, stirred to deep resentment, sorry for the loyal Sam Playford, bitter at Lee Tate, thrillingly conscious that he was not alone in his estimate of the latent potentialities of Rich Ames.

Tanner awoke to the onslaught of the merry blacksmith on his door. Late hours and sleeping indoors were not conducive to early awakening. Tanner had breakfast with his friend, accompanied him to the forge, and presently went on into town. The wide street, by day, presented an interesting spectacle. Normally, and even on Saturdays, a few saddle-horses were hitched to the rails, a wagon or two and a buckboard standing in front of the buildings. But today there was not a space left in the main block. The whole population of the Tonto, at least the northern half of the basin, had turned out to see Lil Snell married. For that matter, they turned out for any wedding. Such events were rare in this isolated community.

Troops of children romped up and down the street, unmindful of their Sunday garb; groups of brightly clad women and girls in gaudy colors paraded from store to tavern, with tremendous interest in the big house of James Snell, where the bride and her contingent were supposed to be mysteriously ensconced.

Cappy had neglected to find out from Sam Playford where he and Rich were located, but he expected to see them at one of the few centers of intercourse. He failed, however, and it took him some little while to find their room. At his knock the door was opened by Sam, whose greeting certainly did not lack relief.

"Howdy, boys!" said Tanner, with good cheer, as he entered.

Rich sat on the bed, clean-shaven, his hair wet and plastered down. If Cappy had expected to find him sullen or thick he was vastly mistaken. Never had Rich appeared so handsome, so cool and self-contained. Again Cappy sustained a nervous shock at the subtle possibilities emanating from the scion of old Texas fighting-stock.

"Hello, Cap!" drawled Rich. "We was just debatin' whether to get outside a gallon of red liquor an' take some shots at Jeff Stringer's boots, or keep sober, lay low, an' watch the whole show. What say you?"

"Wal, I incline to the first, but common sense an' regard for Nesta decide me on the last," replied the old trapper, sententiously.

"Shore you'd fetch Nesta in," declared Rich, almost mockingly. "Damn her lovely face!...All right, Cap, we'll stick to your hunch an' stand a hell of a lot from these hombres. But my Gawd! I'd like to start somethin'! Sam heah is rarin' to. First time he's showed any spunk, Cap. He came boltin' in heah, fire in his eye, a chip on his shoulder. An' then he won't tell me nothin'."

"Anythin' rile you, Sam?" queried Cappy, bending speculative eyes upon the young homesteader.

"Hell yes!" retorted Sam. "But no matter. It's not what I'd like to do. Rich an' me are in bad here with all these Tate followers. But for Nesta's sake I think we ought to see nothin', hear nothin', do nothin'.... An' rustle home quick—tonight before all these hombres are drunk."

"Thet's sense, an' we'll act on it," replied Tanner, decisively. "Not one single snack of liquor! Hear that, Rich Ames, you Arizona gopher?"

"Shore I heah you," said Rich, nonchalantly. "The two drinks I had yesterday will last me a spell. Gee! I thought I'd been kicked by a mule."

"Wal, come on, an' act like a couple of moony

youngsters with their pa," said Tanner, in conclusion.

Whereupon they went out, a quiet, amiable-appearing trio, vastly deceiving, according to Cappy's thought. His admiration for Rich Ames grew in leaps and bounds. Any other young buck of the Tonto would get drunk and start trouble. Rich had developed depth and was the more dangerous for it. They made the round of the saloons, lounged in and out of the tavern, made odd purchases in the store, and rubbed elbows with a hundred or more of the male element. They rather avoided the women, more conspicuous and almost as numerous. Playford seemed aloof. In fact, he could not see any women. Rich was cool, careless, easy-going, almost smiling as he passed the girls, many a one of whom cast shy glances at his handsome face.

It was in Turner's hall that Cappy's sharp gaze set upon young men of the Tate faction, whom he had expected to encounter sooner or later. He did not need to be told that Rich had espied them first.

Turner's hall was the largest place of its kind in Shelby. It had been decorated for the ball that night, and feminine hands had assuredly superintended the arrangement of flags, bunting, autumn leaves, and other gay accessories. This hall was used for all public gatherings. Today it served, as on most days, for the gambling prevalent in the Tonto. Turner's bar was in the adjoining room, into which it opened by swinging doors, now concealed by curtains.

Perhaps two dozen were in the hall, most of them gambling, and others looking on. Lee Tate, with a companion Tanner did not recognize, was watching a table at which sat Jeff Stringer, the sheriff, Slink

Tate, and two cowboys whom Cappy knew but could not place.

Cappy would have passed on, had it not been that Rich halted by the table, with Sam following suit.

"Howdy, everybody!" drawled Rich, in his lazy way.

Lee Tate sneered a voiceless response. He was tall, with olive-skinned face scarcely tanned, dark-eyed and dark-haired, and he looked his reputation with the Tonto women. He appeared older than his twenty-two years, and though dissipation stamped his features it had not yet marred their perfection. He wore dark clothes, high-top glossy boots, and spurs.

Slink Tate might not have been a relative of Lee's, he was so different. He had the face of a surly hound. He lifted sunken, gloomy eyes to Ames, and accorded him a curt nod.

"Hullo, Ames!" spoke up Stringer, in dry, caustic tone. "Sober again, hey?"

"Shore am," drawled Ames. "Reckon I want to see awful clear today."

Cappy plucked at Rich's sleeve and attempted gently to start him on the move. This was atmosphere charged with menace. But Rich did not take the hint.

"Powerful interested in weddin's, hey?" queried Stringer, as he slapped down a card.

"Shore am. My sister Nesta is marryin' Sam heah next week an' we want to get some pointers."

"Haw! Haw!" laughed the sheriff, interested out of his gruffness. "Wal, I'm darn glad you've sobered up. Was afraid I'd have to jail you."

"Say, Jeff, there were a dozen cowpunchers

roarin' around last night," declared Rich, sarcastically. "Why didn't you arrest them?"

"Wal, thet's my business. But they wasn't no pertickler menace to the community."

"An' I am? Ahuh. I see the point," returned Ames. "You shore got me figgered correct."

Cappy had taken a swift glance at Lee Tate the instant Ames made his startling statement about Nesta. Whatever had prompted Ames to launch this retort, it certainly reached home. Lee Tate's face turned a burning red of surprise and rage. During the byplay between Ames and Stringer he stared at Playford, slowly paling.

"Say, Playford," he queried, sharply, in the pause that followed Ames' caustic reply to Stringer, "are you really gettin' married next week?"

Sam rose to the occasion. "Sure am," he said, with innocent importance. "Didn't Nesta tell you?— She hasn't set the day, though. I wanted it on Monday an' Rich compromised on Wednesday. But Nesta will likely put it off till Saturday. Worse luck....Are you congratulatin' me, Tate?"

"Not so you'd notice it," returned Tate, sourly, and distortion of passion disfigured his beauty. "No later than last night Nesta Ames swore to me she was breakin' with you."

"Ha! Ha!" laughed Playford, and there was a ring of more than mirth in his voice. "Do you reckon you can make a monkey out of Nesta, like you have so many Tonto girls? Ho! Ho! ... Tate, she was only givin' you a little of your own palaver. Why, Nesta told me she was goin' to."

"The hell you say!" ejaculated Tate, growing purple.

"Yes, the hell I say," repeated Sam, hotly.

"Well, by God! There are some things she *can't* tell you!" burst out Tate, with dark and malignant significance.

Suddenly Ames leaped like a panther to confront Tate.

"There *are*?" he rang out. "But she'll tell *me*, Lee Tate. An' if you've wronged her in word or deed— God have mercy on you."

Tate's expression changed swiftly. Yet his intensity of amaze and rage had scarcely flashed into a gulping recognition of sinister menace when Ames struck him a terrific blow. The blood flew from his smashed nose. He fell over a table, and it, with bottles and chairs, went to the floor with a crash.

Ames backed to the door, his right hand low at his side, his blue eyes magnificently bold and bright with disdain, scorn, hate. First they transfixed Slink Tate, and seeing that he did not intend to accept the challenge, they included the gaping sheriff.

"Jeffries, I'll be waitin' for you over by the jail," he drawled, with the coolest of sarcasm. And the accompanying thin-lipped smile seemed assurance that the sheriff would not be there.

CHAPTER

4

*L*IL SNELL'S marriage took place late in the
afternoon, hours after the time set. Cappy
Tanner heard a woman, who had access to
the Snell household, announce to eager listeners that
the delay was occasioned by the bride-to-be's jealous
frenzy over Nesta Ames' lovely gown. Lil had consumed part of this period in beseeching Nesta to sell
or loan her the gown, and the rest in raging at Nesta,
who was flint to the appeal.

This dramatic interlude, following the assault of
Rich Ames upon Lee Tate, had Shelby by the ears.

Cappy could not get a peep into the crowded
house during the ceremony, but he did ascertain that
Lee Tate was not present. His overweening vanity,
no doubt, would not permit him to show his disfigured face.

"He's hidin' or he's gone home," declared Playford, with great satisfaction. "Say, Rich, but that was an awful sock you gave him."

"Wal, Tate'll never show up to no dance this hyar night," added Cappy.

But Ames made no comment. He was hard to keep track of, and his friends, after following him around long enough to make sure that he did not intend to drink, lost apprehension on this score. Ames, however, left them plenty to be concerned about. He had spent an hour stalking up and down in front of the stone-walled jail, where crowds watched from a respectful distance. But Jeff Stringer did not approach to make the arrest. Cappy's keen ears registered the fact that the majority of Tontonians approved of Rich Ames. He was liked by all except his enemies. The Tates were hated. Jeff Stringer had many things against him, and that day he lost prestige enough to ruin his future aspirations as a sheriff.

Ames could not keep still for long. Naturally he was nervous, watchful, strained. He alone of the three friends forced his way into Snell's residence, not to be a witness of the ceremony, but to see his sister in the now famous gown. And he came out to Cappy and Sam with a soft, beautiful light on his face.

"O Lord! She's ruined us!" he exclaimed. "Sam, you must see her in that dress if you have to kill somebody....An' you, Cappy Tanner—damn your old wooden haid! The mess aboot Nesta was bad enough before you throwed this gauntlet. But, by Heaven; it's worth it!"

The wedding feast and dance began simultaneously, but neither the dance-hall nor the dining-room could accommodate all the guests at one time.

The hour was late when Cappy Tanner saw Nesta Ames in all her glory. Cappy knew her and yet she seemed a stranger. How queer that a mere dress could make such difference! But it did. Nesta was the despair of all the girls present and the object of adoration to the young men. No such beautiful, radiant being had ever before graced a Tonto ball. Lil Snell had been made a bride, but she did not look a happy one. She looked dowdy and dim beside the lovely Nesta. And Nesta utterly outshone Madge Low, a dark, handsome girl reported the sweetheart of Lee Tate.

Cappy's shrewd old eyes saw through the flimsy disguise of these few girls who hated Nesta, just as they had penetrated to the shallow, evil heart of Lee Tate. Their machinations to undo Nesta, for this great occasion at least, had rebounded upon their own heads. Nesta had her revenge. The young men of Shelby and of all the Tonto mobbed her in their demand for dances.

After a dance she led her partner to Rich, Sam, and Cappy, where they watched from the side. Close at hand she appeared to Cappy the old Nesta, only more mature, lovelier, sweeter of smile. She had forgotten every unhappy moment of her life. This ball and her triumph were enough for all the future. Her face shone like a pearl in a glowing light; her eyes seemed to have turned to dark midnight hue made strangely brilliant by stars.

"Sam, you haven't asked me to dance," she said,

with bewildering sweetness. "Nor you, either, Rich Ames."

"Listen to her!" gasped Sam.

"Nesta, you might just as well be in Doubtful Canyon," drawled Rich, but his eyes held a blue worshiping flash.

"Look at 'em comin'," burst out Sam, indicating the tall young men rushing like wind through the cornstalks.

"I've saved two dances," trilled Nesta, gayly, "the next for you, Sam, and then one for Rich."

Under the glamour upon her, and the obsession of passion or love or revenge, whatever it was that radiated from her, Tanner's piercing affection discerned tragedy. He watched her dance with Sam, the cynosure of all eyes, and then with Rich. Since childhood these twins had danced together. They moved as one, Rich the personification of lithe masculine grace, and Nesta, her heavy-lidded eyes dreaming, dark, seeing nothing, lost in the music and rhythm of the dance.

Cappy Tanner left the hall and wended a sorrowful way to his lodgings. He saw through the hour to unknown calamity. Next morning, an hour after the cold gray dawn broke, he was riding alone back to Mescal Ridge.

Nesta, too, returned late that day, with Sam and Rich, and her mother accompanied by the twins, all weary and spent. Cappy saw them for only a few moments. But next day the serene, even tenor of life at Mescal Ridge seemed to have reinstated itself. Cappy welcomed it, though he sensed it as a lull before a storm.

"Cap, shore I'm drunk or dreamin'," said Rich, when Cappy presented himself at the cabin.

"Wal, you do look wild, but you ain't drunk," rejoined Tanner.

"Nesta came home like a lamb. She's promised to marry Sam, if we'll give her a little time. She's queer. The fire an' glory of her seem daid. It clean stumps me."

"Wal, thet weddin' an' dance would have taken the starch out of most girls—if they'd been Nesta. ...I'm plumb curious. Did she find out you punched Lee Tate's nose into a sausage?"

"Did she? Shore!...The dance lasted all night. Nesta asked Sam an' me to stay. In the mawnin' she cut the Snell outfit. An' as she came out with her things, who should bob up but Lee Tate. He shore tried to detain her, talkin' low. She looked at his busted face an' laughed. By thunder! My blood run cold, then hot. She pulled her sleeve away from him as if he was dirt. An' she swept by, her eyes ablaze, her haid up....An' I reckon that's aboot all, Cappy."

"Wal, wal! Thet clean stumps *me!*" ejaculated Tanner, stroking his beard. "Who'n'll can savvy a woman?—But I say, watch her close."

An astounding thing to Tanner was the way Playford's boast to Lee Tate bade fair to turn into reality. Nesta actually did consent to be married that week.

Tanner went several times to the Ames cabin, but only once did he see Nesta. Then he was shocked. She seemed infinitely removed from the glorious Nesta of the dance at Shelby. She was too apathetic, too yielding, too haunted. Tanner imagined she had resigned herself to a situation which her heart sanctioned, but her conscience opposed.

Sam Playford hung around the cabin apparently in a trance. Mrs. Ames' cheerful and practical preparations for Nesta's marriage augured well for her subtle waiving of a possible slip between the cup and the lip. But she might have known more about Nesta than anyone else. Rich showed increasing strain. He, too, hung around in sight of the cabin. About the only work Tanner saw him apply himself to was chopping wood, which he did desultorily.

Tanner kept to himself for a couple of days forcing himself to necessary labor, if he intended to spend a winter trapping. He would be glad when this marriage business was over. Mescal and Manzanita sought him out the second day, eager to impart the latest news. Nesta did not want to go to Shelby to be married and Sam had ridden in to have the parson come to Mescal Ridge on Saturday.

Indian summer lingered, though it was past the middle of November. The old trapper could not help being aware of the still, smoky blue days, the warmth of sun, the late-blooming asters, the lonesome caw of crow and the melancholy note of thrush, the slumberous waiting solitude.

Saturday—Nesta Ames' wedding day—dawned at last, the warmest, purplest, and most beautiful of those waning summer days. Cappy had vaguely imagined that it never would come. Even now, as he donned his best garb to see Nesta married, he could not drive away a strange presentiment. He had seen a shadow in Nesta's eyes and it had spread to his consciousness.

When Cappy emerged from the gulch into the Mescal Ridge trail he espied half a dozen horses hitched under the three spruces beside the Ames cabin.

A clip-clop of hoofs at a trot sounded up the trail. Sam Playford emerged from the wall of green, and his garb shone bright against that background.

Cappy essayed a merry halloo to Sam, but a piercing scream cut it short.

"What the hell?" ejaculated the trapper. Could that have been Mescal's high-pitched shrill laughter? Playford had checked his horse. He had heard. Suddenly with a shout he leaped out of his saddle and plunged down over the rocky bank.

Then Cappy, thus directed, saw a moving object along the shore of Rock Pool, coming around the huge boulder. Cappy stared, while all his senses save sight seemed held in abeyance. Something flashed silvery in the sunlight. He made out Rich Ames carrying a heavy burden up from the creek. Then he saw Playford crashing through the willows, thumping over the rocks. Cappy's heart gave a great leap, then sank like lead. In a panic he rushed at the declivity below the trail. But as he could not get down there he ran up to where Playford had gone over. His frantic haste caused him to stumble and fall headlong. Jarring contact with rocks, furious threshing into brush, caused no pain he was conscious of. Scrambling up, he hurried across the rough bench, arriving at the sycamores panting, so spent he could not speak.

Nesta Ames leaned back against a tree trunk,

disheveled, limp as a sack, wet from her waist down. A terrible dark blaze burned in her eyes. Playford knelt beside her, wringing his hands, his face ashen.

Rich's back, as he stood bowed as if under a tremendous burden, made Tanner not want to see his face.

"I saw the parson," Nesta was saying. "I lost my nerve. . . . I couldn't go on with the wedding."

Tanner's relief to see her alive, hear her voice, realize she was unhurt, was so great that it seemed the shame and tragedy of her avowal were as nothing. He went forward, to drop on one knee on the other side of Nesta, and take her limp cold hand.

"Lass—lass—" he began huskily, in broken accents.

"Shore that's plain. But *why?*" demanded the brother, grim and hard. Tanner felt the urge to look at him, but had not the courage yet.

Nesta looked at him with unfathomable eyes. She might have lost her courage when it came to the marriage, but she had no fear of Rich, no shame in facing him! She seemed beyond both. Her hand shook, her full bosom rose and fell. Her red lips set in a bitter resolute line.

"Didn't you try to drown yourself?" queried Rich, harshly.

"Do you think I was trying to baptize myself?" she countered, scornfully, her voice gathering strength.

"Answer me!" he ordered. "You slipped out. I saw you. I ran over heah. . . . An' I caught you tryin' to make away with yourself. Didn't I?"

"You shore did," she replied, with steely ring of

voice. "But you might have saved yourself the trouble—and me more than you can guess."

"Tell me why," went on Rich, hoarsely.

"I couldn't go through with it. I wanted to. I hoped to make Sam happy. I loved him.... But I couldn't marry him."

"*Why?*"

"I wronged Sam. I was untrue to him.... Mother wanted me to marry him and keep it secret. But I intended to tell him—soon as I—was his wife."

"How'd you wrong him?"

"I got   mixed up with Lee Tate."

"*Mixed up!* ... Ahuh. You shore talk queer.... Nesta Ames, what you mean—mixed up?"

"It couldn't have been worse," she returned, mournfully.

Rich violently shook his whole supple frame, as if to throw off an enmeshing net. He plumped down on both knees at Nesta's feet and plucked at them with nerveless hands. His face was convulsed in agony.

"I thought I could go on with it," continued Nesta, simply. "I really do love Sam.... More a hundred times than that devil. I didn't mean to be a false wife. I'd have told Sam. And I knew he'd forgive. ... But I wilted—when I found out I was going to have a baby."

"*O my Gawd!*" cried Rich, and he fell forward on his face, to dig his brown hands deep into the moss, to beat the ground with his feet.

Playford flung an arm over his twitching face. Nesta gazed from him to Rich, and then to Tanner.

"Cappy, it's—horrible!" she whispered. "If he'd only let me—drown myself."

"Lass, thet wouldn't help none," said the trapper, huskily. "It's hell on the boys—but I reckon—all right with me."

Rich Ames shuddered. He then seemed to freeze. When he arose Tanner could not bear to look at his face.

"Nesta, I reckon I can kill you," he said, in a singularly cold and bitter voice.

"I wish you would, Rich," she burst out, with a first show of passion. "Then I'd not have it—on my soul....For I cain't live. I wouldn't make way with the baby—I cain't live through it, Rich!"

"By Gawd! you won't, if you were to blame!"

"Of course I was. How could any girl be such—such an idiot—unless she were to blame? But I swear to you, Rich, and to Heaven—that I never knew it would go so far."

"You loved this skunk Tate?" demanded Ames, stridently, as he leaned over her, his jaw protruding.

"No!—No!" she cried, wildly. "That's the horror of it....But I was fascinated ...then—afterward—he had some power over me. I never broke it till the mawnin' after the dance....Oh, too late—too late!"

Tanner found his voice and besought Ames to hear Nesta's story. "Boy," he concluded, "you're pronouncin' judgment too soon."

"Nesta, tell us," begged Playford. "I can't think of you—as bad....But no matter. Tell the truth. We three will find a way out for you."

"Poor Sam!" she whispered, lifting her hand to

touch him. "I must be bad. I *am* bad. And there's no way out for me."

Rich knelt again, this time closer to her.

"Tate won't marry you?" he asked, huskily.

"I don't know. But even if he would, I'd never—never have him."

"Well, you stump me, Nesta Ames," said Rich, throwing up his hands. "Do as Sam wants. Tell us the truth."

"Oh, it's miserable enough," began Nesta, her eyes brooding and somber. "I never loved Lee Tate. But I always felt queer when he looked at me—talked to me—which he came to do this last year.... It all must be because of Madge Low and Lil Snell. Madge is his girl now and Lil used to be. I didn't know till lately how thick he was with them. Madge was a cat, and Lil was jealous of me. They made me so furious I could have killed them. I swore I'd show them I was not a gawky country jake. They said Lee was playing with me. But they fixed it many times when he could see me. I know now they put the job up on me.... Well, it began then. I flirted with him. But I—I didn't give in to him—let him touch me—or kiss me... until one day Lil double-crossed me—rode off and left me with him alone.... He dragged me off my horse—threw me into a pine thicket—and—and had his way.... After that I hated him—but still I couldn't help myself. I didn't want to see him—I avoided him—but when he found me I—I couldn't help myself.... He was like a snake.... That night at the dance I woke up. All I had ever wanted was to show that nasty, dirty Madge Low I wouldn't wipe my boots on her. And Lil Snell—too! They helped Lee Tate ruin me. I saw it. I won Lee from them and their other beaus. I had Lil's husband running after me as hard as any of them.... That was enough. I saw my mistake—the awful cost. Before I left Shelby I laughed in Lee Tate's face—I told him I despised him—would never look at him again. But I lied. I knew his power over me—that he could drag me down again. Still I came home to Sam—to hope and fight.... Then I found out aboot the baby coming. It was—all too—late.... When I—saw the parson coming—I ran to—drown myself."

Playford reached long arms for Nesta, and kneeling still, he lifted her against him.

"Nesta, it's not too late," he said, poignantly. "You poor mad little girl!—All for vanity!—I'll stick to you. We'll never let anyone know."

"*Sam!*...You'd marry me—now?" she wailed, all defiance and bitterness gone from her.

"Yes. We'll go over to the cabin, an' have the weddin'—same as we planned."

"No, no," she implored, suddenly bereft of the hopeless resignation that had been her anchor.

"But, Nesta, you said you loved me?" went on Sam, tenderly.

"Oh, I do—I do!...I never stopped loving you. ...But I cain't risk this!—O my God—if I only dared!"

Rich Ames reached a long arm, to catch her quivering shoulder and turn her face from Playford's breast.

"Why don't you dare?" he flung at her, sharply. "Sam's big an' fine. He's got real love. No one will ever know. Me an' Cappy will keep your secret. The baby will be an Ames.—Why don't you dare?"

Tanner never before gazed upon such woe as wrung his heart then. Nesta could not meet her brother's flaming eyes; she turned from the staunch Playford. And it was to Tanner that she whispered piteously:

"Cappy—he'd hound me—catch me alone some day—"

Tanner choked with misery. He heard Playford sob. But Ames bent over his sister:

"Never in this world, Nesta dear," he drawled, with his old slow, cool speech.

"*Rich!*"

"You heahed me. Come, brace up. Help her on her feet, Sam.... You'll go back home. An' listen. Nesta fell in the creek. An', Sam, you an' Cappy happened along. Nesta was scared. She's pretty shaky. But you'll go on with the weddin'."

"*Rich!*" cried Nesta.

"You heah me, Sam?"

"I ain't deaf, pard," replied Playford, his voice gruff with emotion.

"You heah me, Cap?" went on Ames, inexorably.

"Shore do, lad, an' I'm obeyin' pronto," replied the trapper, as he helped Sam support the trembling girl.

"Nesta, I won't be heah to see you married," went on Ames. There were finality and farewell in his words, a strange note, scarcely tenderness. He made no move to kiss her, touch her, though her fluttering hands were outstretched. "But I wish you happiness with Sam—an' shore, if you're good to him, it'll come some day."

"*Rich!*" she screamed, but it might as well have been to the empty air.

News arrived post haste next day at Mescal Ridge. The rider, a stranger to Tanner, dashed in on a froth-lathered horse, and slid off.

"Howdy!" he said. "Come 'way from the cabin. I got a word for you."

Mrs. Ames, who had been talking to the trapper, after one look at the grave-faced visitor, hurried into the living-room, drawing the wide-eyed twins with her.

"Reckon you're Tanner?" the man interrogated, when they had reached the spruces.

"Reckon I am," replied Cappy, gloomily, in a tone that signified that he wished he could deny his name.

"Where's young Playford?"

"Gone up to his homestead with his wife. They was married yesterday."

"Glad to hear it. I didn't cotton to this job. An' you'll have to tell them."

"Ahuh.... What'll I tell?"

"Ames killed Lee Tate last evenin' an' Jeff Stringer. Shot Slink Tate up bad, too, but he'll recover."

"Tate—an' Stringer—eh?" queried Tanner, with a hoarse little catch of breath between the words. "Wal, thet's awful bad news.... How'd it happen?"

"Nobody knows jest how, but they seen it," replied the rider, wiping his sweaty face.

"Did you?"

"I should smile I did."

"Even break?"

"Shore. Couldn't hev been no evener."

"Wal, thet's good, anyhow....How'd the town take it?"

"Most folks kept their mouths shet, as is a wise habit in the Tonto. But it was easy to get the general opinion. Shelby needed a new sheriff, anyhow. Lee Tate wasn't worth killin', so he was no great loss. There's not many, though, prayin' fer Slink Tate to get well."

"Ahuh. But you said he would?"

"Shore. He won't be no good for a while, mebbe never, but he'll come out of thet shootin' scrape."

"How about—young Ames?" asked Tanner, finding the query most difficult to enunciate.

"Never touched him. He fooled them aplenty an' throwed the slickest gun I've seen these many moons."

"Wal, suppose you tell me all about it, an' then we'll go up to my cabin an' have a drink."

"Aw, don't care if I do. An' let's stroll along right now....I happened to run into Ames last evenin' before dark. He was sober as a judge. After the shootin' there was some figgerin'. No one seen Ames take a drink. Shore he might hev had a bottle on him. But most of us old heads doubt thet. He had dinner at the tavern an' loafed around. Unsociable, though. Jed Lane seen him not five minutes before the fight an' he was sober *then*, too....Wal, I was in Turner's an' the hall was jammed. But I didn't happen to be gamblin'. I was talkin' to old Scotty about my prospect when Ames blew in. Funny thing. I noticed fust off thet though he looked staggerin' drunk his face was white. An' I'd swear no man full of liquor ever had eyes like his. He spotted the two Tates an' Stringer playin' cairds with two men from Globe. It was a stiff game an' there was a crowd watchin' the play. It struck me after thet Ames knowed these men were in there. He swaggered around, lurched ag'in' their table, an' made them sorer'n hell. But nothin' come of thet. Then he wanted to set in the game. They didn't want him an' thet riled him. Plain to me Ames wasn't drunk, though he fooled them fellars, an' he aimed to start a fight.

"'Git out of hyar or I'll run you in!' yelled Stringer, who was a loser in the game, an' pretty testy.

"'Run me in, you————four-flush sheriff. Jes' try it,' said Ames. But Stringer kept his seat, fumin'. He didn't want no mix with Ames.

"Wal, he stood around watchin', an' damn me if he didn't ketch Lee Tate tryin' to cheat. Quick as lightnin' he nailed his hand—an' showed Tate's trick. Clumsy holdin' out of aces! Tate jumped up, roarin'. He figgered Ames was too drunk to fight, anyway, an' he was hot-tempered. He called Ames a lot of hard names, which were shore sent back, with some added.... Wal, the crowd got interested, an' quiet all around. Reckon nobody figgered anythin' but mebbe a little fist fight.

"Slink Tate kept pullin' Lee down in his seat an' Lee kept jumpin' up, gettin' madder all the time. They got to swingin' at each other, an' it's a notion of mine thet Ames didn't punch Stringer by accident. Stringer got up, an' pullin' his gun he swung it by the barrel.

"'Ames, I'll knock you cold an' throw you in jail—if you don't get out.'

"Wal, Ames was leanin' over, leerin' at Stringer,

callin' him a yellow crooked sheriff, when Lee Tate soaked him on the side of the head. Ames wasn't actin' when he fell. The crowd roared.

"Then Tate, bold as a lion now, went after his gun.... My Gawd! but it happened quick. Right from the floor! Ames drawed. But I seen only the flashes of his gun. Three shots, quicker'n lightnin'. Slink Tate's gun went off in the air as he was saggin'. Lee screamed an' grabbed his belly. Stringer dropped like a log.... You ought to have seen thet crowd split an' rush, after the danger was over.

"Ames jumped up like a cat. Drunk? I should say not. With his smokin' gun out he lifted a foot an' shoved Lee Tate off the table, where he hung, bellerin'. Tate flopped to the floor on his back. His hands, drippin' red, flung up. Ames looked to see if he was done fer. Anyone could have seen thet.

"'Tate, heah's to your Arizona,' says Ames.

"Next he had a look at the other two. Slink 'peared a goner, an' Stringer had been shot through the heart. Lee Tate half sat up, a sickenin' sight. Then Ames, shovin' him down with a slow deliberate boot, sheathed his gun an' went out."

S PRING had come to the Wyoming valley where the Wind River wound its shining way between the soaring ranges of snow-crowned peaks.

The eagle from his lonely crag could gaze down upon thousands of cattle, and if he flew across the wide valley, or soared above the center of its long length, from end to end, he could have seen the rolling grassy ridges, the green bottom lands and the vast levels, all dotted with straggling herds.

It was the heyday of the rancher, and therefore that of the rustler, the horse-thief, and the cowboy. Up in the wild notch where the Gros Ventre River crossed from the head of the Wind River Range, or where the Snake River cut through the Teton Range, the Wind River gang had their rendezvous. Down in

Utah, in the canyon fastnesses of the Green River, hid the outlaws of Robbers Roost and the Hole in the Wall. These desperadoes sometimes rode far north along the winding Green River, across the Union Pacific Railroad, to the rich ranch lands of the Wind River Valley. These gangs engaged in conflict with one another more often than with the cowboy posses.

The leagues of this vast area were many, the grass and water abundant, the cattle numberless. But the small homesteader was not welcomed; the stranger without a horse as good as damned. The grub-line riding cowboy was received, but never trusted till he had proved his worth. No good rider ever wanted for a job in that country.

The ranches lay far apart, a day's journey sometimes from one another, yet this was too close. There was not a drift fence in all the Wind River Valley.

The range of Crow Grieve had no northern boundary short of the mountains, but its southern lines were sharply defined by the East Fork of the Green on one side and Wind River on the other. They merged where the rivers joined.

Here, perhaps, was the most beautiful location for a ranch in all that country. Kit Carson, guide for Fremont on his exploring expedition, made camp there in the early days when the buffalo blackened the valley.

The ranch house stood on a high point above the shining rivers where they met. Here the ubiquitous cottonwood trees had been superseded by pines. The green-and-yellow range rolled downhill to the south, and to the north waved by endless slope and swale up and ever upward toward the black Wind River Mountains. Westward, across the dim blue void, the grand Tetons rose white-toothed against the sky.

One day in May the cowboy outfit of Crow Grieve straggled back to the ranch, in twos and threes, some ahead of the chuck-wagon, and others behind. They were returning from Granger, a shipping point on the railroad, where, following the spring round-up— Grieve had driven three thousand head of cattle. It had been a hard drive, ending in a carouse and the fights, under such circumstances, as common to cowboys as any of their habits. They had departed twenty-one strong, and had returned minus several comrades. No contingent of range hands, after a big drive and the accumulation of a winter's wages, ever reached the home ranch intact. Two of Grieve's boys would never ride again. Others had drifted. They veered like the wind, these fire-spirited striplings of the ranges. In this case, after being drunk for a week and then on horseback for another, the main body reached what they called home, sober, broke, several of them crippled, many of them bruised, all of them weary, yet gay as larks. Nothing mattered to the cowboy of that period, except his status with his fellows.

Grieve's quarters for cowboys were famous throughout Wyoming and farther still. The mess cabin had a fine location, far from the ranch house, adjacent to scattered pines, and from it extended a line of small bunk-houses, tiny cabins, each with fireplace, two bunks, and running water. Beyond spread the corrals, the barns, the grain-sheds, the black-smith shop, and other accessories to a great ranch.

Grieve controlled, if he did not own outright, a hundred thousand acres.

Lany Price, cowboy of nineteen, tanned and tawny, comely of face, rode in far ahead of Grieve's outfit. He had reason to hurry. Absence from the ranch had not been to his liking. His wild comrades had gotten him drunk for the first time. There was someone at the ranch he wanted to tell about that, to make excuses for himself.

The door of his bunk-house stood open. A heavy silver-mounted saddle and a neatly folded saddle-blanket lay against the wall. A tall rider in high boots appeared in the doorway.

"Howdy!" he said, pleasantly. "There wasn't anybody heah, so I made myself at home."

"Howdy, stranger!" returned Lany, inclined to be irritated, not that he felt anything but welcome for a visitor, but because he had a reason for wanting to be alone, and an errand he preferred no one to see him perform. But after a second look at the stranger the irritation left him.

"Reckon your outfit is comin' in?" he asked in a slow drawl that made Lany take him for a Texan.

"Yep. Strung out for miles. Our chuck-wagon will beat most of them in. I rustled along. Are you hungry?"

"Tolerable."

"Just ridin' by or aimin' to stop?"

"Reckon I'll stay if I can get a job."

"Spread out, then. Crow takes every rider on, which ain't sayin' he'll last long."

"Ahuh. I heah Crow Grieve is a hard boss. Never hires a foreman. Is that correct?"

"You bet it is. He's bad medicine any time, but after bein' drunk for a week he's hell on stilts."

"Drinkin' rancher, eh? Just sociable-like, or does he like red liquor?"

"Stranger, you're new in these parts," returned Price as he dismounted and unbuckled the saddle cinch.

"Shore am. Wyomin' is aboot the only range I haven't ridden these last six years."

"Where you from?"

"Where'd you say?"

"Texas."

"I was born in Texas, but left when I was a boy."

"My handle's Lany Price. What'd you say yours was?"

"Reckon I didn't say yet," drawled the other.

"So I noticed. Excuse my curiosity," rejoined Lany, with a keen cowboy's appreciative glance at his visitor. He liked his looks, yet had reason to resent this newcomer. "Maybe you happen to be related to Grieve's wife? She's from the South."

"No. So he's married?"

"Yep," said Price, with unconscious relief. "Been married a couple of years. Amy—er—Mrs. Grieve," he corrected, hastily, "is much younger. She's just my age. Nineteen....They have a baby."

"How old is Crow Grieve?"

"Between thirty an' forty somewhere....Well, stranger, I'm seein' after my horse. If you don't want to look around, just make yourself at home."

The stranger contented himself with sitting on a bench against the wall while he looked across the river at the far-flung vista, with eyes that seemed to see far beyond. Presently young Price returned, evidently in a hurry.

"Say, is that your horse in the first corral there?" he queried.

"Yes. Like him?"

"You better ride on, stranger, if you love that horse. What with this outfit of cowpunchers an' the Wind River gang you'll sure lose him."

The rider smiled as if pleased at the covert compliment, but he did not reply. Price went into the bunk-house, to emerge rather hurriedly, carrying a packet under his coat, something he evidently wished to conceal.

"Some of the outfit comin' now," he said, pointing down the wide lane past the corral. "Take them as they come, stranger, an' be mild. Savvy?" Then he strode off toward the ranch house, shining white through the green of trees.

The stranger lounged on the bench, watching the riders straggle in. Apparently to his casual interest these cowboys presented nothing striking. Soon the two-team chuck-wagon rolled by, to be brought to a halt in front of the mess-cabin. More riders put in an appearance down the lane, and by the time Price returned there was a line of saddle-horses, pack-horses, and noisy cowboys all along the front of the bunk-houses.

"Hey, Lany," called a lanky red-faced fellow, pausing with rope in his hands, "is thet thar your sister's sweetheart come visitin'?"

"Hey, Red, you better not get funny," replied Lany, in cheerful banter.

That broke the ice and other sallies intended to

be witty were forthcoming from each side of Price's bunk-house.

"Ho, cowboy, who's the white-headed gent?"

"There's a wild cowpuncher a-lookin' fer me."

"This hyar is Wyomin', stranger, an' we don't see your hoss."

"I am a wanderin' cowboy," sang out a lusty-lunged rider. "From ranch to ranch I roam. At every ranch when welcome, I make myself at home."

Another cowboy intoned in answer:

> "My parents reared me ten-der-lee;
> They had no child but me,
> But I was bent on ramblin'
> An' lit out for the U Bar E."

Price sat down beside his guest and laughed as he named his comrades. "Some pretty decent boys, an' some hell's rattlers, too. Did you ever hear of Slim Blue?"

"Reckon I have," replied the other, with a quiet smile.

"He'll make it hot for you, an' if he keeps on makin' it hotter you can swear he likes you. But don't let on. An' there's Blab McKinney. He's bad stuff any time, but just now he's mean. Got burned in a gun-fight at Granger."

"I know Mac. But you needn't let on. Did he hurt some hombre?"

"Hurt? He damn near killed two fellars. So you know Blab? That's interestin'."

The line of cowboys below Price's bunk-house led their horses off toward the corrals but those above had to pass it, and they were nothing if not curious about the newcomer. Each one emitted some characteristic remark, which brought only a slight pleasant smile to the stranger's keen tanned face. The last cowboy stalked up, bow-legged, dusty, with jangling spurs. He had a lithe slim figure, striking because it gave the impression of strength and suppleness not usual in a man so thin.

"Here's Slim Blue," whispered Lany Price. "He always wears a blue shirt. Whatever you do now, don't dodge!"

Blue possessed a remarkable face. It resembled a desert that had been scoured by fire, avalanche, lightning, rain, and wind. He was so burdened with rider's paraphernalia that he had only a thumb free to indicate the quiet figure sitting next to Price.

"Lany, has your paw come to see you?" he queried.

"No. Stranger blowed in," replied Price.

"Good day, Mister Blue," spoke up this stranger, pleasantly.

"Who'n hell told you to call me Mister Blue?" demanded the cowboy, belligerently.

"Nobody. It's your shirt. I saw you comin' four miles away."

"Is thet so?" queried Blue, sarcastically. "So you're *thet* sharp-sighted, huh? Wal, now, how good can you see with one eye swelled shut?"

The stranger leaned back with his sinewy brown hands clasping one knee. His wonderful eyes, a flashing blue, seemed to bear out his assertion.

"Cowboy, see heah," he drawled, in a lazy, cool way, most deceptive. "You've had a long drill, an' I reckon you're weak in more'n your mind. Better get some nourishin' food under your belt an' a night's rest before you talk that way to *me*."

Blue's jaw dropped. His face could not have grown any redder, so it was impossible to tell whether this remark had infuriated or confused him.

"Much obliged, stranger," he replied, curtly. "You're orful considerate. But I jest can't take all thet advice. I'll be back to ask you suthin'."

The cowboy ahead of Blue had halted to listen to this colloquy. Facing ahead, he yelled: "Whoopee! Nuthin' goin' to happen atall! Aw no!"

They hobbled along to the corrals. Lany Price turned speculative eyes upon the stranger.

"Excuse me if I got you wrong, stranger," he said, apologetically.

"Shore. Reckon I've made mistakes," was the smiling reply.

"It'd be great if Slim Blue has made one an' I'm darned if it don't look like he has," replied Price.

"Mebbe he has. It happens now an' then. How aboot this Slim Blue? He struck me all right."

"As good a fellar as you'd meet in a week's ridin'. Slim's just cantankerous. He got licked in Granger. An' he's always cross when we get home. Always jumps every new rider."

"Ahuh. I've met up with a heap of his kind. Do you want to risk this heah courtesy you're showin' me? You needn't, you know. It's shore decent of you. I know this game. An' if I didn't get a place with Grieve you'd come in for some cussin'."

Young Price regarded his interrogator with keener interest, and after a moment's study he replied: "I'm not any too—too well liked. You see, the boss an'—an' his wife have been pretty nice to me, an' that's made some of the outfit sore. But I'll risk makin' them sorer."

"No, you won't, La—what'd you say your name was?"

"Lany. Lany Price."

"Well, Lany, you leave me to my fate," replied the stranger, ruefully. "But so far as Slim Blue is concerned, you shore want to be around when he comes back."

"I'm goin' to. An' I reckon, if you'll let me, I'll take a chance on standin' by you."

"Thanks, Lany. But you just wait."

Some time later the strange rider, having patrolled a beat in front of the corrals for a reasonable time, approached the mess-house, where on the wide comfortable porch a dozen or more cowboys lounged. They quickened as he stalked up, nonchalant, with that pensive little smile. He made a singularly striking figure.

"Do you-all reckon I'll get thrown out askin' for a meal heah?" he queried, drawling the words.

The cowboys stared. That question might be taken for insolence.

"See hyar, Texan, air you insultin' Wyomin'?" asked a stalwart rider.

"No offense. But course I cain't tell. I was just hopin' you're not all like Slim Blue."

"Haw! Haw! An' why're you hopin' thet?"

"Well, I never met no riders like him. Asked me

if I could see to shoot with one eye swelled shut....
He scared me terrible."

"Huh, you look it, stranger," replied the big cowboy, shortly.

The stranger approached the open door and
called:

"Hey, cook, can a poor rider who's starved an'
broke get a feed heah?"

"You bet. When I yell just knock over some of
them hawgs an' come a-runnin'," replied the cook.

"Hyar comes Slim now," remarked one of the
loungers. "Gee! ain't he sassy-lookin'?"

The stranger went forward to the front of the
porch, stepped off, and as he sat down his gun
bumped heavily upon the wood. Far down the road
behind Blue limped another cowboy, coming slowly.

Slim Blue, espying the stranger, swerved out and
came round the porch to confront him. Then the
loungers on the porch sat up with interest.

"Stranger, I reckoned you'd be gone," announced Blue.

"Nope. I'm powerful hungry, an' the cook told
me I could get a feed heah if I'd knock over a couple
of the hawgs."

"Wal, I'm orful sorry,'cause you won't be able to
eat very good—with *two* eyes swelled shet," said
Blue.

"You won't take any advice?" drawled the
stranger as he stood up.

"Not from any tidy, clean, pretty strangers. Jest
goes ag'in' the grain."

"Too bad. But I reckon a fellow ridin' into
Wyomin' ought to expect worse. I'm shore apprecia-

tin' that you left off your gun," replied the stranger as he unbuckled his belt, heavy with gun and shells. He laid this on the porch, and the gun-sheath, old and black, bore a letter A in silver.

"Slim," said one of the cowboys, "your personal dislikes ain't nobody's bizness, but it riles us to have you give Wyomin' a black eye."

The stranger stepped out from the porch and throwing aside his sombrero, thus disclosing a handsome head of light shiny hair, he said: "Blue, I've heard of you."

"Is thet so? Wal, you're actin' damn queer, then," growled Slim.

"Shore is one of the happiest moments of my life," drawled the rider.

Blue, swinging his fists, rushed in. The rider suddenly moved with incredible swiftness to one side. His left arm shot out and his fist took Blue over the eye in a solid thump that all but upset him. Then the rider, swinging round with his right, took the cowboy squarely in the abdomen with a blow that sounded like a loud *bamm*.

Blue, his face swiftly changed into one of awful contortion, began to sink down, his hands pressed to his body, his wide-open mouth issuing his expelled breath in one loud explosion.

The cowboys yelled in glee. Blue sank to his knees. Lany Price, standing on the edge of the porch, called low: "Look out! Here comes MacKinney. He's Slim's pard."

Just then the last cowboy arrived on the scene. His Irish name suited the forceful step, the honest ugly face, the gray eyes wide and sharp upon his friend Blue. Manifestly he had hardly taken a look at the stranger.

"Slim, air yez laffin' or croyin'?" he demanded, plainly perplexed. Blue evidently heard, but could not get breath enough to reply.

"Blab, he's prayin'," spoke up the big cowboy from the porch. "Prayin' the Lord to forgive his on-civil tongue."

"Wot's happened?" flashed MacKinney, plainly nettled by the remark and the laugh following.

"Nuthin'. The strange gent jest slugged Slim in the gizzard."

Then MacKinney fastened those flaring gray eyes upon the stranger. They opened wider. They stared. They popped. His whole expression suddenly changed to one of incredulous joyous recognition.

"Howdy, Mac!" drawled the stranger.

"Fer the luv of Heaven!" burst out MacKinney. "It ain't *you*?"

"Shore is, Mac. An' plumb glad to see you."

"*Arizona Ames!*" ejaculated MacKinney, verifying a recognition that did not seem credible. And he rushed to embrace the stranger in a manner that harmonized with his speech. "Of all the surprises, this shure is the best. Why, mon, I thot you was dead."

"No, Mac. I'm still tolerable alive."

MacKinney, with his arm round Ames' shoulder, addressed the amazed group on the porch. "Fellars, meet my old pard, Arizona Ames. Shure you all rim-imber me tellin' about him? When I rode fer Rankin—with the toughest outfit that ever stretched leather."

"Arizona Ames!" ejaculated a cowboy.

"Wal, Blab, we sure do."

"Howdy, Ames! I reckon you ain't sich a stranger as Slim took you fer."

That latter remark caused MacKinney to wheel. There knelt Blue, still ludicrous, but recovering.

"Wot the hell, Slim? I forgot you."

Slim shook his fist at Ames. "Y-you k-kicked me—in—the belly," he gasped.

"No, Slim," replied Ames. "Shore I only gave you a little tap on the knob. An' then a punch where you're weak. Didn't I say you needed some nourishment?"

Lany Price called out, "Here comes the boss."

Little attention did anyone else give the approaching buckboard.

"Y'u—did," replied Blue. "But lickin' me—ain't no satisfaction.—Blab, I'm requirin' yore gun."

"My Gawd! Slim, you're crazy," broke out MacKinney, suddenly recovering. "You don't want to try to throw a gun on this fellar!"

"The hell you say. I reckon I do."

"But, mon, this is an old pard of mine," protested MacKinney.

"Orful sorry," returned Blue, stubbornly, though he seemed impressed. And he got up. "You've double-crossed me, fer you swore I was yore only pard."

"Shure I did. But, Slim, this was years ago. I thought he was dead."

"Wal, it's orful sad, when two old pards gits reunited like thet. But you jest won't only think it about him this time. You'll know."

"But, Slim, did you hear who this fellar is?"

"No. An' I don't care a damn. He said my mind was weak—"

"It shore is."

"Wal, if it'll gall you so to lose this ole pard, make him apologize," rejoined Blue, blusteringly.

Ames, with a winning smile, held out his hand. "Shore I apologize. I was only foolin'. I had to say somethin', didn't I?"

"You must hev felt thet way," said Blue, reluctantly shaking hands. "But I'll overlook it.... So you're an old pard of Mac's?"

"Glad to say I am."

"Wal, Mac never had but one pard, besides me, thet was wuth a damn, an' he got shot. So I reckon I ain't jealous. What's yore name?"

"Ames," drawled the rider.

"*Ames?* ... Not thet Arizonie pard?"

"Shore am, Slim."

Whereupon Slim Blue turned to MacKinney and roundly cursed him. "——, you'd let me commit suicide!"

The buckboard with its two occupants halted opposite the cowboys, and a man of fine physique jumped out. He was under forty, dark-skinned, with hair and eyes as black as the wing of a crow. His face showed the blotches of recent dissipation. He had a bold, virile presence.

"What's goin' on here?" he demanded, in a loud, authoritative voice.

Only then did the three cowboys become aware of his advent on the scene.

"Howdy, boss!" said Blue, in a tone that Ames did not miss.

"You been fightin'?"

"Nope, not me, boss. I only got hit."

"A blind man could see that. Your eye's all swelled up. Who hit you?"

"Wal, boss, as I was in the wrong an' got my just deserts, I reckon thet doesn't make any difference, does it?"

Ames took a forward step. "You're the rancher, Grieve?" he asked.

"Yes. I don't recollect seein' you before."

"Hardly. I'm a stranger in Wyomin'," returned Ames, quietly. "I rode in today, an' was waitin' around when your outfit came. Blue, heah, wanted a couple of punches at me—cowboy-like—you know. I accommodated him. That's all, sir. No hard feelin's."

"I'm glad somebody rode in with the nerve to punch him. . . . Were you waitin' round to see the range boss?"

"Yes, sir."

"Well, that's me. I don't run a foreman. What you want—a job ridin'?"

"Shore do, if you have one."

"You're hired. Report to me for orders," rejoined Grieve, brusquely, turning on his heel.

"Hould on, boss," broke in MacKinney. "Shure you'll loike to hear this is an ould pard of mine?"

"Mac, I suppose that'd be a reference, if I needed one. But I never care what a cowpuncher has done or been, or whose friend he is. All that counts with me is how he works for me."

"All the same, boss, you shure ought to know this pard of mine is Arizona Ames," continued MacKinney, stubbornly.

"*What?*" exclaimed Grieve, his single query coming like a bullet. His crow-black eyes set upon Ames as if back of them a singular and inexplicable instinct was working.

"My pard is Arizona Ames."

Crow Grieve took a step back toward them, with that black penetrating gaze fastened upon Ames.

"Cowboys give each other handles that fit," he said. "I've had Montanas ride for me an' Nebraskies an' once a gun-slinger who called himself Nevada. But no Arizonas. An' I happen to have heard of one. Do you call yourself Arizona?"

"No, I don't," returned Ames, almost coldly. "But I cain't help what others call me. An' I'm bound to admit that name is hard to shake."

"Why'd you want to shake it?" queried Grieve, suspiciously.

"Well, it's not because I've anythin' against Arizona or Arizona has anythin' against me. I don't like bein' reminded of Arizona—that's all."

"You rode for Rankin once?" asked Grieve.

"Yes."

"How long?"

"Reckon all of two years."

"Up till his death?"

"Yes."

"Did you see him shot?" inquired Grieve, coming closer, his eyes like black coals.

"I reckon I did."

"Then you know who did it?"

"Well, Mr. Grieve," drawled Ames, with a sort of cool, disdainful ring in his voice, "naturally if I saw him shot I saw who drew on him."

"It doesn't always follow. Men on that range got shot from cover. If I remember correct, no one was ever supposed to have seen Rankin shot."

"You may remember correct, but you have it wrong. *One* man shore saw the job done."

Grieve drew back with sudden slight violence and his black eyes rolled.

"Excuse me," he said hastily. "I'm gettin' personal. But Rankin was a rustler an' once he cleaned me out of every hoof I owned. Whoever shot him did me a good turn."

Whereupon he whirled as on a pivot, and jumping into the buckboard, called to the driver to go on, leaving a variety of expressions on the faces of the cowboys.

MacKinney bent piercing gray eyes upon Ames, as if the recent exchange of words had opened up thought-provoking vistas.

"My Gawd!" blurted out Slim Blue. "Did I hear Crow Grieve apologizin'?"

"Blab," called a comrade from the porch, "I reckon we all figgered you the damndest liar on the range. But—"

"Hey, stranger, are you ready?" yelled the cook from the door.

"Shore am," shouted Ames.

"Knock 'em over now. Ready. One! two! three!— *Come an' get it before I throw it out!*"

Arizona Ames led the stampede into the cabin, where the whoops and yells and laughs, the pound of boots and jangle of spurs, suddenly ceased.

6

ARIZONA AMES was a typical character of his period. Every range from the Pan Handle to the Black Hills, and as far west as the Pecos, had its Ames.

The cowboy was a product of Texas and an evolution from the Mexican *vaquero*. When cattle in great herds began to be driven north over the Chisholm Trail, to Abilene, to Dodge, and thence north, west, and east the cowboy was introduced to the world. He multiplied with the rapid growth of the cattle industry. He came from the four corners of the United States, and beyond. At most he was a boy not yet out of his teens; but the life of the range, the toil and endurance demanded by cattle-raising, the border saloon, the gambling-hell, the rustler, developed him at once into a man, and one that eventually made the West habitable.

Wild and free, untamable, a jolly and reckless individual was the average cowboy. Naturally the times developed the vicious, hard-drinking, gun-throwing cowboy, but he was in the minority. All of them, however, shared a singular quality which must have been a result of their picturesque, strenuous, and perilous lives, and this was an unquenchable spirit. Cowboys, as a rule, were fire-eaters. They were simple, natural, elemental, and therefore heroic. They performed the most tremendous tasks as a matter of the day's work, without ever dreaming that they had essentials of greatness.

And here and there, on every range, there rode a cowboy like Arizona Ames, in whom united all these qualities except viciousness and drunkenness, and to which was added the individual trait that made him stand out from his fellows. Seen truly, they were all remarkable. But that one added trait seemed to exaggerate the others; and in Arizona Ames it was a magnification of the spirit, that made the lives of all cowboys significant.

He was quiet, but he could be gay. He would take a drink with his fellows, but he had never been known to get drunk. He would lend his last dollar and then borrow from a comrade to help the one who sought him. He always took the hardest, darkest, coldest watch; and most of the jobs hated by cowboys fell to him. His horsemanship and skill with a lasso, and other tricks of the trade, left no room for the ridicule and banter so common to cowboys. Then his swift and unerring use of a Colt added the last notch to the admiration of whatever outfit he rode with. Gunmen on the frontier usually were avoided to a greater or less extent, especially those who bore the name of killers. But seldom did these remain cowboys. Nevertheless, there were many bad cowboys who would shoot at the drop of a hat, and these did not long survive.

The reputation of Arizona Ames either preceded him wherever he roamed or arrived with him. And it was such that any honest cowboy liked him; and any dishonest cowboy, or, for that matter, any man known to the range as shady or notorious or mean, felt instant antagonism towards him. MacKinney told the vague range rumors about the fights attributed to Arizona Ames. Rankin had been shot and presumably by Ames, but nobody had seen the deed, except Ames himself, and he never admitted that he had killed the rustler. Tales had drifted from all over the West, one particularly bloody one from Arizona, which had given him his name, but none of them could be verified by any of these Wyoming riders. The more mystery about Ames, however, the more these cowboys gave him credit for.

Ames had not ridden out the month of May before almost every cowboy of Grieve's outfit had bullet holes in his sombrero, physical proofs of Ames' prowess with a gun. One by one they pestered him in every way to induce him to shoot at a hat tossed into the air. He was good-natured and he liked to bet.

"Dog-gone yu, Arizonie," complained Slim Blue, one day. "I jest don't believe yu're so good with a gun."

"Say, you blue-shirted Jasper!" Ames had retorted, "shore I don't care what you believe."

"Wal, I reckon not. But s'pose for instance some purty gurl rides into our outfit—say as purty as Grieve's wife. An' you an' me lock horns over her! I'm darned if I'm a-goin' to throw a gun on you if you can shoot like Mac says you can."

"Slim, if the pretty girl comes you can shore have her," replied Ames, patiently.

"Hell, cowboy! Air you a woman-hater?"

"Not altogether exactly."

"Dog-gone!—One of these heartbroken cow-punchers, huh?—Wal, I might want to fight you fer some other reason. So I'll bet you ten dollars to five that you can't hit my hat in the air."

"Slim, I hate to take your money."

"Wal, you needn't."

"All right, then, Slim. I'll take your bet," Ames had replied, tossing aside his cigarette and rising. "How many shots will you give me?"

"Reckon as many as you kin shoot while my hat is in the air."

"Sail it up. Straight now," said Ames, backing away.

Blue had tossed it straight and high, enabling the marksman to get three shots. Upon examination three bullet holes were found in it, two in the crown and one in the rim.

"Hell, cowboy!" ejaculated Slim, in disgust. "One would have been enough. An' hyar you spoil my hat. You put only one in some of the other fellars."

"Slim, shore you need a lot of convincin'," laughed Ames.

"Wal, you shootin' hombre from Arizonie," replied Blue, reluctant with his admiration. "I jest ain't a-goin' to pick no fight with you."

Ames had taken up his quarters in the bunk-house occupied by Lany Price. This occasioned the first friendly row. Blab MacKinney insisted that Sam Perkins get out of his bunk-house and let his own partner, Ames, come in. Sam told him that with all due deference to the genteel and beautiful Ames, they could go where it was hot. Then Slim Blue tried to oust Lany out of his own house and install himself there. Ames decided each argument as fast as he came to it. And he remained with Lany.

It seemed that the more Ames tried to avoid circumstances with latent possibilities the more they gravitated to him. He had not long shared the cabin with Lany before he divined there was something on the mind of that young cowboy. Like many boys Ames had worked with, Lany was the son of a poor rancher, a capable rider, a wholesome character, with an ambition to get on in the cattle business.

Work, for the present, on the Grieve ranch was rather light, owing to several causes, chief of which was that the rancher had just sold out most of his stock and was awaiting a consignment of cattle from Texas. This was expected to arrive at the latest in June or July. The outfit, therefore, had only odd jobs to do, and not any night work at all. They got thoroughly rested and in good humor again. In leisure hours they played poker, lolled around smoking and joking, and for cowboys had a mighty good time.

Crow Grieve was the most unlikable cattleman Ames had ever met, let alone ridden for. He drove hard bargains with smaller cattlemen, an unpardonable crime in the eyes of cowboys. He paid less wages than most ranchers, though this was obviated to some extent by the comfortable quarters he provided. Obviously he put no trust whatever in cowboys, which condition might have arisen partly because he had never been one himself.

The second day after Ames' arrival MacKinney had delivered an illuminating remark.

"Arizonie, let me give you a hunch," he had said. "You're a handsome cuss. Reckon they don't come handsomer, among cowmen, anyway. An' you've got somethin' more. Wal, don't look at the boss' wife."

"Why not? I'm not blind. I heah she's a beauty. An' shore I cain't hurt myself lookin'."

"Wal, you damn idjit, I know you're all right. But if you want to stay on hyar with me don't go fallin' off your hoss in front of Mrs. Grieve's. Savvy?"

"No, Blab, I'm darned if I do."

"Arizonie, you shure always used to rile me, an' now you're beginnin' again. Listen.... Amy Grieve is a beauty an' if you ever seen a hungry-eyed gurl, she's one. Why, them big eyes of hers will haunt you. Two years ago Grieve went south. Louisiana, I reckon. Anyway, he came back with this girl. His wife an' not more'n seventeen! If I ever had a peep at an unhappy gurl—wal, it was then. We boys had our idees. Along comes a puncher from Texas. He told us enough to get us figgerin'. Shure Grieve had got hold of this gurl through her family or relatives owin' him money, or somethin' loike. Wal, afther a toime she perked up. Then came a baby. She seemed to bloom up. An' lately she's foine. I seen her the other day."

"Mac, isn't life hell?" ejaculated Ames, poignantly.

"Shure it is, you dom fool. But it could be wuss. An' thet's why I'm givin' you a hunch to avoid Amy Grieve. Shure as sheep come home to roost she'd fall in love with you. She *likes* cowboys. Aw, I can tell. Any fellar could. An' you can bet your bottom dollar she doesn't love thet black buzzard, Grieve."

"Blab, you're shore blabbin' a lot," returned Ames, seriously.

"Wal, if it was anyone else I swear I'd keep still. But you know dom well, Arizonie, how things sort of lodge against you an' stick."

"Now you're talkin'."

The story had peculiar interest for Ames, such as would have actuated most cowboys, to see Amy Grieve. Romance and tragedy not his own had kept step on his trail. The oftener he saw Crow Grieve the sorrier he felt for the young wife.

Not long after that, while he was rummaging around in the drawer of a rude table in the bunkhouse, a small photograph came to light under some of Lany Price's letters. It bore the likeness of a young girl not more than sixteen—a sweet rather weak face, with most audacious eyes. A name in ink stared up at Ames. Amy! The photograph had been taken in New Orleans.

Ames regretted the incident, for which he certainly could not blame himself. What was Lany Price doing with a picture of the boss' young wife? Ames decided to give the youngster the benefit of a doubt. Cowboys were sentimental. Lany might be merely dreaming. On the other hand, he might be seriously involved in an affair that would have grave consequences for him. Ames put this later thought out of his mind.

He had taken a liking to Lany Price. The young fellow was virile enough, but not exactly a rough, raw cowboy. On that account he came in for considerable of the teasing. However, they all liked Lany.

The day came when Ames had to blind himself to certain indications, doubtful though insistent. Lany had spells of depression. He would mope around, gloomy and cross. Then all of a sudden he became radiant. This last manifestation, coincident with Crow Grieve's departure for South Pass, seemed too significant for Ames to overlook. It was another of those cases where fatality seemed thrown upon him.

"Heah good news from home, Lany?" inquired Ames, genially, after supper.

"No. Come to think of it, haven't heard for ages. Darn Visa, anyhow!"

"Who's Visa?"

"My sister. She's the dandiest girl. I'd like you to meet her, Arizona. She's a dandy-lookin' kid, full of fun, an' good as gold."

"Shore would like to," replied Ames.

"Arizona, you've got a sweetheart?"

Ames shook his head, smiling a little.

"But you've had one?"

"No, I cain't say I ever had—what you'd call a regular sweetheart."

"Funny! A wonderful-lookin' fellow like you!—You must be lyin'. Have you a sister?"

"Yes," said Ames, dropping his head.

"Does she write you?"

"Shore. Once in a long time. But then she writes a long wonderful letter."

"That makes up. Visa likes me, but she's not much good as a letter-writer. What's your sister's name?"

"Nesta."

"Nesta? Sounds nice to me. Is she young?"

"I reckon so. I feel awful old, but I'm not really. Nesta is just my age. We're twins."

"You don't say!—Then she must look like you?"

"Shore. They used to say they couldn't tell us apart, when we were little, anyway."

"Gosh! She must be a looker! You're the finest-lookin' person I ever saw—unless it's Am—Mrs. Grieve."

"Thanks, Lany," rejoined Ames. "I'll show you a picture of Nesta." Whereupon he lifted his bag to the table, and searching therein he found an old wallet, from which he extracted a carefully wrapped photograph.

"She was sixteen then," said Ames as he handed the picture to Lany.

That worthy ejaculated, "Lord!" His eyes shone with pleasure. "Arizona, course she's married?"

"Yes, an' happy, thank God," returned Ames, his sudden emotion contrasting strangely with his former casual mood. "Sam, her husband, is doin' fine. He'll be a big rancher before long now. But I was broke four years, sendin' them money. . . . They've got two kids. Twins!—An' the boy is named Rich after me. That's my right name."

Lany handed back the photograph. His eyes held a dark, far-seeing shadow. "My Gawd! It'd be great to—to be married—an' happy, like that," he said, speaking as if to himself.

"I reckon it would," agreed Ames.

From that hour circumstances and thoughts multiplied for Ames. He could not obviate them. Lany Price stayed out late that night, and apparently no one but Ames was any the wiser. Ames heard him slip in noiselessly, in his stocking feet. Long sighs attested to something more than a need of slumber. Lany sat on his bunk, half undressed, absorbed in thought that made him oblivious to his surroundings. A bright moon outside cast light into the cabin. Ames could see Lany sitting there—saw him step to the window to look up at the moon, rapt and sad.

All this repeated itself the next night, with the details augmented, if anything. Ames deliberated. If young Price was in love with Amy Grieve, which assumption seemed incontestable, he simply invited death. Crow Grieve was the kind of a man who could horsewhip a cowboy for looking at his wife and kill him for but little more. Now Ames did not know the youthful wife, and though he sympathized with her, he could not be sure she was not to blame. On the other hand, Lany Price was too fine a young man to be merely a target for a fierce and jealous brute like Grieve. It occurred to Ames that this rancher rubbed him the wrong way—a thought which, once crystallized, made Ames restless. He sought to cast it aside. Finally he made up his mind to ascertain, solely in the interest of this foolish boy, if he were actually meeting Amy Grieve.

Therefore, he did not return to the bunk-house after supper, but took a stroll among the pines. Darkness settled down soon after. The moon would not rise till late. From the gloom of the pines he watched both the road and the walk leading to the ranch house. His vigilance, not to mention the woodsman's instinct developed during his hunting years, enabled him to catch Price stealing through the pines. At a safe distance Ames followed, just keeping the dark figure in sight. Price went round to the side of the ranch grounds, through the orchard, where he disappeared. Ames cautiously moved forward, and presently in the starlight he espied a slight form in white pass through an opening. It was that of a girl, swift and eloquent of motion, bound for a rendezvous. The only other woman in Grieve's employ, Ames knew, was the housekeeper, who was old and heavy.

Soberly Ames retraced his steps, reluctantly accepting his misgivings and vastly concerned about Price. But he persuaded himself this was none of his business, and then had to do battle with his conscience. Still, he had not yet actually caught the cowboy with the young wife. Suppose he took Lany to task, only to discover he had blundered! But though he tried to convince himself, Ames knew he had not made a mistake. He went back to the bunk-house and fell asleep before Price came in.

Next morning Ames seized upon a favorable opportunity to say: "Mawnin', Lany. It runs in my haid somehow that you keep late hours."

Lany protested that he did nothing of the kind.

"Excuse me, cowboy. I'm a funny kind of a sleeper. Always dreamin' an' heahin' things. I shore thought you came in late every night—since the boss has been away."

Ames drawled this casually, careful to have his back to Price. Evidently the cowboy was so startled, so confused, that he scarcely knew what he was saying. He made too many explanations. He lied clumsily, and he betrayed himself to Ames.

On the following day Grieve came back from South Fork, not yet sober, and rancorous over some real or supposed wrong done him by a rival cattleman.

He led the cowboys a miserable life. Two of them quit, one of them after being knocked down by the rancher. MacKinney interfered to prevent gun-play.

"Boss, I shure ain't presumin' to criticize you," said MacKinney, "but if you're keen on rakin' the outfit loike this you won't have none left. An' you've got a bunch of Texas steers comin'."

For a wonder, Grieve did not resent this speech and made himself scarce. That night the cowboys congregated at the mess-cabin, for the most part a disgruntled outfit.

"Wal, he's a———nigger!" exclaimed Jake Mendal, dourly.

"I hit him fer my wages an' when I git them you watch me hit the trail," said Boots Cameron. "I'll starve to death before I'll ride fer this two-bit of a rancher."

"Fellars, the wust about Grieve is thet he keeps owin' you back pay. An' if you quit you don't git your money. I've a mind to do somethin' so he'll fire me," added Sam Black, the eldest of the outfit.

One by one the other old hands aired their grievances. Ames had been six years on the ranges, riding with many outfits, and never had he heard a cattleman arraigned as was Crow Grieve.

"Shure he's a hawg!" spat out MacKinney. "Some puncher will bust his black jaw one of these hyar days."

"Huh! An' git bored fer thet. Crow Grieve has throwed a gun on more than one cowboy," replied Jem Gutline.

"Wal, he might throw a gun on the wrong fellar," said Slim Blue, darkly. "Fer instance, suppose he tried it on Arizonie?"

"I wisht to Gawd he would," said someone.

"Arizonie, why in the hell don't you say somethin'?" railed Blue.

"You boys are shore sayin' a lot. My two-bit talk wouldn't count much," returned Ames, calmly.

"Thet's so. Talk is cheap. But if you chipped in with a word or two I reckon we'd all feel you was with us," added Blue, pointedly.

"If I hadn't made friends heah I'd shore ride away, money or not."

"Pards, thet's shure talk from Arizona Ames," said MacKinney.

Then the Irishman fastened his narrow slits of blue eyes upon the working face of Lany Price.

"Cowboy, you're shure mum as a clam. An' I'll bet you hate Grieve wusser than any of us."

"That so? Reckon I've no more reason than any of you," returned Price, with annoyance.

"Haw! Haw!" roared MacKinney, derisively.

"You damn Irish Mick! What do you mean—givin' me a horse laugh like that?"

"Shure I don't mean nuthin', Lany," rejoined the Irishman, with sarcasm.

Price, red in the face, flounced out of the cabin, and he did not come back for the meal.

Later that week cattlemen drove in to confer with Grieve. They received scant courtesy, and one of them, a rancher who had started as a cowboy, delivered some pertinent remarks in the hearing of Slim Blue. Then another of the cowboys, who happened to be in the confidence of the housekeeper, informed the outfit that Grieve was having hell with his wife. She wanted to go home.

Shortly after this incident Grieve left, driving the buckboard himself. That he would depart without leaving many and stringent orders was unprecedented. It gave rise to wild speculation on the part of the cowboys. They joyfully took advantage of this omission and did very little work.

Ames took a lonely ride, simply to get away from the ranch, up high somewhere in the timber. He saw the gradual disintegration of Grieve's outfit. Hard drinking eventually ruined any rancher, irrespective of domestic troubles. Ames felt stir in him the familiar longing to ride away from this ranch, as he had ridden from so many others. But he did not want to desert Lany Price. That young cowboy was due for disaster. Often Ames had been prompted to broach Lany's secret. Still, he had never done so. On this ride Ames resolved not to let it go longer. There would be opportunity soon, for in Grieve's absence Lany would probably grow bolder, if he did not run wholly true to the habit of lovers in a distracted situation.

"Shore it's aboot time for me to have some bad luck," soliloquized Ames, meaning that in the nature of events he would likely be involved soon. He rode down the trail. Early summer had brought out the aspens in full foliage. How the green leaves fluttered! He never saw aspen leaves that he did not think of Nesta. Was this Amy Grieve another love-torn girl, frail and fluttering as one of these leaves of aspen?

Down through the pines his quick eye caught a glimpse of a white horse. If he were not mistaken, that horse belonged to Lany Price.

"By Heaven!" muttered Ames. "Shore I felt it this very mawnin'. Now will I turn tail or go face them?"

The beautiful bench below was not a long ride from the ranch. Two trails led up to it, by different routes. Ames had several times seen Amy Grieve riding, but never close at hand. Her horse was certainly not white. Lany's was. Ames would have wagered anything he owned that the two had met up here on this lonely bench. It roused his ire. They were out of their heads, and perhaps they were guilty of more than he had heretofore suspected.

Ames dismounted and, leading his horse over the soft trail, which gave forth no sound, he went on under the pines and through the aspen thickets.

Presently in a glade he espied two horses, both saddled, but riderless, bridles down, nipping at the grass. He dropped his own bridle and went round a corner of green, almost to bump into a huge log.

Not ten steps farther, on the other side of this log, leaned Lany Price, his back to Ames. He was talking low, disconnectedly, earnestly. He had a girl clasped in his arms. Hers were wrapped tight round his neck. Her face pressed close to his cheek, his hair dark against her chestnut curls. Her eyes were closed, her cheeks stained with tears.

Ames had a wild impulse to run before those eyes unclosed to see him. But just that first look at her changed his preconceived ideas.

Under his boot a twig snapped. The girl's long dark lashes flew up. Velvety humid eyes, large and beautiful, stared uncomprehendingly, widened to startled amaze, then dilated in sudden realization and fear.

SHE cried out, and unclasping her arms from round Lany's neck, she violently broke from his embrace.

"O my God!" she exclaimed, and the shaking hand that pointed at Ames swept on to her parted lips.

Lany stood a second as if turned to stone. Then he sagged and lunged, to whirl with gun extended, his face fierce, his hair up like a mane.

"Howdy, Price!" said Ames, coolly, suddenly stiff at sight of that gun.

"*Arizona!*" gasped the cowboy, distress edging into his wild expression.

"Shore is. An' I'm tellin' you this heah is an accident. I just happened along."

"Damn you! Accident? You expect me—to believe that?" demanded Price, hoarsely.

"Lany, if it wasn't an accident you'd never have seen me. Use your haid now."

"No matter. Anyway, I've got to kill you!"

"Think quick, boy," flashed Ames, sharply, "before you make it worse. Shore you've no call to kill me. I'm your friend."

"Friend? . . . Gawd!—if I could only—believe you!" panted the distracted youth.

"Lany—who—is he?" faltered the girl.

"He's the new rider I told you about. Arizona Ames."

"Arizona Ames?" she echoed, and her halted consciousness seemed to be laboring over the name.

"Yes, miss. I'm Ames," interposed Ames, moving up so only the log separated them.

"Don't you—know me?" she asked.

"I've a hunch, but I cain't be shore."

"I am—Mrs. Grieve."

"Glad to meet you," returned Ames, doffing his sombrero. "Sorry it's not under—happier circumstances."

"Arizona, it's no use," burst out Price, passionately. "Hard as it is—I've got to kill you. . . . No man can see what you did—an' live!"

"Shore is pretty tough, Lany," said Ames, forcibly. "But look me in the eye, boy. An' if you cain't trust me—why, you can throw your gun. Only, I warn you, Lany, I'm shore liable to beat you to a trigger."

The cowboy shook with the violence of his emotions as he endeavored to meet the piercing gaze

Ames bent upon him. He had manliness, yet he seemed pitifully weak.

"Arizona, I don't care—about myself," he said, breathing hard.

"Shore I know that. You're thinkin' aboot Mrs. Grieve's honor. Well, Lany, it's as safe with me as if I were you."

Price's gun arm lost its rigidity. His face worked.

"Lany, you mustn't kill him," spoke up the girl. "It'd be murder."

"What's a murder to me? I'd shoot the whole outfit to save you from ruin."

"Dear, I told you I'm ruined already," she returned. "For I'll not live a lie any longer. I hate Crow Grieve. I mean to tell him the truth."

"O Gawd—no!" cried Price. "He'd choke the life out of you."

She reached for Price's nerveless arm and dragged it down so that the gun dropped out of sight. Then, tottering a little, she put both hands on the log to steady herself, and leaned to gaze seekingly into Ames' eyes. If she was gaining assurance, Ames was certainly readjusting wrong impressions. In an ordinary moment she would have been more than pretty. Here, white as marble, with great dark velvet eyes of tragedy, with red tremulous lips parted, with throbbing throat and breast, she was wonderful to look at.

"Lany, I trust him," she said, quietly.

The moment of ended strain was poignant for Ames. To have to kill or disable this love-maddened boy would have been a terrible thing. Ames slid his legs over the log and sat between Lany and the girl, his hand going to the boy's shoulder and his gaze to her.

"Thanks. I reckon I'm glad," he said, feelingly. "Now, listen, folks. I've known for weeks aboot you two bein' in love. An' I'm afraid some of the outfit suspect you. MacKinney is on, I'm shore, but there are some things Mac doesn't blab. I can keep him from it, anyhow."

"You knew—Lany and I were—in—in love?" queried the girl, with a slow blush.

"Well, I wasn't so shore aboot you lovin' *him*. He was out of his haid. But I knew you were meetin' him, an' I confess I had some pretty queer notions about you. A young woman—still in her teens—with a baby! It shore looked bad. Reckon it looks bad yet, only somehow, seein' you with Lany, an' heahin' you, makes it different."

"You are Lany's friend?"

"Shore. An' I've been layin' awake at night, tryin' to find a way to help him."

"Arizona, I—I love Lany terribly," she confessed. "But I—I have not really been untrue to my husband."

"Shore you haven't," replied Ames, loyally. "Reckon Lany had me plumb scared. When a man's horrible in love you cain't just tell whether he's good or bad. But, Amy, since I've seen an' heahed you, I've aboot made up my mind you're *good*, all right, but terrible young an' wild an' unhappy."

Faith and kindness worked upon her to the havoc of composure.

"Oh—Lany!" she sobbed. "He gives me—

strength and hope....My self-respect was bleeding to death....He will help us."

"I shore will," declared Ames, binding himself to he knew not what. He drew the weeping girl to him until her drooping head rested on his shoulder. "Now, Lany, you tell me."

Price heaved his gun back into its sheath, and when he lifted his face it showed drawn and wet with tears.

"Arizona, it'll look so—so foolish to you," he began. "I saw Amy the very first day she got to Wyomin'. It was at Granger, where I took the rig to drive Grieve home. She looked at me—an' life hasn't ever been the same since. I fell in love with her—just like I'd fallen off a cliff. I didn't dream of it then, but she fell in love with me, too....I swallowed it—took my medicine. I kept out of her way. If I'd been half a man I'd have gone away. But I wasn't big enough for *that*. Luck was against me. Twice we were thrown together—alone. One whole afternoon I drove her back from Stillman's ranch. We talked for hours. I could tell she was unhappy an' she—she liked me....Then one day, up the river, I found her sittin' on a rock. She had fallen off her horse an' she couldn't walk. Her horse went off somewhere. I couldn't find him; I—I didn't try hard. I tried to help her on my horse. She fell into my arms. That was too much."

Lany wiped his wet face with unsteady hands.

"I carried her home—an' on the way it—it all came out. I told her I was crazy over her an' I'd have to leave Wind River. She wouldn't hear of it. She was in love with *me*....My Gawd!...Since then we've met. Not often at first an' most at night. But lately we had to see each other more.... Then today Amy frightened me out of my wits, as well as put murder in my heart. Grieve is a drunken beast. He beats her. He loves to hurt her!...She's a slave girl. An' she swore she'd not stand it any longer. She swore she'd tell him the truth an' leave him. She would have done that long ago but for the baby.... When you came I was tryin' to persuade her to keep our secret, to stick for the baby's sake. I'd go way off an' never see her again."

Ames kept silent a moment after Lany's disclosure ended. What he felt most was great relief. Then a sadness pervaded his spirit. Everywhere he roamed life seemed like this, and love a glorious and awful thing. The only love he had ever known—that for Nesta—had brought agony, and a sleepless regret, but it was nothing to what overwhelmed these lovers. In the face of it he quailed. How could he help them? What was right and what was wrong? Then he felt the girl's head stir. And in her movement and the face she raised Ames sensed a blind and unreasoning trust in him—that shackled and bound him. Her eyes were as different from Nesta's as eyes could well be, but they burned with the same beauty, the same brooding tragedy through which hope shone.

"Well, well," he began, somehow finding the old cool drawl, "that's not such a terrible story. Why, I reckoned it'd be worse. You just fell in love. God Almighty is most to blame....But, come to remember, you two were pretty close when I come up an' caught you."

"You caught us, all right, Arizona," admitted Lany, hanging his head.

"Amy, you were huggin' Lany somethin' scandalous," went on Ames, just talking for time and perhaps to tease a little.

"Yes, I was, and I'm not ashamed," she retorted, bravely. "I've kissed him a—a million times.... What would you expect, Arizona Ames?"

"Lord! I shore don't know," returned Ames, pensively. "I never had no wonderful girl love me. An' I'm afraid I've missed a lot."

"You must have run away from girls," she said.

"Shore I did. Runnin' away from girls—an' everythin'—is aboot all I've done for six years.... Well, to come back to your story. It's not so terrible, except aboot Grieve bein' a brute. Is that so, Amy?"

"Yes, it is."

"I could tell he's a hard drinker. But I've known men who drank a lot an' yet were not so bad."

"Grieve drinks *all* the time," she declared, scornfully. "It's his life. Whisky is his very breath. There is never a half hour, except when he's asleep, that he doesn't leave off what he's doin'—to go out or in—to come back with that queer little cough. Very often he gets dead drunk. That's the best part of it, for then I can put him to bed. But when he's half drunk, then he's—he's—oh, what can I call him?" she burst out, in ringing passion. "A beast who paws me—tears my clothes off! Beats me! A dog! A nigger!"

The last epithet had in it all the contempt, the hate, the inevitableness of the Southerner's point of view.

Ames felt the leap of his blood. He did not dare

look down at her, but gazed off through the pines, at the gathering of golden clouds over the mountains. He heard Lany's heavy breathing.

"Amy, are you shore you're not exaggeratin' some?" he queried, at length.

She broke away from his gentle hold.

"Look, Arizona Ames!" Swiftly she opened her sleeve to roll it up, exposing a round white arm the beauty of which was marred by black and blue fingerprints. "Look!" she went on, tearing her silk blouse open at the neck, and pulling it aside to reveal a dark bruise on the rounded swell of shoulder. "Is that exaggeration? Shall I take off my boots and show the marks of his kicks?"

Ames cursed under his breath.

Lany shook himself out of his amaze and horror.

"Amy, you never told me *that*!" he raved.

"I'm telling you now," she retorted, defiantly.

"You were afraid—I'd kill him?" panted Lany.

"I was. And now I hope you do." Then all of a sudden she was in his arms.

Ames had to sit there and endure their crying over each other, their forgetfulness of him, their scoldings and tender reproaches, their evidences of heartbreak.

"Don't mind me, folks," he said, finally. "Only, time's shore a-flyin'."

Lany, still holding the girl in his arms, turned with a face which thrilled and awed Ames.

"Arizona, for her sake, tell me what to *do*!"

"I reckon nothin' right pronto," replied Ames, bluntly. "An' shore keep away from Amy till we figure what you can do."

"I can't keep away. When I try she—she sends for me," said Lany, despairingly. "This mornin', for instance. Mac gave me a job to tend to, an' Amy sends me a note by the housekeeper's boy, askin' me to meet her up here."

Ames threw up both hands.

"Mrs. Grieve, you shore take risks—"

"Don't call me *Mrs.*," flashed the girl, in petulant passion.

"Very well, then, Amy. You oughtn't have done that."

"But I'm a human being," she protested.

"I reckon you are. Terrible human. All the same you don't use any haid."

"I can't live—I won't live without seeing him."

To Ames she seemed subtly dangerous then, beautiful and irresistible, a strange creature that any man would have risked his life for.

"But you're courtin' death," said Ames, gravely. "If you're found out—an' it's reasonable shore you will be—Crow Grieve will kill Lany. An' if he didn't kill you, too—well, you'd be worse off than daid."

Her face blanched at this and her eyes sought Lany's face. "I—I don't care *what* he'd do to me. But if he killed Lany I—I'd murder him with my own hands."

"Ahuh. I believe you've got the nerve to do it. ...Amy, you're forgettin' your child. You're not fair to him. Or is it a boy?"

"A girl, Arizona. Golden curls, blue eyes—you'd never believe it was Grieve's child."

"O Lord! A girl! An' she'll grow up to be like Nesta an' you!"

"Who's Nesta?" asked Amy, curiously.

"A twin sister of mine....Sweet as a flower, wild as a doe!"

"Arizona, we're gettin' nowhere," interposed Lany, desperately.

"Lany, shore there are only two places you can get with a woman. One's heaven, where I reckon you've been lately. An' the other is a place you're goin' if you're not damn careful."

"You mean he's goin' to hell?" asked the girl, sorrowfully.

"I shore do, Amy."

"He won't go alone," she said, simply.

Ames had long realized that he was dealing with fire and powder in these two young people. He dropped off the log and began to pace to and fro. Presently the girl came to him, slipped a hand under his arm.

"You're distressed, Arizona. I'm sorry. Perhaps you'd better keep our secret and let us fight it out alone."

"You poor kids! I reckon I cain't do that."

"Oh, you are good!" she exclaimed. "I never had a brother. Your Nesta must have loved you ...Arizona, you know I can't stand Grieve much longer. I couldn't even if Lany was not in it at all. Don't you see that?"

"Shore I see it."

"I must take baby and go away where he can't find me."

"How old are you, Amy?"

"Not yet twenty. But I feel a hundred."

"You're not of age. You're not your own boss,

especially if your folks gave Grieve a guardianship over you."

"Father did just that. He *sold* me to Grieve. He owed him money. But I've never believed father could have done it if he'd known what Grieve really is."

"Ahuh. Then Grieve could drag you an' the child back. If you'd stick it out till you're of age an' then leave, you'd have the best of him."

"More than a year!" she shuddered. "When now I know what love is?—It's impossible, Arizona."

"Ahuh. I reckoned as much," rejoined Ames, with a grim little laugh. "Let's sit down. I'm gettin' weak in the laigs.... Come heah, Lany."

They sat down together under a pine tree, Ames strangely brooding, Lany miserable and hopeless, the girl white with resolve.

"I think I'll run off," she declared, solemnly. "If he catches me—I'll end it all for the baby and me."

"Arizona, you see?" burst out Lany. "See what I'm up against? She'd have done it before but for me."

"You're shore up against a lot, cowboy," agreed Ames as he let the yellow pine needles sift through his fingers. "But we shore won't let Amy go that far."

"Arizona, you don't savvy my lady love," said Lany, making a sad attempt at humor. "You couldn't stop her with a team of mules."

"How aboot that, Amy?"

"If I once got started you never could," she asserted.

"Well, young folks, as I see it—aboot the only hope for you is to wait until Crow Grieve is daid."

"But he is still young and healthy. He'll live many years," protested Amy, taking him literally.

On the other hand, Lany Price turned a deathly white.

"How long is he goin' to be away?" queried Ames, ignoring her protest.

"I never can tell. When he says a week he comes back before. When he says a day or two he stays longer."

"Amy, is he suspicious you might be—"

"Suspicious—jealous, oh, he's hatefully both!" she cried. "Of *any* cowboy."

"Not particularly of Lany, then?"

"I don't know it, if he is. But he's cunning. I'm in a perpetual state of fear, both when he's home and away."

"Well, for a girl who's scared to death all the time, strikes me you've got nerve," drawled Ames.

"Nerve! I've no more nerve than a rabbit. And I'm an awful liar, too, Arizona."

"Aw no. Shore I cain't believe that."

"I'm a liar, anyway."

"Amy," spoke up Lany, with loyal repudiation, "you might have had to lie to Grieve, but you never have to me."

She let out a little peal of silvery mocking laughter. She was bewildering to Ames.

"Haven't I, though? I'm all a lie.... Why, Lany, I brought about those accidents when you were with me alone. I fell in love with you and I swore I'd make you love me or die.... That time you carried me home in your arms!—I found out where you were going. I followed you. I drove my horse away and waylaid you. I pretended to be hurt when I wasn't at all. When you tried to put me up in your saddle I fell into your arms. On purpose! And then when you thought you had to carry me and you did carry me! And before you knew it you were kissing me!"

"Oh, Amy," returned Lany, at once wretched and happy.

Ames rose to his feet. "I reckon that's not the kind of lies men count. If the lyin' is done for them! …Now do as I tell you. Say you won't tell Grieve nothin'. You'll be awful careful aboot meetin' Lany now while your husband is away. An' when he comes back you won't meet Lany at all or send him notes."

"Till when?" she asked, rising with her hands on her hips, her eyes singularly bright on him.

"Say as long as Grieve is away an' while he's home next time."

"Arizona, I promise. Cross my heart," she replied, smiling, and after she had suited the action to the words she proffered her hand. "And during this time you'll find some place where I can hide or you'll take me yourself—or hit upon a way to help me and Lany out of this terrible mess?"

"That's *my* promise, Amy," he replied.

"How aboot you, Lany?" he asked, turning to the cowboy. "Shore you'll help Amy to keep this heah promise?"

"Arizona, I swear—I will," rejoined Lany. His lips were pale and he swallowed hard.

"All right, children, I shore feel better," drawled Ames. "I'll leave you now. An' I advise you don't stay up heah till mawnin'. It's comin' on sunset now. It oughtn't take you long to say good-by. Fact is, I don't know nothin' aboot kisses, but allowin' a second or so for each one, an' reckonin' on four or five hundred—they wouldn't take so long."

Lany laughed to hide his embarrassment.

"Arizona, I didn't think you could be sarcastic," said Amy, disappointed, and she swayed toward him, a dangerous little gleam in her big eyes.

"Gosh! Now I've played hob!" ejaculated Ames, realizing his effort at naïveté had fallen somewhat flat.

"You think we're young fools?" she queried.

"Aw no, Amy, not quite that."

"You ridicule kisses. Arizona Ames, I've a notion to kiss you," she averred, backing him against the log.

"Do it, Amy," said Lany. "Show him. The darned cowboy never has been kissed."

"Have you, Arizona?"

"I reckon, years ago at parties an' dances. An' the sister I told you aboot—Nesta, she used to kiss me. But, Amy, I never had a sweetheart."

"Arizona, I think that the most amazing thing," said Amy. "And I believe you." She took hold of the lapels of his vest and looked up sweetly, half in fun, half in earnest, with a woman's gratitude for his sympathy and championship, and also with a woman's subtle instinct to defend her sex. "I'm going to kiss you, Arizona."

"Please don't, Amy," he returned, hastily, in tremendous embarrassment, trying gently to get away.

"Shut your eyes, coward," she commanded.

"Lord! if you're goin' to—I—I reckon I got to see you," he exploded.

"Arizona, I'm deadly in earnest. I'll pretend to

be the sweetheart you'll win some day. Oh, you will! Lany and I hope you'll feel what we feel now."

With heightened color she stretched herself, then had to jump to reach his lips, which she kissed full and soundly.

"There, Arizona Ames!" she exclaimed, sliding back to the ground, a little scared, but still audacious.

"Now you've done it," said Arizona, and vaulting the log he hurried away round the thicket to his horse. Mounting, he cut off the trail to avoid meeting his young friends again, and was soon beyond the glade, headed down into the thinning forest.

Through openings between the pines he could see the green slope, the shining river below, the wide range, and the black mountains rising to the peaks crowned in gold and white, and above, the flaming sunset clouds.

"Poor kids!" soliloquized Ames, shaking his head sadly. "No more to blame than two chipmunks!... Lord, what a girl! Just like Nesta—only so different in looks. An' she kissed me. I wish she hadn't....No, I shore don't. If I ever meet a girl like her my name will be mud....Heigho!...I'm always huntin' trouble. My feelin's run away with my haid....An' it's a shore bet I'll have to draw on that black bastard, Crow Grieve."

CHAPTER
8

WHEN Ames rode into the ranch that evening his line of future conduct seemed to have been arbitrarily arranged, as if by the fates.

During supper, at which Lany arrived late, subdued by spent emotion, Ames was preoccupied. Later he avoided his friend, and passed hours with the cowboys, evincing a sudden and unusual curiosity about Crow Grieve, prompting innumerable stories of the rancher's hard-fistedness, his niggardly doling out of wages, his peculiar habit of always holding back the balance due a range-hand, his distrustful nature, and lastly, his cruelty to horses. These were Grieve's common and well-known traits, such as, especially the last, were unforgivable by cowboys.

"Dog-gone it," said Slim Blue, as Ames stalked

out. "What's eatin' Arizonie? It's not like him atall."

"How do we know what Arizonie's like? He ain't been hyar long," returned a comrade.

"But Mac's told us."

"Aw, Mac blabs too much. I reckon Arizonie is jest goin' sour on the boss. We all got thet way, sooner or later, didn't we?"

"We plumb sure did. But somehow it 'pears kinda different in Arizonie."

Next morning Ames called upon the house-keeper, Mrs. Terrill, a buxom widow of forty, who was not averse to mild flirtations with cowboys.

"Mrs. Terrill, I shore been stayin' away from heah," drawled Ames, in his nicest way. "The boys been tellin' me aboot you. Handsome widows are my especial dish."

"You cowboy cannibal," she replied, gayly. "You're a handsome devil yourself. I'll bet you only want cake or pie out of me."

"Shore I'll take a piece. But I just ran up to say howdy, an' ask if you know when the boss is comin' back."

"Laws a-mercy! Are you sweet on the young missis, too?"

"Me? Naw! I like 'em all broken in. High-steppin' fillies are shore too hard for me to ride."

"You're the first cowpuncher I ever heard say anythin' like that. . . . No, I ain't sure when the boss will be home. I'm hopin' it won't be soon."

Mrs. Terrill liked to talk and Ames was an inspiring listener. He was to hear much about the sweet and patient Amy Grieve and her adorable baby. And from that it was but easy to lead the woman to talk about Grieve. "Sure you'll get your money," she had answered to Ames' query, "but only when he's good an' ready to pay."

Ames worked upon her feelings then, and her evident devotion to Amy. The housekeeper, growing confidential to this earnest-eyed and soft-voiced cowboy, waxed eloquent. As her tongue loosened, she imparted many things, among them a hint that there was one cowboy to whom young Mrs. Grieve was not indifferent.

"How does Grieve treat this girl?" asked Ames, with great sympathy. But here the woman's volubility ceased, and from her sudden restraint Ames gathered more significance than if she had actually given instances of Grieve's brutality. Ames left the housekeeper, darkly satisfied with his interview. Amy Grieve had not exaggerated. The testimony of disinterested people, however, was what Ames required in the stern court-martial going on in his mind.

Ames encountered MacKinney on the road near the bunk-house.

"Shure was lookin' for you, Arizonie," he said, genially.

"Haven't got a dollar," replied Ames, surlily. "I'll have to borrow, myself, if Grieve won't shell out."

"Borrow! Who's hollerin' about money? I ain't. But I'll lend you some."

"Thanks, I'll wait till I see the boss."

"Shure you'll wait longer till you get all thet's comin'.... Arizonie, some of the outfit's gotta work a little. There's a corral fence to fix up, an' some shinglin' to do. Wanta help me?"

"Me blister my hands an' pound my fingers?"

queried Ames, in magnificent scorn. "I should shore hope to smile not!"

"Say, you Arizonie Injun," expostulated Mac-Kinney, in surprise, "since when did you begin shyin' at work?"

"I reckon aboot this heah minute," rejoined Ames, moodily, and passed on to leave his old friend standing in the road, scratching his head in perplexity.

That night Ames slumped in late to supper, minus his habitual cool and pleasant amiability. He swore at the cook, who appeared too surprised to retaliate, a lack exceedingly rare with that individual. Ames' keen ears caught a drift of conversation outside on the porch.

"Lany, what's ailin' Arizonie?" asked one of the boys.

"Haven't seen him for 'most two days," returned Price, in surprise and concern. "Anythin' the matter?"

"Wal, he ain't like himself, lately."

"Somethin' workin' on Ames," vouchsafed one.

"I jest guess yes. But I've no idee what."

"Aw, he's gettin' sore at the boss."

"Mac, is this old pard of yours one of these punchers who has quiet drinkin' spells, when he ain't sociable?"

"My Gawd, no!" declared MacKinney. "Soberest pard I ever had."

"Wal, if you ask me," spoke up Slim Blue, "I'll tell you Arizonie has got somethin' on his mind."

"Mebbe it's Amy Grieve," said another, so low Ames all but failed to catch it.

"Nope. So far as I know he's never even seen her."

"Say, Lany, has Arizonie seen the boss' wife?"

"I guess so. Once, anyway," replied Price, awkwardly.

"Once is enough."

"Boys, when I looked into them bootiful eyes of hers I felt a turrible wrench. An' I've had an ache under my breast-bone ever since."

"Wal, Saunders, thet ain't no compliment to her. Anythin' wot wore skirts would give you aches."

"Bill, your hunch is wrong. It takes a gurl without skirts to give Saunders the aches. Last time we was in South Fork there was a show in town. An' a gurl with a shape like peeled corral poles did a trapeze act. You'd a' thunk Saunders had collera morbis."

"Haw! Haw! Haw!" roared the cowboys in unison.

Ames finished his meal and stalked out on the porch.

"Say, have any of you suckers an idea how soon that———of a Grieve will be back?" asked Ames, curtly, as he bent his head to light his cigarette.

No one replied promptly. This was strong raw talk, even for a tough cowboy. But coming from a rider of Ames' repute, it fell with a shock.

MacKinney stirred the uneasy silence, his boots coming down from the porch rail with a thump.

"Pard, we shure ain't," he said. "Figgerin' past performances, I'd say he'd drive in tomorrow. An' shure no fellar to brace. If you'll excoose the loikes of me—Arizonie—I'd advise—"

"Aw, blab away, Mac," said Ames, as the other hesitated.

"Shure this ain't no blabbin' matter," returned MacKinney, testily. "You ain't in no humor lately to tackle the boss."

"An' why not?" demanded Ames, coolly. "If you an' the rest of your yellow outfit haven't the guts to call this man, Crow Grieve, it shore doesn't follow that I haven't."

MacKinney lapsed into amazed silence, his jaw dropping, and manifestly his memory active.

"Listen to me, Arizonie," spoke up Blue, with cool and deliberate force. "I reckon to you we are a purty yellow bunch an' mebbe thet crack is desarved. But the way Mac and I figger, an' thet holds fer most of us—Grieve is a nasty, aggravatin' fellar to rile. Wot's the sense in it? We've got purty good jobs. An' if you crawl to him you get along an' you can always draw a little money. Mac was tryin' to tell you this, an' thet the wust of callin' Grieve would be y'u'd jest have to back it up."

"Bah! That black hombre is white-livered inside."

"Wal, Arizonie, we-all jest hope you'll go slow. Not thet any of us care a damn fer *Grieve*!"

"Much obliged, Slim. I shore appreciate that," replied Ames, with sincere warmth. "I'm askin' you to overlook that mean crack. Reckon my nerves are on edge."

As Ames left the porch to stroll away down the dark road Slim Blue's voice trailed to him, but not its content. Ames had deliberately planted a germ among his fellows. Lany was the only one who might suspect Ames of deceit, and he was so absorbed with the enchanted hours that he could not cease his dreaming.

Next day Ames rode out on the range to call upon the "nester," or squatter, who was the only individual of that nature remaining on Grieve's holdings. He was a stolid Norwegian named Nielsen. He had homesteaded a little valley of fifty acres on a creek that flowed into the river. There were a hundred such places on the range under Grieve's control, all more or less fertile, suitable for farms. In fact, some of them had been put under cultivation by the squatter type of pioneer, poor men who had to start with an ax, a plough and a horse. Grieve had run all of them off except Nielsen; and because he could not intimidate the Norwegian he had grown bitter toward him. Ames merely wanted to substantiate range rumor.

He found Nielsen to be the kind of pioneer who would in the long run do more for the West and cowboys than Grieve would. Nielsen had a pretty homestead, a comely wife, and several sturdy youngsters. He could live off the little farm and the meat he packed down from the foothills, but he was standing still. He could not get ahead at ranching. If Grieve had been a square man he would have permitted Nielsen to run his few head of stock on the range near by. But the Norwegian had to drive his cattle up into the foothills, where wolves killed the calves, and rustlers took every two-year-old steer he raised. Nielsen admitted he could not hold on much longer. His simple statement of facts put Grieve in no good light.

Ames respected the Norwegian, and liked the

patient-faced wife, and the merry children, with whom he made friends.

"So Grieve fenced you off his range, eh?" mused Ames, thoughtfully. "Who built that fence?"

"It ain't much of a fence," replied the squatter. "Grieve an' two of his boys put it up in a day. But it cuts me off, except from the river."

"Do you remember who those boys were?"

"Yes. Tall fellar they called Carpenter. He was killed in South Fork a year or two ago. The other is Brick Jones. He's still ridin' for Grieve, but I don't know if he is in your outfit. Brick rode out here a couple of times after that an' annoyed my wife."

"I know Jones. He's workin' at the ranch. Kind of a hand Grieve likes.... How aboot him annoyin' your wife? What'd he do?"

"Not much. Tried to get sweet with the wife. Next time he'd loaded on a little rum an' he was in a wrastlin' mood."

"What'd you do, Mrs. Nielsen?" asked Ames, of the wife, who stood by, listening.

"I ran in and barred the door," she replied, smiling. "I like cowboys, but not that red-head."

"Nielsen, you've a fine little farm heah an' I advise you to hang on," drawled Ames, and patting the bright head of the youngest child he rose to go.

"You do?" inquired the homesteader, his face lightening. "That's kind of you. We're mighty discouraged. I've some little money banked. Been savin' it to buy stock. But I'm afraid. An' yet we hate to pull up an' leave here."

"Hang on, then. But don't buy yet awhile. Wait," said Ames, and then he gave Nielsen a steady gaze.

"Shore I reckon somethin' might happen to Crow Grieve."

"Happen!" exclaimed Nielsen, staring.

"Shore. Life is awful uncertain for men like Grieve. He might fall daid any minute."

"Cowboy, you're talkin' queer for one of Grieve's riders," said the squatter.

"I don't ride for Grieve. I used to, but no more."

"We hope you ain't leavin' without tellin' us your name."

"Well, I am forgetful. My name is Ames. They call me Arizona ... Good-by, folks. Stick to the range an' send these dandy kids to school some day."

Ames rode away, feeling a warmth of satisfaction at the hopes he had evidently kindled in the breasts of these toiling pioneers. Kind words were easy to find, but he reflected grimly, sometimes they pledged him to things difficult of accomplishment.

Soon his mind reverted to his problem at the ranch, and he realized that it had ceased to be a problem. During his visit with Nielsen he had severed his connection with Grieve. For Ames, decisions often came through events as well as long cogitation. Crow Grieve was a stumbling-block to the progress and happiness of worthy people. Many men were like that—stones in the path, weeds to tangle weary feet—thorns that lacerated and poisoned.

"Shore I just cain't savvy Grieve," mused Ames, as he rode along.

Dust clouds down on the range set him to wondering if the advance guard of Grieve's expected herds had arrived. Soon he espied a long string of cattle moving up toward the corrals.

Ames put his horse, Cappy, to a lope, and in half an hour reached the ranch. When he rode round the barns to enter the wide open square between them and the bunk-houses his quick eye noted many things. Grieve had returned; dust and noise emanated from the corrals; cowboys were crossing the open toward the mess-house; several buckboards stood with teams hitched to the rail; a group of men in plain garb were conferring on the porch. And lastly Ames observed with surprise that Mrs. Grieve was sitting alone in the farthest buckboard. She held the reins and appeared to be waiting.

If adventure gravitated to Ames, and circumstances evolved around him, it was equally certain that situations seemed to be set for him by fate.

Ames rode up, dismounted, and throwing his bridle he took off his sombrero to make Mrs. Grieve a bow, a little prolonged and over-graceful.

"Good mawnin'," he said, with a reassuring smile. "Shore there's a lot goin' on around heah an' me missin' it."

"Good morning to you, Mr. Ames," she replied, brightly, and she blushed becomingly. "But it's really afternoon. You're not the only one late for lunch."

He put a gloved hand upon the dashboard, deliberately placing his back to the men on the porch. Ames needed only one glance at Mrs. Grieve to reassure himself. She was thoroughbred, a little puzzled and obviously excited at his approaching her, and withal pleased. No doubt she wore a mask of pride and smiling composure for the world, and it was hard for Ames to pierce to the tragedy and terror of the girl who had only a few days ago besought him so wildly.

"Reckon Grieve is back?" he asked, in lower tone.

"Yes. Surprised me no end," she replied, likewise in low voice. "He's sober. Brought friends to stay over Sunday."

"Fine if it only lasts," he drawled. "Shore fetched some cattle, too, didn't he?"

"No. The first herd of Texas longhorns got here," she said. "Oh, they're such wonderful cattle. I drove down to look them over. And when I got back Mr. Grieve had arrived."

"Where is he now, Amy?"

"On the porch, glaring like a black-eyed owl. But you stay here by me!"

"Shore. An' while I'm heah I want to ask somethin' of you. There's a squatter family up the river. Name is Nielsen. He located before Grieve got control of the range an' he won't be driven out. Grieve has fenced him in, an' has just aboot ruined him. There are three dandy kids an' the mother is a nice woman. They're awful poor. Now, Amy, I want you to promise you'll go up there—some day when you're boss heah—an' help them—be their friend."

"Boss heah!" Amy seemed so strangely struck that she even imitated Ames' accent.

"Don't stare at me like that, you big-eyed child. I asked you to promise."

"Promise?—Certainly I—I will," she returned, hurriedly. "What's this squatter's name?"

"Nielsen. He's a Norwegian an' so's his wife. But I reckon they've been heah in this country pretty long. They're Americans, shore, an' the West needs that kind."

"Arizona, I can feel trouble in the air," she said, still lower, her casual glance on the men behind Ames. "But don't you dare move."

"Me move?—See heah, Amy, I been 'most dyin' to tell you somethin'."

"What?" she inquired, with misgivings.

"Do you remember what you did to me the other afternoon?" he queried, mischievously.

"I'm not likely to forget, Mr. Ames," she returned, with mock aloofness.

"Are you shore? I mean aboot what you swore you was goin' to do—an' Lany told you to show me— an' what I reckoned I didn't want?"

"I am perfectly sure," she rejoined, blushing.

"Funny aboot that. I was shore wrong, Amy. I did want it. An' when I leave heah I'm goin' to ride all over the West till I find a girl like you. An' then I'll get a million—same as you gave Lany."

"What a wonderful compliment to me!" she exclaimed. "I hope you mean it, Arizona. . . . But—when you leave here! What do you mean?"

The gravel crunched under vicious footfalls. Ames leisurely turned. Grieve stalked over, a tinge of red under his dark skin, his large black eyes bright with amazed suspicion and anger.

"Howdy, Grieve!" said Ames, lazily.

"I wasn't aware you were acquainted with my wife," he declared.

"Shore I'm not. Course I know her by sight. I was just askin' her to be good to some friends of mine up the river. Squatter family by the name of Nielsen."

"You're damned impertinent."

Ames had his cue in that. As if he had been stung he jumped clear of the buckboard.

"Who's impertinent?" he flashed, in hot loud tone. The sudden anger he meant to simulate actually became real with the explosion of his words. His deliberate intent to attract attention to Grieve more than succeeded.

"You are," replied Grieve, fuming, though plainly Ames' swift change was a surprise.

"I'd like to know why?" shot out Ames, still louder. "I shore see no call for you to insult me before your wife an' guests, not to say these gapin' cowpunchers. I was only askin' Mrs. Grieve to be good to some friends of mine. You ask her if I wasn't."

"Amy, is that so?" demanded Grieve, turning to her.

"Certainly. What did you think?" returned Amy, coldly. And with the paling of her face her eyes grew larger and darker.

"Do you know this cowboy, Ames?" went on her husband, jealously. "Who introduced him to you?"

"No one," she retorted.

"See heah, Grieve, you cain't bullyrag her on my account," interposed Ames. "I never was introduced to her. I just saw my opportunity to help some friends of mine. Mrs. Grieve has got a reputation for bein' good to poor people."

"Suppose she has. It's none of your business. The nerve of you—bracin' her here!"

"He was very courteous and polite," interposed Amy, solicitously.

"You shut up," snapped Grieve. Every word

edged him in deeper, which fact augmented his temper. He failed to gauge Ames' motive, though he sensed some undercurrent here.

"Thank you, Mrs. Grieve," said Ames, gratefully. "But I reckon you needn't apologize for me."

"Ames, if you address her again I'll—I'll bust your abby jaw," declared Grieve, stridently.

Ames regarded the irate rancher in silent disdain. There was a restless movement of feet upon the porch, and husky whispers among the cowboys. Grieve's temper had precipitated a situation extremely exasperating to him and which, despite a looming portent, could not be obviated by one of his intolerant nature. Certainly he had no fear of Ames, but there seemed to be something he could not understand. The steady eyes of the cowboy, with their blue gimlet-like flash, only inflamed him the more.

"Ames, I don't hire you to ride around huntin' up poor squatters," he went on. "You just made that up or an excuse, so you could speak to my wife."

Ames calmly and irritatingly lighted a cigarette.

"An' you're fired," exploded Grieve, with what he thought was finality.

"Shore I'm not fired," returned Ames, quickly.

"What?" The rancher's voice grew thick. "I say you're fired."

"You cain't fire me, Crow Grieve."

"The hell you say!"

"Shore. I beat you to it. I quit."

"When did you quit?"

"Reckon it was this mawnin'."

"Bah! You're just braggin'. You windy cowpuncher."

"I shore can prove it, Grieve. I told Nielsen this mawnin'."

"All right. I'm damn glad to be rid of you."

"Well, *that's* a question. You're not rid of me yet. Not till I get my money. An' if what I heah is correct I'll get that aboot Christmas after next."

"I won't listen to you," shouted Grieve.

"You shore will."

"Get off the ranch!" yelled Grieve, hoarse with rage, and he started to pass.

Ames struck him a quick light blow in the breast, not violent, but sharp enough to halt him in his tracks. Then Ames shoved him out of line with the buckboard, where Amy sat rigid and white.

"Listen, Grieve, an' when I get through tellin' you why I quit—you can go for your gun."

The ringing voice, with its thin icy edge, left utter silence. Some of the older cowboys, notably Slim Blue and MacKinney, had sensed this climax. Grieve certainly had not, and his black face turned livid. His guests, whom Ames now also faced, hastened to get from behind.

"Ames, you're plumb sure—I'm not packin' a gun," blustered Grieve. His shaken nerve was recovering.

"No, I'm not shore," snapped Ames, curtly. "I didn't look. I hoped you were. An' if you're not—well, you can borrow one, or go home after your own."

The bitter raw challenge shot into Grieve's teeth. The lawless and inevitable West spoke through Ames.

"I quit this mawnin' because I wanted to tell you just what a skunk of a rancher you are, Crow Grieve," went on Ames, in a derision that gained rather than lost from its cool biting drawl. "Shore suits me fine that your beautiful young wife is heah—an' your guests—an' your cowpunchers. For once in your life, Crow Grieve, you're goin' to get called. I'm only sorry for one thing an' that is I cain't cuss you—call you every low-down name known on the range. Reckon I cain't cuss before a lady."

Ames threw down the cigarette which a moment before he had taken from his lips.

"Grieve, it's been my bad luck to meet a lot of rotten cowmen," went on Ames. "But I never run into your beat. You're a cheap, two-bit, stingy buyer of cattle an' hirer of cowboys out of jobs. You're no rancher. If you had any guts you'd be a rustler. I reckon you steal a calf now an' then from poor devils like Nielsen. An' your fencin' him in, so he couldn't range his few haid of stock—of all the dirty jobs I've seen that's the dirtiest. Nielsen's kids looked starved. An' heah you throw out money for whisky like a drunken millionaire....An' 'most as bad is the way you hold on to the wages of decent hard-ridin' cowboys. I've learned how many a cowhand has ridden away from heah without the money he'd earned an' that you owed. Forty miserable dollars for a month of work, day an' night! ... Grieve, you're a drunkard— a sot!—You're a black-faced buzzard! ...You're shore a nigger! An' you've got the soul of a nigger!"

As the breath-arresting denunciation ceased at last, Grieve, swaying with passion, lunged round the buckboard toward the porch. He stumbled in the convulsive violence of his step and nearly fell. When he got on the porch he turned a hideous blotched face.

"*Get out!*" he hissed.

"Shore. When you pay me my wages," taunted Ames.

"You'll rot before you get a——dollar from me," panted Grieve, and like a bull he plunged back on the porch, toward the door of the mess-room.

"Hey, somebody slip him a gun," yelled Ames, in a high-pitched voice.

All the movement there was among the few men still left on the porch was not forward, but backward. Grieve headed into the open door.

"Come on, you nigger prince of the range!"

The rancher slammed the door behind him.

Ames stood motionless, strained for a moment, then he relaxed. Presently Grieve appeared, stalking away under the pines. He had gone through the cabin. Then Ames walked over to his horse, and as he took up the dragging bridle he shot a flashing glance at the girl huddled down in the buckboard, her face as gray as ashes.

A little while later, when Ames sat in his quarters smoking and thinking, Lany Price arrived.

"Hello, Arizona! Where you-all been?" he inquired, cheerfully. Manifestly he had neither seen nor heard about the exciting incident that had just been concluded.

"Me? Aw, I've been foolin' around," drawled Ames. "Rode up to call on that nester, Nielsen. An, when I got back heah seems like there was a heap goin' on."

"I guess. Boss back, sober for a wonder, with some cattlemen. One of them is Mr. Blair. I've worked for him. An' that bunch of Texas longhorns—they sure got my eye. I'd just give my left leg to own them."

"Lany, you'll shore need your laig. An' I reckon you'll own that herd or one like it before long."

"Arizona, are you drunk?" ejaculated his friend.

"I'm as sober as an owl. Feelin' fine, though. Just had a nice talk with Amy Grieve."

"If you're not drunk, you're crazy," cried Lany, jumping up.

"Well, I'm shore not drunk. An' I didn't dream it aboot Amy. My, she looked sweet an' pretty! She's got class, Lany. I reckon she's too good for you."

"You talked to Amy!"

"Shore, just a few minutes ago."

"Where?"

"Right out in front of the mess-house, before Grieve, his visitors, an' the whole durned outfit." ·

"*No!*"

"You bet. She was in her buckboard alone, an' I waltzed up, tipped my hat, an' braced her. Talk aboot your thoroughbreds! She was tickled to death to have Grieve see me there. Well, I made her blush, an' among other things I told her I was daid wrong aboot not wantin' that kiss she gave me, an' I was shore goin' to hunt for a girl like her an' get a million kisses, same as she gave you. Oh, boy, but you should have seen her face!"

"Arizona, you're a perfect devil!" ejaculated Lany, divided between ecstasy and horror.

"Gosh! I'm jealous of you, Lany!" drawled Ames. "But, fact is, my main reason for speakin' to Amy was to ask her to befriend these poor Nielsens up the river."

"Arizona, she can't befriend a poor sick horse anymore," declared Lany. "She always was doin' some kind thing. But Grieve found out an' shut down on her."

"Shore I made a point of Amy helpin' the Nielsens when she's boss heah."

"Boss—heah!" whispered Lany, incredulously, his eyes suddenly fixed.

Thump of boots and jangle of spurs outside interrupted the conversation.

"Hey, pard, air you home?" called a rather husky voice.

"I reckon, if you come careful," returned Ames.

Slim Blue entered with his hands up, and behind him came MacKinney, pale of face, if he showed no other sign of perturbation.

"Put your hands down, you damn fool," ordered Ames, sharply.

"Wal, you said come careful," replied Blue.

"Set down on the bed, boys. I reckon I want to watch the door."

"Natural, but it ain't necessary. Grieve won't come out to meet you an' he hasn't one single man hyar who'd do it for him, even if he had nerve enough to face you."

Lany crashed down off the table. "My Gawd! fellars, what happened?"

"Boy, you go back in the corner an' listen to men talk."

MacKinney leaned against the bunk and gazed sorrowfully down on Ames.

"Shure now you've played hell."

"How so, pard?" drawled Ames.

"Same old story. You mosey into camp, make all the fellars loike you, an' then you throw a jolt into us—an' ride away."

"Mac, I'm heah yet, an' if I've got Grieve figured correct you-all won't be lonesome for my society very pronto."

"Slim an' me shore didn't bust in hyar to argy with you, Arizonie," replied MacKinney. "We jest wanted to tell our stand. Every hand on the ranch knows how you called Grieve. An' every darn one of thim is scared an' tickled stiff. The Texas punchers have heerd, too, but as they're strangers they ain't takin' sides. Grieve's guests rustled away, plumb disgusted, if nuthin' more. Blair's an old cattleman. I heerd him say to one of thim other visitors, 'Wal, one way or another it's the end of Grieve on this range.' —an' they left. By tomorrow it'll be all over the country, fast as hosses can trot."

"Ahuh. Reckon it'd have been better if Grieve hadn't showed yellow," remarked Ames.

"Wal, the suspense would have been over," laughed MacKinney, grimly.

"Arizonie, you're a cool joker," put in Slim, admiringly. "Don't you jest give a damn?"

"What aboot, Slim?"

"Wal, I don't jest exactly mean about Crow Grieve," rejoined Blue, sarcastically.

"One way or the other you'll have to leave us, Arizonie, an' thet's what Slim is beefin' about," went on MacKinney.

"Friends always have to part, some time or other," said Ames.

"Arizonie, I'm quittin', an' Mac is, too, an' I'll bet

most of the outfit is. We'll never ride for Grieve again."

"How aboot your money?"

"Aw, to hell with thet. We don't need no money."

"Shore sorry to bust up the outfit, boys. I don't see no call for that."

"Niver mind us," interposed MacKinney. "But listen, pard. I'm shure advisin' you to ride in to South Fork an' wait fer Grieve there. Sooner or later he'll come, fer he has to have his licker. Then he can't avoid you. But hyar in his own back yard.... It shure ain't safe, Arizonie. Grieve is a hunter, you know. The rifle is his long suit. Shure he'll plug you from a distance."

"Reckon I was figurin' aboot that," replied Ames. "Wal, I'll hang around a couple of days, anyhow, so he cain't say he chased me away."

"Wal, so much fer thet, Arizonie," concluded Slim. "You want to watch like a hawk. An' it's a safe bet some one of us will have an eye on Grieve, whenever he comes out of the house."

The cowboys lounged out, leaving Ames sitting there, watching through the door. Then Lany Price, white and shaken, accosted Ames.

"You—you done this for Amy an' me!"

"Done what?" growled Ames.

"Picked—this—fight," faltered Lany.

"Me! What's wrong with your haid, boy? I didn't pick nothin'."

"Yes, you did. I see it all now. Your ridin' up to Nielsen's. I know Nielsen an' his wife. She's a strappin'-big handsome woman.... I never told anyone, Arizona. Not even Amy! But Grieve tried to make up to Nielsen's wife. An' when he got flouted he shut down on Nielsen.... Then your bracin' Amy before Grieve an' all of them. Oh, you're a cute one. You knew Grieve would see red—yell at you—or hit you. An' that'd give you a chance to call him....An' you made him crawl before the crowd! An' Amy!—Gawd! I'd like to have seen it! But she'll tell me."

"Lany, since you're such a darn smart boy an' have such a weakness for me—suppose you take a hunch from what Slim Blue said, an' keep your eye peeled. Shore I haven't got eyes in the back of my haid."

"I will, by Heaven!" declared Lany, desperately, and stalked out of the bunk-house.

Thereafter when Ames left his quarters he did it guardedly. Pine trees and thickets, sheds and corrals, fences and rocks, all came in for careful scrutiny. Careless men with enemies sooner or later suffered for it. Ames was not careless. He changed his seat at the mess-table, so that he could watch both doors. He had a preoccupied air, but a keen observer would have noted his intent, unobtrusive watchfulness.

The following day, just before supper time, while most of the outfit were lounging at the mess-house, Ames sauntered up the middle of the road, from the direction of the corrals.

When he reached the porch he encountered Brick Jones, a red-headed, lean-faced cowboy, lanky in form and lackadaisical in manner.

"Jones, I shore been lookin' for you," drawled Ames.

"Have ye? Wal, I ain't quite been returnin' the compliment," grinned the cowboy, though it was plain that surprise and anxiety possessed him.

"Reckon if I punched you in the nose, good an' hard, you'd go for your gun, now, wouldn't you?"

"Wal—I—guess I would—if ye didn't knock me—cold," replied Jones, his lean face losing its red. "What ye sore at me fer?"

"You helped build that fence shuttin' in Nielsen, didn't you?"

"I did an' I hated the job, Ames. But a puncher can't pick his work."

"He shore cain't, if he works heah....All right, you're talkin'. Now how aboot Nielsen's wife? You treated her pretty low-down."

"Aw, hell, I didn't nuther," hurriedly retorted Jones, growing red as a lobster. "Thet ain't so, Ames. You got it wrong. She's a big nice-lookin' woman, an' she smiled so pleasant—wal, I reckoned she was plumb took with me. An' I made a little love to her. I might have been sort of loony, for I'd been drinkin', but I thought the lovemakin' went with her. So I rode up again, an' thet time—wal, if grabbin' a woman an' wrastlin' her some is low-down, I'm shure guilty. But she smacked the stuffin's out of me an' barred me out."

While the listening cowboys guffawed their delight Ames looked long at Jones, evidently satisfying himself as to his status.

"Ahuh. Well, Brick, I reckon you're more loony than low-down," concluded Ames. "An' if you want to shy at a fight with me you'll go up there, knock down that fence, an' apologize to Mrs. Nielsen. Savvy, cowboy?"

"I ain't deef, what else I am," returned Jones,

surlily. "Ames, I ain't achin' fer a fight, but you're givin' me a hard choice. I've got to throw up my job."

"Shore. Most all the boys have quit. So you won't be lonesome."

"Mac, is thet so?" queried Jones, plainly impressed and bewildered.

"It shure is," replied MacKinney, blandly. "Arizonie quit, an' then Slim an' me an' all the fellars who sat in on the little show yestidday. You missed it, Brick. We're loafin' around now, waitin' fer a new boss."

"Grieve sold out or suthin', huh? By golly! I sort of felt there was a mystery."

"Haw! Haw!"

"Brick, you hit it plumb center," put in Slim Blue. "Grieve is sold out!"

"I'm gettin' a hunch an' I reckon I need to be gettin' in out of the wet....Hyar, Arizonie, if you'll shake on it, I'll ride up to Nielsen's tomorrer, lay thet damn fence flat, an' tell Mrs. Nielsen I was a low-down conceited jackass of a cowpuncher."

That night Ames went to bed early. The day had been warm and fine, and the cool wind from the heights had not yet blown down to waft away the sultry air and silence the melodious trilling of the frogs.

The window was open. Little did Crow Grieve dream the use to which windows in bunk-houses might be put when he amazed the range by their installation. Ames' ear, developed in the backwoods, caught a faint swish of grass on a woman's skirt. Then a soft footfall outside. He was slipping off the bed when a light tap-tap sounded on the window frame. He knelt and whispered, "Who's there?"

The night under a clouded sky was dark, but he made out a darker form moving from one side.

"It's Amy," came a low whisper.

"Good Lord!—What is it?"

Cold hands caught his as they rested on the sill. But they did not tremble.

"I've been barred—in my room, all—day," she whispered, catching her breath twice, "or I'd have—got you word. Grieve went out before daylight—this morning. I didn't think till late today—to look for his rifle. It was gone. Then I realized he was out hiding somewhere, waiting for you. He just came in. I heard him stamping—and swearing in the kitchen. He was hungry. So I slipped out of my window—"

"Amy, you're shore a brave kid," he whispered, fervently, squeezing her hands. "But you shouldn't have taken such a risk. Run back now."

"Is Lany here?" she asked, in eager, thrilling whisper.

"No. He hasn't come in yet."

"Give him this." She loosened one hand and drew a letter from her bosom.

"Arizona, for God's sake—watch out!" she ended, in an eloquent, broken whisper. Then like a noiseless shadow she stole away in the gloom to vanish.

Ames gazed at the letter to assure himself of reality. "Shore she's a game kid!" he muttered. "Takin' a chance with that black devil—to warn me! An' to fetch a love letter to Lany."

Ames laid the letter on Lany's pillow, and unbarring the door he went out, and bent slow steps up and down the lane. Presently he reëntered and carried out his pack and saddle, which he deposited just round the corner of the cabin. Then leisurely he proceeded in the direction of the pasture where he kept his horse.

The gray gloomy hour before dawn found Ames stealing under the pines toward the ranch house. At the first streak of daylight he was in the shadow of the trees, opposite the wide gate of the courtyard. Imperceptibly the light brightened. A faint rose color appeared in the east, out beyond the misty sleeping range.

A door shut somewhere. Ames bent like a watching, listening deer. Then slowly he straightened and stiffened, as if to spring.

The bulky form of Grieve appeared in the gateway. Under his arm he carried a rifle. He moved cautiously, without noise, like a hunter. He looked up and down the lane, waited a moment. Then swiftly he started across for the shelter of the pines.

Ames stepped out, his gun leaping up.

"Mawnin', Grieve!" he drawled.

Grieve jerked in terrific shock. An instant he froze. Then as the mad blaze of his eyes set on Ames he shrieked a curse of terror and hate. Up he swept the rifle. Ames' shot broke the action. The rifle burst red and boomed, then appeared to spin in the air, while the heavy bullet spanged among the branches.

Grieve took short steps, falling all the time, to plunge like a stricken bull. He struck the ground hard, and such was his tremendous muscular energy that his bent body stretched with the rapidity of a released spring. His black hat bounced and rolled. He flopped to his back with a loud expulsion of breath.

Ames stooped over the ghastly face. In a last black flash of consciousness Grieve's eyes rolled on his foe, changed their appalling frenzy, grew blank and set.

A few minutes later Ames rode down the lane, past the silent bunk-houses, out toward the range, which was awakening to rosy beauty in the morning light. He did not look back. At the turn in the road he dropped his bridle over the pommel and bent his head to light a cigarette.

"Well, Cappy," he drawled to the horse, that shot up his ears, "reckon this ought to feel familiar to you. So go along. We'll shake the dust of Wyomin'....I shore hope Nesta never hears aboot it."

CHAPTER
9

*I*T WAS summer down under the glaring red cliffs—that strangest of desert formations, Hurricane Ledge. Hot, windy, dusty, it seemed hell to the lonely lost rider who faced it.

From the Grand Canyon this irregular and lofty upheaval of rocks, yellow and gray and red, with its black specks of timber, extended north across the Arizona line into Utah.

In all Ames' long ten years of wandering from range to range he had never seen the like of this sublime and desolate Utah. And he was glad that circumstances had driven him to ride into it. How strangely and tremendously a contrast to his beloved Tonto Basin! In his mind's eye he could see the pine-black ridges, the rushing amber brooks deep down between, the sycamores shining in the sun, the floating golden maple leaves, the purple-berried junipers, the craggy slopes rising to the Rim, gold and black against the blue. He could see the deep Rock Pool of Tonto Creek, that eddying dark hole from which he had rescued Nesta—now so long ago, yet so vividly remembered. Dear old sweet Nesta, with her hair like sunlight and the twin blue-star eyes! It would have been worth a great deal to see her again—this last had been the third attempt in ten years—but there were men still living who waited and watched for his return. It would have been sheer wild joy to give them satisfaction, but such a move would not have been for her happiness. She was happy, the last letter had said—two years and more ago—and Sam was prosperous, and the twins well. Little Rich was big and sturdy and took after his uncle, loving the forest trails and the brown brooks.

"Shore I'd like to see that lad," mused Ames, and he wondered if he ever would. At every turn it seemed that risks and hardships multiplied for him. He had entered Arizona again from New Mexico by way of the White Mountains, and at last, when he reached the Cibeque a camp-fire chat with a chance rider had turned him north again on the long trail.

He stopped at Williams, a lumber camp, where he bought supplies and traded one of his horses for a pack-mule. Venturing into a saloon, something he seldom had done of late years, he had been recognized by one of four gambling men. "Arizona Ames!"

Ames did not know the fellow, who was evidently a rider, and neither an enemy nor a friend. Ames said, "Howdy!" and passed on. At the corral Ames addressed the lad who had taken care of his horse.

"Hey, sonny, where'n the devil would you go if you wanted to lose yourself?"

" 'Crost the canyon," replied the lad, with bright shrewd glance. "Utah an' the Mormons. You'll never be found or knowed there."

"I'll take your hunch an' you take this," said Ames, flipping his last dollar.

The ride down Havasupi Trail into the great gorge, the swimming of the Rio Colorado, river of red silt, the climb up the perilous Shinumo, and out through the wilderness of the Siwash—two weeks of tremendous effort found Ames without pack-horse or supplies, hungry and worn, lost somewhere over the Utah line.

It did not worry Ames to be lost. Nothing mattered very much. Everything save death had happened to him—death and love, the former of which had been ever a step back upon his trail, and the latter something which had strangely escaped him. But he felt always that Nesta had filled this need, ever since he could remember the little bright-haired twin sister.

Nowhere in all the West that he knew or had heard of could he have ridden with such growing pleasure as here in this stark region of purple depths, of hot barren wastes, of bold-colored windy heights. If the Mormons prospered here they were indeed wonderful people. One sweeping glance over a vast sage-dotted level, or down into a wild rock-and-brush-choked canyon, or up an endless yellow slope that climbed to the bleak heights of red dome and ragged peak, was sufficient to acquaint Ames with the meager nature of this country.

He rode on, hoping to run across a sheep trail, a cattle trail, or a horse track, that might lead to camp or ranch or hamlet. He had salt and deer meat in his saddle-bags, and he had been nearer starvation than now, but he felt a continual gnawing in his stomach.

The spotted sage plain glared under the noonday sun; yellow whirling dust-devils spread aloft like colossal funnels riding inverted across the desert; sheets of sand sifted along the ground, rustling at the brush; low down on level glaring flats deceitful mirages appeared as if by magic, only to vanish; and the wide distance showed isolated mesas and long promontories running out from the hazy horizon, and walls of pale red rock and saw-toothed pink cliffs rising against the copper sky.

Hurricane Ledge blocked the west from Ames' searching view. Far down at its southern end showed the dim zigzag line of the canyon, dark and somber and mystic.

Ames rode on. There was nothing else to do. He headed north as nearly as he could judge by the sun, and this direction would take him across the brow of Hurricane Ledge. It would, he grimly muttered, unless the gale blew him and his horse off their course. The hot blast appeared to be rushing up from the canyon, and obstructed by the Ledge, it whined and moaned harder and fiercer over the desert of sand and sage. He did not see enough grass to nourish a goat. And the hour came when he let his intelligent horse choose the way, while he protected his eyes from dust and his face from stinging sand. No doubt this hurricane wind rose with the sun, increased all day, and died out in the evening. It was incumbent upon him to let the horse seek shelter.

Toward the middle of the afternoon the horse left the sand for rocks. Ames ascertained that he had crossed a trail and turning into it was going down. Soon low walls shut off the wind and dust—a welcome change. Ames wiped his wet face and smarting eyes. Another relief followed closely—he rode down into shade.

He had entered a narrow rough gulch that rapidly grew deeper and wider. Ames discovered that his horse was following fresh tracks in the trail. Ames dismounted to see what he could make of these tracks, soon calculating that four shod horses had passed by, some hours before.

Whereupon he mounted again, to ride on with growing interest in this canyon. Ames believed he had descended some thousands of canyons, never one of which resembled this. A mile from where he had entered it the walls were a thousand feet high, and in another like distance they had doubled their height. Moreover, they were insurmountable. Broken in places, splintered, caverned, grandly sculptured, with blank vacant spaces, and again overhanging ledges, nowhere did they offer opportunity for man or horse to climb out. The floor was level, except where slopes of talus and ruins of avalanche reached out from the walls. A dry wash, with low banks, wound down the center of this gorge. What little grass there was appeared to have been scorched by the sun. The sage had suffered the same blight. The only green that enlivened this glaring rent in the rocks came from a cactus here and there.

It was the nature of canyons, even in the desert, to slope gradually down to where water ran and grass grew. Ames would have been satisfied to take this chance, irrespective of the horse tracks he was following.

Time and again his quick eye had caught sight of striking marks on the cliffs, mostly in the shadow of ledges. Presently the trail passed close by a cavern, on the yellow walls of which showed vividly a number of blood-red hands. Ames stopped.

"Dog-gone my hide!" he said, plaintively. "Am I seein' things?"

He got off to investigate. The blood-red hands were of paint, perhaps deposited there in centuries past by aborigines or cliff-dwellers. They were small in size, perfect in shape, the fingers spread wide. These hands had been dipped in red paint and pressed against the wall. Who placed them there? What did they signify?

"Funny old world," he soliloquized. " 'Most as bad now as it was then, I reckon. Shore any darn fool would savvy what they meant then. But I'm just wonderin'. Maybe this is a hunch for me to back-trail.... Tough on me to have a lot of bloody hands stuck in my face. But my conscience is clear."

Ames rode on, and from that cavern every few rods of this remarkable gorge gave evidence of prehistoric habitation. Hieroglyphics in black and yellow, crude figures of birds, snakes, animals, of which Ames recognized deer and bear, spotted level walls in every protected place. But no more in red!

Likewise the gorge gave evidence that it had been used as a burial-ground. Small graves low down along the base of the walls consisted of stones cemented by some red substance harder than rock. These graves were short and narrow, and all of them had been broken into. After a while, however, Ames noted that there were many sealed graves, like mud-wasp nests, high up above his head. And these had not been despoiled. That excited his speculation, and presently he concluded that during the years or centuries since the upper graves had been cemented, the canyon floor had eroded down to the level upon which he now rode. They had once been at the base of the wall.

Sunset and then twilight put an end to Ames' diversion. It was about time for him to find a place to camp. Patches of grass had begun to show along the walls, and thickets of scrub-oak, and in rocky recesses of the stream-bed gleamed pools of water. A little farther down, Ames concluded, there would be a good place for him and his horse to spend the night.

He did not, however, get much farther. The canyon made a turn, opened wide, with a break in the right wall, where under the bulge of rock a camp fire flickered out of the shadow. Presently it disappeared behind huge sections of cliff that had tumbled down. The trail led round them. Ames expected to be hailed, yet kept his horse at a natural trot.

"Hands up!" rang out a harsh command.

With one action Ames reined his horse and elevated his hands.

"Shore. Up they are," he replied, peering behind an obstructing rock.

A tall man, bareheaded, in his shirt sleeves, stepped out with gun leveled.

"Who air you?" he demanded.

"I'm nobody to hold up, you can shore bet on that," answered Ames, with a dry laugh.

"What you want?"

"Well, most particular I yearn for a cup of hot coffee an' a hot biscuit."

His drawling cool speech in the face of the extended gun had evident effect.

"An' then what?"

"Bed, by gosh! if it's only hard rock," declared Ames, fervently.

"Face round...now get off," ordered the man, curtly.

Ames was extremely careful to comply with this command.

"Keep your hands up an' go on ahead."

"Which way? Reckon I see two trails," said Ames.

"To the right."

Ames complied, and after a few steps passed an obstructing rock to be greeted by a bright camp fire. The dark forms of three men stood expectantly. Packs and saddles were scattered around under a projecting ledge of rock, the smoke-blackened roof of which afforded evidence of many camp fires. As Ames drew closer, he caught sight of unrolled beds, from which he deduced that this was a camp of some permanence.

"Heady, look this fellar over," spoke up Ames' captor.

Ames halted at a significant touch from behind. He stood in the firelight. A lanky man in ragged garb stepped up, and aside, so as not to block the light. Ames looked into cadaverous face and gray hawk eyes.

"Steele, I never seen him in my life," said this man, called Heady. "He ain't no Mormon."

Whereupon Ames' captor stepped round in front, to disclose to Ames a swarthy crafty face, eyes like bright beads, and the tight-lipped mouth and hard jaw of a man who kept his own secrets.

"Wal, so much fer thet," he said, slowly, and he lowered the gun. "Amos, what you an' Noggin make of him?"

The other two of the quartet half circled Ames, the first a ruddy giant, bearded and unkempt, and the second a lean little man, past middle age, with a face like a ferret.

"Steele, he's a Gentile cowpuncher," said Amos, "an' you scared the hell out of us fer nuthin'. Haw! Haw!"

Whatever the ferret-faced individual thought he kept to himself.

"Wal, give an account of yourself," continued Steele.

Ames realized that he had, as often before, fallen into bad company. Slowly and easily he lowered his hands, and replied with manner that suited his movement.

"Shore. Short an' sweet. For reasons of my own I haided across the canyon, down Havasupi. Lost my pack-mule an' supplies swimmin' the river. Climbed out by the Shinumo Trail. Then I got lost. Natural enough, for this heah's bran'-new country to me. I kept haidin' north. When I hit this gulch the dust was blowin' fierce, an' I started down. Never saw your tracks till I got to the bottom. That's all.... Quit raggin' me an' give me somethin' to eat an' drink."

"Wal, we all have reason of our own fer things. I ain't over-inquisitive. But what's your name?"

"Ames, if that's any good to you."

"Ames? I don't know. Sounds queer."

"Reckon that's because it's my right name. They call me Arizona Ames."

"Arizona Ames? Sounds still queerer. I'm good on faces, but pore on names.... Wal, set down, Ames, an' pitch in. We got plenty of grub, an' Amos sure can hash it up."

"Thanks. Will you let me tend to my horse?"

"Wal, I'll throw your saddle an' turn the hoss loose. Plenty of grass an' water below."

"He'll shore be as glad as I am heah," responded Ames, and espying a wash-basin and a bucket of water he gave his hands much needed attention. "Oh, my, but the Lord can be good to a fellow when he just aboot give up!"

"What you ridin' into Mormon country fer?" asked Heady, curiously. "Know any Mormons?"

"Only Mormon I ever knew was a wild-horse wrangler," replied Ames, as he bent his stiff, sore legs to sit down before the spread. "Finest chap in the world. But he stole a girl I was aboot to fall in love with."

"Haw! Haw! Sure Mormons are hell on stealin' gurls, if nothin' else," averred Heady.

Then Ames paid strict attention only to eating, though he was aware of Steele's return. He ate prodigiously, to the delight of the big cook and the amusement of the loquacious Heady. Steele did not have a small appetite himself, and the ferret-faced Noggin munched his food, listened, and watched without comment.

"Any smokin'?" asked Steele, at the end of the meal.

"Got the makin's," replied Ames.

Presently all save the cook had comfortable seats round the fire.

"Arizona Ames?" Steele questioned himself again, with puzzled beady eyes on Ames. "Wal, I don't reckon I ever seen you, because you're the kind of a lookin' fellar easy to remember."

"Shore I forked a horse everywhere, except in Utah," replied Ames.

"Thet's a fine hoss of yours," said Steele, with a zest of appreciation not lost upon Ames. "What you call him?"

"Captain. Cappy for short. Named after an old friend, a trapper I used to know."

"Not sich a bad name. How long you had him?"

"Aboot seven years. He's mine."

"Would you sell him?"

"Say, man, did you ever love a horse?" queried Ames.

"Only weakness I ever had—lovin' *hosses*," rejoined Steele, and this sally fetched guffaws from Heady and Amos. Noggin watched the fire with half-lowered, ferret eyes.

Ames casually dropped his own eyes, to hide the leap of his thought. He let the remark pass, and he decided to act and talk as best he could the part of a rider not too keen and of ordinary experience.

"Lookin' fer a job?" asked Heady, during a lull in Steele's monopolization of the conversation.

"Yes an' no," answered Ames, and he knew that was a clever remark.

"Mormons need good riders, but they pay poor wages," said Steele.

"Reckon if you were a Mormon you'd shore not say that," laughed Ames.

"Me an' Amos an' Noggin hyar are genuine Christians. But Heady is a Mormon. So be careful how you sling your gab around. Haw! Haw!"

Heady dropped his gaze. The remark did not go well with him. Ames, used to watching the play of men's features and the light and shade in their eyes, saw that Heady betrayed regret or remorse for something that had passed.

"I'm flat broke an' I'll have to take a job with a Mormon—or anybody who's not too damn particular aboot references."

"You can sell your hoss. I'll give you a hundred, an' my hoss to boot," said Steele, with the persuasiveness of the born horse-trader. Also it bore a note that jarred on Ames.

"Thanks, Steele. I'll consider it," returned Ames, thoughtfully. He knew how to handle this situation, and he made a quick jump at conclusions.

"We're from Nevada," vouchsafed Steele, confidentially. "Me an' Noggin are pardners, an' Amos is our cook. We lost a string of hosses over on the Virgin. They've been druv down in this canyon country. An' we hired Heady to guide us around. But, Gawd! you might as well hunt fer a needle in a haystack."

"Wild stallion lead your horses off?" asked Ames, innocently, when he knew perfectly well that Steele was lying.

"Hoss thieves," replied Steele, shortly. "Are you one of them trackers thet can foller unshod hosses over rocks?"

"Nope. Shore wish I was," lied Ames, coolly. "My horses are always fat."

"Haw! Haw! Which means you spend most your time trackin' an' you'd rather see their ribs?"

"You shore hit it on the haid," replied Ames, stretching and yawning. "Steele, I'm so tired an' sleepy I cain't stay awake. Will you mind if I turn in heah?"

"You're welcome."

"Where'd you throw my saddle an' blankets?"

"Right thar," returned Steele, pointing. "I can spare you a blanket. You won't need none over you in this hole. Hotter'n hell."

Ames made his bed just out of ordinary earshot and he lay down with a loud groan. As a matter of fact, he was weary and heavy-eyed, but not so much so as he desired it to appear. Presently he gave a capital imitation of an exhausted man snoring. But really he was listening with all the power of remarkably sensitive and trained ears.

"Arizona Ames? Where'n hell did I ever hear thet name?" Steele muttered, in a considerably lower tone.

"Wal, you must have heard it somewheres on-usual or you wouldn't put sich store on it," replied Amos.

"I'd say in Salt Lake City jail—if this fellow

wasn't an honest cowboy," said Noggin, in a voice suited to his face.

"Honest? Why, Noggin, thet puncher is as crooked as your nose," averred Steele.

"Fine judge of men you are!" ejaculated the other, loud in contempt. "If you was otherwise, would we be hidin' here?"

"Not so damn loud!" flashed Steele, irritably, and with the authority of a leader. "You might wake him up."

"Small matter. What're you goin' to do about him, anyhow?"

"Wal, for one thing, I want thet hoss," returned Steele. "I ain't seen his beat in a month of Sundays."

"He talked like a man who cared for his horse. You'll have to steal him and that might not be so easy. Unless—"

"He'll trade all right, with a little urgin'," interrupted the leader, complacently.

"You want things so bad you fool yourself," rejoined Noggin, in his thin-edged voice. "You'll have to do some strong urgin' or I'll miss my guess. What's more, this stranger who calls himself Arizona Ames may be otherwise than he pretends."

"Arizona Ames!—Dammit! thet name rings in my ears like a bell. I must be gettin' old.... What you mean, otherwise?"

"When you marched him up to this camp fire, with his hands high, he was too damn cool and sharp-eyed to tickle my fancy."

"Ahuh!—Wal, he was a cool one, at thet. But what if he is?"

"He changed so gradual that I never noticed till after supper. And it's made me think."

"So much the better if he's on the dodge. We'll find out, an' if he is, let's take him in with us."

"Advise against that strong," replied Noggin, vehemently.

"Why? We could use a couple of slick hombres."

"You're the boss. And my last word is be careful he's not too slick."

"Noggy, you'd throw cold water on your grandmother's coffin," said Steele, in disgust.

"I'm goin' to bed," rejoined the other, and his hobnailed boots scraped on the rocks.

A silence ensued. The camp fire crackled. Some one of the men threw on a stick of wood and the sparks flew upward. Down the canyon an owl hooted dismally.

Then Steele changed his seat for one closer to Heady, and a good deal of their low conversation was indistinguishable. Ames caught some of Steele's phrases such as, "To hell with Noggin."—"I'm runnin' this outfit."—"Morgan's hosses."—"Too big a bunch."—"Lund or Nevada."—"Figgerin' hard."— "Get across Canyon."

Heady had little to say in reply. Soon the two men followed the others to bed. Ames lay thinking, and watching the flickering shadows of the firelight. There did not appear to be any doubt that he had fallen in with a band of horse-thieves. Steele was easily gauged as a crooked Westerner of long experience. Ames regarded Noggin as the more dangerous. Just where Heady, the Mormon, fitted into this band Ames could not see, but he was inclined to the opinion that Heady was being persuaded or intimidated. For the rest, Ames thought they were planning to rob a Mormon rancher, probably named Morgan. The drove they might corral would probably be too large to drive off to Lund or Nevada, and they wondered if they could get them across the Canyon. Ames, remembering the trails he had traversed and that boiling red river, and the awful roar of the falls below where he had swum his horse, grimly believed the thieves would find just retribution if they attempted it. Here Ames shifted to the references made to his horse, and that set in motion another train of thought not favorable to Steele's chances for longevity. Lastly Ames pondered over what he should do on the morrow. Finally he gave it up. So much had to be left to the hour itself. Then he fell asleep.

Ames awakened early, but he was the last to get up. Sleeping in his clothes and boots, nights on end, was not conducive to a comfortable feeling in the mornings.

"Wal, if you feel like you look, I reckon you didn't lie about thet trip across the Canyon," was Steele's greeting.

"Trip wasn't bad," replied Ames. "It was hustlin' so fast an' then losin' my bed an' grub that knocked me up. I'd like to rest heah today, if you don't mind."

"Glad to have you. I'd like to know how to cross the Canyon. You're pretty damn good or else orful lucky. But, come to think, you had a real hoss."

Ames grasped the drift of the horse-thief's thought, but he offered no reply to that speech. Hot water and a shave, neither of which he had had for weeks, helped considerably toward comfort, not to say appearance. Steele gave him an appraising glance.

"Humph! Damn queer I don't remember you, *if* I ever seen you."

"Thanks. I'm takin' that for a compliment."

"Wal, you can, an' no mistake."

"Mawnin', men," said Ames, cheerfully, to the others.

Noggin was the only one who did not reply in like vein. Daylight seemed to accentuate this little man's crafty face, as it did the swarthy evil of Steele's. The cook was a jovial blond giant, likable even if he was a horse-thief. Heady appeared to be a broken man, one who might have seen better days.

"Amos, I'm shore gamblin' you never learned to cook in cow camps," said Ames, at the conclusion of a hearty breakfast.

"Not much. I learned in a hotel in Missouri, if you want to know."

"That so!—Well, I'm not bein' inquisitive, but I'm shore wonderin' how you ever came to be shootin' biscuits heah."

All of them, except Noggin, enjoyed a hearty laugh.

"It's a sad story, Ames," replied the cook.

"Don't tell me," said Ames. "I might be moved to inflict mine on you."

Without being asked, Ames set to help at the camp tasks, which he had observed appeared to be left to Amos. It was after he had chopped and split a spruce log that Steele remarked:

"You was raised in a timber country."

"How'd you figure that?"

"Plain as print. Seen it in the way you swung an ax."

"Steele, I can tell you where *you* was raised."

"Bet you can't."

"Shore won't take your money, but I'll bet you."

"Wal, where now?"

"Kentucky."

"How'n hell did you guess thet?" queried Steele, astounded.

"It was the way you said, 'hoss.' "

"Wal, you could have won my last dollar.... You're an interestin' sort of fellar, Arizona Ames. I notice you pack thet gun pretty low. An' it 'pears to kind of grow on you."

"Habit, I reckon. I've had to sleep with a gun so long."

"Ahuh. Air you as handy with one as you air with an ax?"

"Lots handier," replied Ames, smiling. He saw that he had Steele frankly curious and Noggin openly suspicious.

"Can you put six shots in the ace of spades, at twenty feet?"

"Steele, I can split the ace of spades, *edgeways*, three shots out of six."

"Air you braggin' or foolin'?"

"Neither."

"Wal, I pass. Hittin' the ace face up is my best, an' I always thought I was good."

"That's fair shootin'."

At this juncture Noggin entered the argument, and not with the agreeable badinage which characterized Steele and Ames.

"I'll bet you fifty you can't," he interposed. Whatever his motive was, cunning prompted it.

"Fifty what?" queried Ames, in a different tone of voice.

"Dollars."

"I haven't got even one dollar. But I'll bet you my gun to a cigarette, if you'll throw up your hat I can put two bullet holes in it before it comes down."

Before Noggin could reply Steele cracked a hard fist in his palm.

"Arizona Ames, I've placed you!" he shouted, in loud acclaim.

"Have you? Just where, now?" rejoined Ames, with no appreciable interest.

"Thet brag about shootin' holes in Noggin's hat gave you away. I got you, Arizona Ames," said Steele, forcefully, with leering grin. "I remembered your name, but I knowed sure I'd never seen you."

"Well, you're talkin' a lot about placin' me," drawled Ames, coolly. "But you're shore not sayin' much."

"Wal, give me breathin'-room....It was four years ago, this very month. I remember because they had a big Fourth of July time in Laramie. I was hittin' south an' stopped at a little cow town on the border of Wyomin'. What was thet name?"

"Reckon I can help you to remember," returned Ames, dryly. He saw that Steele had a line on him, not creditable, and it served his purpose to help out with the identification. "How aboot Keystone, at the haid of the Medicine Bow Range?"

"Aha!—Keystone? Thet sure was it. An' I remember them Medicine Bow hills, fer I got chased into them."

"Shore, Steele, it's a small world, for me, anyhow. What'd you heah about me at Keystone?"

"Wal, there was a young cowpuncher about to marry a gurl, daughter of a rancher. I ought to re-member them names, but I don't. Anyway, the very mornin' of the weddin' day, which was when I rode into Keystone, this cowpuncher was arrested by some sheriff's deputies fer rustlin' steers or sellin' rustled steers, I forget which. He swore he hadn't done it—thet another fellar had, an' rung him in. Wal, I heerd the story, they was takin' him along when a rider on a grand buckskin hoss.... By Gawd! Ames, this hoss you rode in hyar last night is thet very hoss...."

"Go on with your story. Your pards are listenin' fine, an' I'm pretty keen to heah the rest myself."

"Wal," went on Steele, "this rider, who was *you*, Ames, held up the deputies, an' proved they had the wrong fellar because *he* was the right one. Would they mind lettin' this cowpuncher loose, so he could go an' git married? An' if they wanted to risk tryin' to arrest *him*, come on.... Haw! Haw!—Ames, you shot your way out of town an' escaped."

"But how do you connect that job up with me?" queried Ames.

"Simple as a-b-c. There was heaps of talk in town. If thet rider was Arizona Ames—an' there were some who swore he was—how'n hell did it come he only crippled two or three of them sheriff deputies? Fer thet hombre, Arizona Ames, could shoot. He could shoot holes in a sombrero—*thrown up in the air!*"

"Steele, it shore is a small West," drawled Ames. "I'd like to know if that cowboy got married. His name was Riggy Turner."

"Thet's it. I remember now. He sure did git hitched up. The town might hev had a circus."

Like a ghost of the past this almost forgotten episode in Ames' eventful career now rose to confront him. It was what he considered the only black mark attached to his name on all the ranges. But Riggy Turner really had been the guilty one and Ames had been innocent. Turner's first offense, so easy to drift into those days! How many cowboys fell simply because it was so easy to do and to conceal! Ames had found it out too late. But he had given this boy Turner a cursing he could never forget and had extracted a solemn pledge, for the sake of the girl who loved Turner, that he would never transgress again. They had hoped to avoid arrest for Turner, but had made no attempt to dodge it. Then Ames had ridden down upon the deputies and the stricken cowboy with the result Steele had narrated.

"Steele, your memory isn't so poor," remarked Ames. "But are you shore aboot one thing? Did the folks in Keystone think it was just accident the range officers got off only crippled?"

"Why, course they figgered it thet way," rejoined Steele, surprised.

Ames edged a half-burned stick into the fire with the toe of his boot. He had no more to say. It had amused him, yet made him a little wistful to recall the incident.

Steele stroked the scant dark hair on his lean chin. "Wal, Arizona Ames, you might do wuss than throwin' in with us."

10

AMES had expected such a proposal and was prepared for it. Steele had accepted him at the valuation of the gossip of Keystone, augmented by the vague hints Ames had seen fit to let slip.

Noggin, however, saw through Ames, or at least powerfully distrusted him, or more remotely a possibility, he actually knew Ames by repute. Ames realized he must be wary, yet seem natural.

"Steele, I told you I didn't have a dollar," presently replied Ames.

"Wal, you don't need none."

"What's your deal?" asked Ames, pointedly.

"Hosses."

"How many?"

"Two hundred head or thereabouts. Fineblooded stock. All broke. Just about ready to be druv to Salt Lake, fer sale."

"Where are they?"

"Over hyar on a Mormon ranch, on the Santa Clara. They belong to a Mormon named Morgan. He lives in St. George. Heady hyar used to ride fer him."

"What's your idea?" coolly went on Ames, lighting a cigarette.

Noggin made a nervous movement that caused a quiver to run down Ames' arm. This thief with the eyes of a ferret needed to be watched.

"Steele, are you goin' to give up your insides to a stranger?" he demanded.

"No, I ain't," replied Steele, testily. "But I'd like Ames to throw in with us."

"I object. I'll not have that."

"An' why not?"

"I've got several reasons. First one is we don't know this man."

"Wal, *I* know him, enough to suit me."

"Do you intend to tell him who we are?"

"Hell! We're no better than he is. Fer thet matter, mebbe we're not as good."

"Steele, you've the mind of a child," returned Noggin, fuming. "I mean, are you tellin' him our business?"

The leader turned to Ames.

"Arizona, what'd you take us fer? Now come out with it pronto an' straight. This Noggin is so damn smart, I'd like someone to take him down a peg or two," replied Steele, his swarthy face heating up. "I took you fer a cowboy on the dodge fer killin' or stealin'. An' I had you figgered correct as you've not denied it."

Ames surveyed the four men, while he withdrew his cigarette. He was keen enough to see that Noggin made note that he used his left hand for this purpose.

"Steele, I reckon I didn't do much figurin' till just the last half hour or so," replied Ames. "But since you tax me I'll come clean. I take Heady heah to be a Mormon wrangler out of luck an' willin' to be roped into any sort of a deal. Amos there is a good fellow gone wrong long ago, who doesn't care one way or the other . . . An', Steele, I figure you as a boss horse-thief, like as not Brandeth himself. I've long heahed of that Nevada outlaw chief."

"Wal, I am Steele Brandeth," replied the other. "An' I'm powerful curious to know what you thought of Noggin."

"Reckon not much," replied Ames, his eyes on that worthy. The response to this terse remark would establish in Ames' mind what he had to expect. Partly he looked for gun-play, and thought it would be better now than later. All he ascertained, however, was that Noggin knew him and would never risk an even break with him. Brandeth saw as much, too, for a derisive smile wreathed his coarse lips.

"Wal, you've tagged us, Arizona, an' now let's git back to hosses," he said. "If you'll help me on this deal I'll give you one-fifth of the hosses. The way we do, when we git a bunch, is to cut the deck, ace high, fer first pick, second pick, an' so on. Then each of us picks the hoss he thinks most of. Layin' aside a little luck fer first pick, a fellar's hoss-sense is what tells."

"You're shore a gamblin' horse-trader," observed Ames.

"Steele, you can't split this deal up anymore," declared Noggin, aggressively. "You owe me nine hundred dollars on our last deal, an' you're makin' it up on our next."

"Noggy, you're not goin' to git thet all back on this deal."

"I am, or there won't be any deal," retorted Noggin, his eyes like glint of flint.

"There won't?...How so?"

"I'll block it."

"How in thunder would you do thet?" shouted Brandeth.

"I'll think it over."

"Wal, you'd better," said Brandeth, soberly.

The little man left the camp fire and disappeared among the huge boulders.

"We're stuck hyar, anyhow, so Noggin has time to cool off," went on the leader. "This time I ain't a-goin' to give in to him."

"Looks like a stubborn fellow," remarked Ames.

"Stubborn as a mule, an' some other ways, too ....Ames, if you hadn't been Arizona Ames—he'd have drawn on you."

"I was a little worried," admitted Ames.

"Haw! Haw! You looked it....He's shot a number of men. I'm sorry he took a dislike to you. An' I'm not double-crossin' him when I advise you to—Aw, hell! I'm wastin' my breath tellin' you sich things. But you know what I mean?"

"Boss, we're most out of meat," put in Amos.

"Say, we're a bunch of hawgs. I'll go fetch the hosses, an' we'll ride up on top."

"Reckon you can let my horse alone. He needs rest an' so do I," said Ames.

Presently Ames found himself in camp with only the Mormon. Ames was quick to grasp that his reputation had made him an object of great interest, to say the least, to Heady. Ames talked agreeably and with friendliness, aiming to draw the fellow out. That achievement did not necessitate any wit or subtlety. Ames' first impression strengthened, and it was not long before his feeling changed from contempt to pity for the apparently outcast Mormon.

"Who's Morgan?" asked Ames, at length.

"He's a rancher up St. George way. Raises hosses on the Santa Clara an' cattle on the Virgin."

"Rich Mormon?"

"Laws, no! Jim Morgan used to be pretty well off. But he's given away so much an' been robbed so often thet he's no longer rich. When he loses them hosses he's goin' to be poor."

"Given away so much? What you mean? I had an idea a Mormon never gave up anythin'?"

"You Gentiles get a lot of ideas thet are wrong. Mormons are generous, for the most part. Jim is a kind old man. If you'd rode into his place, same as you did here last night, he'd have taken you in, just the same as if you was a Mormon."

"Well, I like that. Shore it's a dirty trick to rob such a man. Don't you think so?"

"You needn't tell these men, but I sure hate to see it done," returned Heady, lowering his voice.

"Why are you goin' to help—or do you intend to?"

"Thet's the plan. I met Steele Brandeth over in Nevada, an' he talked me into it."

"Ahuh!—Well, you needn't tell these men, but *I* think you're a damn fool," said Ames, with his most impelling smile.

"But I've got to eat."

"Shore. So do I....Have you any family?"

"Yes. Wife an' two kids," replied the Mormon, haltingly. "But I haven't been home in a year. I did a bit of rustlin', an' got scared, though nobody seems to know."

"Nice wife an' kids?"

"Too nice fer me."

"Are they poor?"

"They couldn't be nothin' else."

"An' you once rode for this Jim Morgan?"

"I did. An' I could get my job back, I'll bet.... An' now I'm guidin' a gang of thieves to the canyon where he keeps his hosses hid.—Hell of a note, ain't it?"

"Do you want to know what I think aboot you?"

"Yes, I'm tolerable anxious."

Ames took a long pull at the cigarette, blew out a cloud of smoke, and then suddenly fastened eyes of fire upon the Mormon.

"A man who has a nice wife an' two kids, an' who will go out an' help rob his employer, an' I reckon his friend, is a———!...—!—!—!"

When the string of profane range epithets had scathingly passed Ames' lips the Mormon had a sort of shriveled appearance.

"Well, you asked me," went on Ames, in ordinary tone. "Is this heah Jim Morgan a Mormon with more than one wife?"

"No. Jim never had but one, an' only three children. They're all livin'. But the son left home an' never come back. He's heerd of occasionally—not much good. Reckon thet hurt the old man. One daughter is married an' the other lives with him. She won't leave him, though they say she's had many chances to marry. She refused a bishop of her church an' thet made trouble fer her father. But he couldn't change her."

"What's her name?"

"Lespeth."

"How old is she?"

"Twenty-one or so. Big lass, an' good fer sore eyes. She can do a man's work, an' handle a hoss— say!"

"Mormon cowgirl?" mused Ames, with interest. "That's a new one on me. Does she like horses?"

"Like ain't no word. She loves hosses. It's goin' to be hard on her, when we steal thet bunch. Her own hosses run with them, an' when we drive thet canyon we'll clean them all out."

"Reckon you an' I know how she'll feel," concluded Ames, rising. "I'm goin' to take a look at my own horse. Have you seen him?"

"Yes. When I was packin' water up. He took my eye. You seldom see his like in Utah. . . . An' he's sure took Brandeth's eyes!"

"Say, Mormon, are you just talkin' or givin' me a hunch?" queried Ames, sharply.

"I—er—jest talkin'," replied the other, hastily, averting his glance.

Half a mile down the canyon Ames found his horse grazing on fairly good grass. Cappy appeared less gaunt, which fact afforded Ames satisfaction. There were other horses in the wide park, though none near at hand.

Ames repaired to the shade of the wall, and finding a grassy nook between two boulders and screened by sage, he sat down to rest and think, and perhaps take a nap.

He had been in worse predicaments than this of falling in with horse-thieves and being taken for something as bad. Nevertheless, he could conceive that the situation might give rise to unpleasant complications.

"Dog-gone!" complained Ames. "If I'd stayed at the bottom of the canyon, shore some kind of a mess would have bobbed up. Reckon I don't know what to do with this heah one."

A solution easily arrived at was to decide to wait a day or so longer, and then, seizing an opportunity such as this hour, to saddle Cappy and ride away. That, he frankly told himself, would be the wisest course. If he lingered with Brandeth, sooner or later there would be some kind of fight. He pondered wearily over the disturbing fact that almost any combination of men gave rise to friction and strife. He had never seen a cow outfit or heard of one that was free of trouble. How much less chance of peace among rustlers, horse-thieves, outlaws!

"Either I stay or go," he said, aloud, and was a

little disgusted with himself that he did not imme-
diately decide upon the latter. Whereupon he asked
himself why.

Sometimes these lucid intervals of self-penetra-
tion were illuminating to Ames. Nevertheless, here
he was irritated. Had not ten years of wild life satiated
him with antagonism and conflict? Evidently he re-
sented Brandeth's conviction that he was a self-con-
fessed cattle-thief. This ferret-eyed Noggin, more
gambler than anything, rubbed him the wrong way.
Noggin had heard more about him than Brandeth; he
might even have seen him somewhere, on one of the
numerous occasions when trouble had thrown him
into prominence.

Ames felt sorry for the weak Heady, who had
easily been dominated by the forceful Brandeth. And
he gritted his teeth at the thought of Brandeth and
Noggin stealing the last stock of a rancher who had
been rich and who through generosity and adversity
had fallen to low estate. Then the Mormon girl who
loved horses and who would not desert her old father—how this thrilled Ames! Someone had to do
these things—to be the buffer and the anchor, to
serve and sacrifice.

It was the thought of this girl, Lespeth, that decided Ames to linger with the horse-thieves and in
some way or other circumvent them. The least he
could do would be to ride over to see this Mormon
breeder of fine horses and to tell him of the plot to
rob him. But that did not satisfy Ames.

He pondered over the problem for a long time.
Meanwhile the drowsy heat and silence of the canyon
began to lull his senses. Lizards ran out of the niches

of the cliff to peer at him with jewel eyes. A scaly dusty rattlesnake glided into the covert of the sage. Now and then he heard the silky metallic rustle of the wings of a rushing canyon swift—strange bird of the rock walls. White clouds crossed the blue stream between the rims above. Then color and movement and sound gradually faded into slumber.

When he awoke his face was moist and his hair damp. He had slept through the heat of the day, and the shadow on the opposite wall of the canyon showed that the sun had slanted far on its westering journey.

Ames arose and leisurely made his way back to camp. Some moments before he reached it he espied the four men, and had not progressed all the way when he grew aware of a changed atmosphere. Noggin paced up and down at the back of the shaded cavern like a ghoul. Amos did not wear his cheery smile. Heady looked blank. And Brandeth seemed to be chewing the end of bitter chagrin.

"Where you been?" he growled at Ames.

"Right down heah. Slept my haid off."

"Noggin swore you rode off to double-cross us with Morgan."

"Ahuh. Didn't you see my horse?"

"Reckon I was oneasy till I went out an' seen him. I knowed damn wal you'd never leave him."

"I shore wouldn't be separated from Cappy," drawled Ames.

"Many a fellar has felt thet way about life, too," responded Brandeth. "There's many things oncertain, Ames."

"Yeah, I've noticed that. An' one of them is the dispositions of men."

"Haw! Haw!—Air you always so cool an' smooth?"

"Me? Gosh, no! I get terrible upset. An' over nothin' sometimes."

"Wal, me an' Noggin have split," announced Brandeth, spreading his hands.

"You don't say? Hope it's not on my account. If so I can mosey along. I'm fair rested an' my horse will do."

"Wal, you was the snag we struck fust. But it turns out you haven't got much to do with it. Noggin used you as an excuse."

The individual mentioned heard this reference to himself, for he wheeled in his pace.

"Brandeth, if you tell that cowboy any more you're a locoed damn fool."

"Wal, I'll talk if I like, an' you can go to hell," returned the leader, sullenly.

"I'll bet you a hundred that when I arrive *you* will be there ahead of me."

"Wal, then, as I ain't got long to live, I'll shoot off my chin," retorted Brandeth, sarcastically. "No, Ames, you ain't the bone of contention. It all came out today. Noggin made this plan. He's a hoss-dealer, an' buys up hosses, where he ain't recognized. Reckon St. George an' south Utah air yet to make his acquaintance as a hoss-thief. Fer Noggin's long suit is to sell a bunch of hosses to some rancher, an' then steal them back. Me an' him haven't worked long together. He had a gang over in Nevada an' they fought among themselves. Wal, Noggin jumped on me with a wild idee. He once bought some hosses from Morgan, couple of years ago. Paid high fer them. But whatever his trick was, it fell through. Morgan knows Noggin under another name. Now Noggin wants to take Heady with him an' ride over to Morgan, an' make him an offer fer the *pick* of his hosses. This is only a trick to git the gurl, Lespeth—"

"Who's she?" interrupted Ames, in apparent surprise.

"Morgan's daughter. They say when a Mormon gurl is purty an' handy she sure is both. Wal, Noggin has seen this gurl a couple of times, an' he's stuck on her. She was extraordinary sweet to him, he says. Heady, hyar, who knows the Morgans, says Lespeth is thet way with *any* man. Reckon thet makes no real difference to Noggin. His plan is to git the gurl an' her dad to take him to see the hosses. The rest of us air to meet them down in thet canyon, wherever it is. We'll take *all* the hosses."

"Oh, I see. An' what aboot Morgan an' Lis— what'd you call her?—Lespeth?" drawled Ames, knocking a cigarette on end. Apparently for him such plots were commonplace.

"Wal, thet's where I hedged," went on Brandeth. "Noggin says likely the one hoss-wrangler Heady seen on Morgan's ranch would go with them. He'd have to be shot. Then Noggin plans to knock the old man on the head—pretend not to kill him on account of the gurl—an' take her off with the hosses. Ames, what's your idee of this deal?"

"Reckon just what I'd expect of Noggin," replied Ames, with strange timber in his voice. That was the instant wherein his consciousness fixed upon a determination to kill Noggin.

"Wal, thet ain't answerin' me. You're purty deep, Arizona," went on Brandeth. "Anyway, I'd have agreed to the deal if Noggin would call off the debt I owe him, instead of grabbin' my share of the hosses. But, no, the damn weasel-eyed little hawg! He wants the gurl, his half of Morgan's stock, an' enough of mine to square the debt. So I bucked. An' we split."

"Too bad. Reckon Noggin is not very reasonable. Cain't you talk him out of it?"

"Haw! Haw! *You* try."

"Hey, Noggin, come out in the sunlight," called Ames. "Your eyes may be sharp in holes, but mine are poor."

"What do you want?" returned Noggin, and it was certain that Ames had struck him differently from Brandeth.

"Well, I reckon that depends on you," said Ames, enigmatically.

Noggin came out of the shade, guardedly, his eyes like pin-points, his nervous hands low.

That short walk defined his nerve and his ability to Ames, neither of which was extraordinary. Still he could be taunted or driven to draw, if Ames wished to force the issue then. This, however, was only in the background of Ames' thought.

"Brandeth has told me aboot the deal you want to work on Morgan," began Ames, as a preliminary.

"I heard him," snapped Noggin.

"Reckon I figure you're some unreasonable."

"I don't care what you think. You're not in it."

"Well, I haven't refused yet."

"No. An' I notice you haven't jumped at the chance, either."

"Noggin, I never jump at chances. I'm considerin' Brandeth's offer, an' if I do accept, your wantin' the earth may stick in my craw."

Nothing was any more certain than that this man seemed trying to pierce through Ames' armor to the truth.

"All right, Ames. *When* you accept, I'll lay my cards on the table," replied Noggin, and turned his back.

BRANDETH evidently evidently took Noggin's statement as favorable to a reconciliation, or if not that, to a split that would present a new phase of the complicated situation.

"Wal, take your time, Arizona, but don't you be onreasonable, too," he said. "I ain't pushin' nobody."

"I'm thinkin' a lot, Steele," replied Ames, agreeably, and that was true.

"My pore head is near busted," confessed the robber, plaintively. "I never could stand much worryin'. An' I'm sure glad it's over....Heady, you rustle some firewood, an', Amos, you throw some grub together."

The shadows lengthened and deepened. The gold slipped up over the rim wall. Twilight gathered quickly, unusually thick. Low long rumble of thunder broke the oppressive silence.

"Say, was thet rock slippin' somewheres or thunder?" queried Brandeth.

"We're in for a storm," replied Heady.

"Good. It'll cool the air, fill up the water holes—an' hide our tracks."

Ames deducted from these words that Brandeth had decided upon action. Presently the cook called them to supper. Meanwhile darkness set in, black as pitch between the walls of the Canyon. Thunder threatened and muttered and rumbled far in the distance. Noggin did not speak during the meal, nor afterward. Brandeth made a civil remark to him, which he ignored, and presently he thumped out of camp, to disappear in the gloom. This procedure drew a doubtful wag of Brandeth's head.

"Ames, can you always back-trail yourself?" he queried.

"If I cain't I'll eat my chaps," laughed Ames.

"Wal, could four men drive a bunch of hosses down into the Canyon, an' swim them acrost the river, an' out up on the other side?"

"Four men?" asked Ames.

"I said *four*. Me an' you an' Heady an' Amos."

"Shore we could, if the horses were not wild."

"Swimmin' the river now. Is thet some hell of a job?"

"It's no fun. But with plenty of time, an' workin' up the bank to take advantage of the current—which I didn't do—it could be done."

"Was the Colorado high?"

"No. An' it was fallin'."

"How about grass an' water?"

"Poor for a couple of days. Then once in the brakes the finest any horseman would want to see."

"Ahuh.—Wal, Ames, I reckon the Providence thet protects hoss-thieves sent you to me. Heady knows all this country from Hurricane Ledge north. But we couldn't figger on south because he'd never been over it.... Could we sell hosses across the Canyon?"

"In Arizona? Mormon horses? Say, man, you could sell a thousand, an' no questions asked."

"Amos, have we got two weeks' grub?" called Brandeth to the cook.

"With some meat we can stretch it to three weeks, boss."

"Heady, see hyar," said Brandeth, to the wide-eyed Mormon. "This camp you say is our base, an' only a day's ride to Morgan's canyon corral?"

"Yes, it's the best hidin' hole I know," replied the Mormon. "It ain't often any riders happen in here."

"If we decide to drive south instead of north, would it be out of our way to come back hyar?"

"No. It'd be safer," returned Heady, with an eagerness which betrayed his fear of the north. "I know a trail below where we can climb out. Wild-hoss hunters used to work in an' out there. They had a narrow place fenced in. We could drive the stock down there, an' out by here the next day. After thet Ames would have to guide you."

"Ahuh. Wal, we'll crawl out before daylight tomorrer, an' do the job—Noggin or no Noggin," concluded the chief, in stubborn relief.

"Reckon we're in fer a storm."

"Won't thet be all the better? What you think, Arizona?"

"Whenever I steal any livestock I always like fallin' weather," replied Ames, nonchalantly. "I shore aim to hide my tracks."

"Ames, why in the darnation cats couldn't you say thet in front of Noggin?"

"Noggin? Huh! I'd prefer he keeps on thinkin' whatever he thinks."

"Wal, thet is, you're a two-face hombre. You're not on the dodge. You're one of these wanderin', line-ridin', adventure-huntin', gurl-lovin', gun-throwin' cowboys!"

"Gosh! but he shore flatters me. I'm glad,'cause I was afraid he thought worse."

"Arizona, I don't mind tellin' you I ain't over well-acquainted with Noggin. He owns up thet ain't his real name. I've a hunch he's Bill Ackers. You've sure heerd of him?"

"Name doesn't sound as if I just heahed it first. An' who's Bill Ackers?"

"Wal, he's all of Nevada thet's no good. A secret, long-armed, high-hat gambler who don't stay no-where long. Who gambles while he makes deals. They say he has a slick gang. But I never seen Ackers. Noggin claims he has."

"Why don't you spring it on him, sudden-like— an' watch his face?" asked Ames.

"Never thought of thet. It's not a bad idee."

The return of the individual whom they were

discussing precluded more talk. Ames went off to his bed, with the intention of lying there a while to listen. But he preferred to sleep somewhere in a safer place, which he had been careful to pick out that day.

Contrary to usual custom, Brandeth maintained silence. The cook and Heady conversed in low tones while packing supplies.

"Packin' up, eh?" snarled Noggin, at length, as if goaded.

"You've got sharp eyes when you want to see," replied the chief. An edge of aloofness hinted of alienation.

"When are you leavin'?"

"Before daylight."

"Where are you goin'?"

"Wal, I was talkin' it over with Ames. An' we're goin' over hyar in the Siwash to gather wild flowers."

"Ha! Ha!" laughed Noggin, with brutal suggestion. "I'll tell you, Brandeth, if you had this Arizona galoot sized up correct you'd think gatherin' flowers was most damn appropriate."

"Thet so. An' why?" rejoined the other, gruffly.

"Figure it out. You've no more imagination than sense."

"Wal, I never laid no claim to be extra bright."

"I asked you where you're goin'?"

"I heerd you."

"Heady, what're you packin' that grub up for?"

"Boss' orders. We're goin' to hide these packs up in the cracks of the rocks."

"What for?"

"Somebody might ride along tomorrer. It happens once in a blue moon. An' we'll need the grub if we drive out across the Canyon."

Noggin hopped like a huge ant upon a hot griddle.

"Brandeth, you're double-crossin' me!" he shouted.

"Wal, seems to me it's t'other way round. But I'm goin' after Morgan's hosses, an *if* I have luck I'll drive them acrost the river."

"You are like hell!" shrieked Noggin.

"I am like hell!"

"Who made this deal? Who outfitted this gang?"

"Reckon you did. But you never told me the straight of it. I ain't squeamish, an' dead men don't take no trails. Reckon, though, I shy at the gurl end of it. So I'm goin' to do my own way."

"What am I goin' to do?"

"Don't ask me riddles. Haw! Haw!"

"Brandeth, that Arizona tricker put you up to this."

"Hell, no. Can't I have an idee of my own? You shan't blame Ames. You've only yourself to blame."

"Is Ames goin' to guide you across the river?"

"He says he can an' I reckon he will. But he hain't promised yet."

"I can go plumb to hell?"

"You can go plumb to hell."

"Ho! Ho! If that isn't rich? Suppose I tip Morgan off?"

"Thet wouldn't be healthy if I ever found out," replied Brandeth, darkly. "But you can't block us. It's half a day longer to Morgan's ranch than to the Canyon where he hides them hosses."

Noggin cursed impotently, eloquent of his realization of the fact Brandeth sardonically imparted. That ended the quarrel, and in Ames' estimation any further possible friendship between the two men. This afforded Ames immense gratification. If he knew such men they would destroy themselves. Neither of them had exhibited any marked quality of greatness. In such a situation as this, Rankin would long ago, and at the first sign of antagonism, have shot his way out of the difficulty.

Both Noggin and Brandeth went to bed, and soon afterward the other two followed suit. The dying camp fire sent ghostly shadows upon the cavern walls. Soon the last flickering light died. Ames waited until he was sure the others had fallen asleep and then noiselessly he gathered up his blankets and felt his way to the place he had selected. There he composed himself to safety, and the comfort of sleeping without keeping one eye open.

Lightning flared across the purple sky and a wind moaned through the Canyon. Raindrops blew in under the shelving rock to wet his face. The sultry air had cooled and the sage gave forth a damp fresh fragrance.

Ames, owing to his long nap during the day, and the thought-provoking climax these robbers were precipitating, was wakeful part of the time. He slept on and off till the dark hour before dawn. The ring of an ax assured him someone was up. He lay yet awhile, thinking. The brooding desert storm still hung over the Canyon. It had not broken.

With his mind refreshed by rest Ames went briefly over the contingencies most likely to arise. It was altogether possible that Brandeth and Noggin would come to a deadlock, and obligingly erase themselves from an ugly scene, of which Ames had already wearied. If they did not—! Ames left it sufficient to that moment.

The thud of hoofs attested to the bringing in of the horses. That roused Ames with a jump. With the blankets under his arm he worked his way along the cliff and soon saw a bright camp fire. When he reached it he found that neither Noggin nor Brandeth were up yet. Amos had a cheery word for Ames. Soon the horses were pounding the ground just outside the cavern and could be seen dimly in the edge of the flare of light.

Ames hurried to find his horse. Cappy whinnied before Ames espied him. Whereupon Ames led him to one side, and returning for saddle and bridle soon had him ready for travel. Then Ames sought the cook.

"How aboot some grub to pack?" he asked, and straightway had hard biscuits, salt, meat, dried apples, and a canteen thrust upon him. This genial cook had taken a liking to him. Ames made a mental reservation that he would remember it.

Brandeth appeared at the camp fire, grim and silent, brushing his long unkempt hair. He spoke once, to order Heady to saddle his horse. Noggin arrived from a direction opposite that from which Ames had looked for him, a circumstance which Ames vowed would not happen again. How almost impossible to exercise eternal vigilance! Habit was more powerful, in the long run, than the most implacable of wills.

The cook yelled lustily, and was instantly cursed

by Brandeth, who had not begun this day amiably. Then the men ate standing, hurriedly, and with never a word.

"Let's git out of this," ordered Brandeth.

Ames, standing back, caught the expression of both Brandeth and Noggin, in the firelight. His lips tightened and a current quickened down his frame. What fools they were! How blindly set on their selfish ends! One and probably both of them would not be blindly set upon anything at the close of that day.

"Air you goin' with us?" demanded Brandeth of Noggin.

"You know——I am," came the terse reply.

"How far?"

"That's my business."

"Ahuh. Wal, you can keep company with our Mormon guide," concluded Brandeth, sarcastically.

The dark hour before dawn had passed. A dim pale opaque gloom possessed the canyon. Ames mounted and rode out behind Brandeth, who had followed his guide and Noggin. Amos brought up the rear.

Ames, once in the saddle, behind the man he desired to watch, relaxed from tense strain. The hour had not yet struck. But he divined that he was not riding forth on a horse-stealing expedition, but a stark tragedy, in which he was exceedingly likely to become involved.

A smell of rum assailed his nostrils. It bore witness to a custom of such men, to fortify their courage and augment their passion by a false stimulation. Ames' dark meditation elicited the cold fact that if he were about to force an enemy he could ask no more of fortune than for him to drink.

Compared with those of many wild cowboys, gun-fighters, rustlers, and other notorious characters Ames had met in his ten years of wandering, his own experience, his actual encounters had been few and far between. But they had been dominated by a clear sight, a clear head, and a nerve as keen as wrought steel.

"Else I wouldn't be heah," he muttered to himself.

They rode at a trot down the canyon, over a good trail that followed the meanderings of the wash. The day broke gloomy, drab, under clouds that hung low over the ramparts. Soon the wide chasm narrowed to sheer perpendicular walls, where darkness was loath to surrender. The grass was thick and heavy; water babbled over rocks; deer went crashing through the sage. When the riders came to a fence of poles Ames remembered its significance, and understood why Brandeth called back to Amos, "Shet the gate."

Once again the canyon opened to grand proportions. Clouds hid the tips of magnificent towers. Heady got off his horse to lead him up a rocky slide. Noggin looked upward, then slowly followed suit.

"Git off an' climb," said Brandeth.

Ames had no hatred of slopes, as Brandeth's tone made clear he had. Soon they were toiling up a zigzag trail, seldom used, full of stones and ruts; and it was noticeable that Brandeth kept at the heels of Noggin. When Heady halted, which was often, they all had to do the same. The horses heaved; the men panted. No one spoke again during that long strenuous hour to the top.

But once up, they all more or less exploded; and Ames' contribution was an irresistible encomium to the astounding and magnificent scene which burst upon his gaze.

He faced the east, out of which weird and wonderful red rays shone from broken massed clouds. The desert floor heaved away, divided by a ruddy track of light, in shape if not in hue resembling a moon track on waters. The sun had not yet cleared the horizon, and the strange effulgence it spread seemed not of earth. Hurricane Ledge towered into the storm clouds, which apparently gave it a false height, and a peculiar effect that Ames could liken only to the approach of a hurricane. A sinister pale red sheen enveloped the distant mesas and buttes, a veil that was unreal and beautiful.

Thunder rolled out of the east, heavy, detonating; and wicked, forked lightning zigzagged across the purple cloud. There was no breeze to fan the hot faces of the panting men. The early morning had a sultry, muggy weight, oppressive in the extreme.

It seemed unnatural that no word was exchanged on the rim of the canyon before the riders mounted. Ames gazed back into the hole. The strange lights affected even it, magnifying the depth and its stark nudity. They rode on, and all the phenomena of storm and desert gathered strength. Ames tried to assure himself of what was true—that he only faced sunrise during a storm in a bleak and terrible region of the earth.

They came soon to where the level desert bulged

into the base of Hurricane Ledge, that had loomed, yet seemed far away. By the time they had rounded its northern point the sun had risen to burn through the clouds. West of the Ledge, opened up the gulf of the canyon country, vast and awful at that moment. North sloped and spread and rolled and upflung that barren splendor of the earth called Utah. Far away black peaks and pink walls stood up, and endless lines of desert wandered away from them.

Suddenly Ames became aware that the guide had halted.

"Trail splits here," he said, pointing. "This one leads to the hoss canyon, a good four hours' ride, downhill. An' thet fork leads to Morgan's ranch, twice as far, but better goin'."

"Ahuh. So I see," replied Brandeth. "Partin' of the ways!"

The undercurrent of his tone, caustic as vitriol, rather than the content of his words, directed all eyes upon Noggin. Ames suddenly reverted to the deadly issue that had hung in the balance. In a flash the moment had arrived. Brandeth had flung the gauntlet in his partner's teeth.

Noggin baffled Ames. If he had worn a mask, which was now off, he presented on the moment a more impenetrable man than before. Unfortunately, the brim of his hat shaded the wonderful eyes which Ames had never trusted.

Brandeth slipped out of his saddle and in one stride stood clear. Yet Ames felt that he was too close to him. Those ferret-eyes of Noggin's could command his movements as well as Brandeth's.

"Steele, will you compromise on the deal?" asked Noggin.

"Wal, I ain't much on compromisin', but what's your idee?"

Noggin's horse was mettlesome, but any cowboy could have seen that it was not only his spirit that kept him on the move. Did Noggin want to line up those four men? The idea seemed preposterous to Ames, but he grew acutely curious. From something that emanated from Noggin's manner or appearance, Ames conceived an impression which operated upon him as subtly as actual menace. Indeed, the place, the hour were menacing.

"I'll go with you for half your share as well as one-fourth for me," said Noggin.

"No....And *one-fourth!*—Say, can't you count? There's five of us."

"Only four. Ames will change his mind when he finds out that I'm...Bill Ackers."

"Bill Ackers?"

"I am."

"Ha! I'll bet you Ames won't care a hoot if you *are* Ackers. No more than me!"

"Ask him if he's goin' with us."

Ames recognized craft here utterly beyond the ruffled Brandeth. And he had an inspiration. Noggin's game was not yet clear, but most certainly it was inimical to the leader of that quartet. Noggin had read Ames' mind, or else he knew absolutely that Arizona Ames would not lend himself to horse-stealing. Brandeth should never have matched wits with anyone, most certainly not Noggin.

"Ames, tell the beady-eyed little skinflint you

care no more'n me fer Bill Ackers, an' thet you're goin' with me," said Brandeth, irately.

"Sorry. Noggin's coppered the trick. I'm not goin'," drawled Ames.

"Not goin'!... When'd you change your mind?"

"I never intended to go."

"——! Git off thet hoss!" Brandeth screeched, reaching a swift hand toward Ames' bridle.

Noggin's gun crashed. Ames saw Brandeth's fierce expression set. Go blank! Ames pitched sheer out of his saddle. Scarcely had he moved when Noggin's gun crashed again. Ames struck the ground hard on both hands. That enabled him to spring over even as he flopped on his side. On the instant he saw Brandeth fall. Cappy plunged away to disclose Noggin, his gun high, hauling on his frightened horse. In a flash Ames drew and shot. He hit Noggin's horse. It screamed and bounded convulsively, to fall and throw its rider.

Noggin plowed in the dust. With marvelous, terrible agility he waved up with the momentum of his fall. Half up—half turned! Then Ames' leveled gun spurted flame and boomed. Noggin whirled clear round, flinging arms high. His gun spun up—fell—and went off while yet he seemed stiffening in grotesque position, without support. Then he slumped down.

Ames leaped up and watched Noggin a moment. One of the horses snorted and there came a pounding of hoofs on rock. Then Ames strode over close to Noggin—looked down to see him twitch and lie still. His gun lay some paces away. Amos had evidently ridden some rods off and stopped. Heady was riding back toward where Brandeth lay prone on the ground.

Ames sheathed his weapon and beckoned for the men to approach. Amos came slowly. Heady rode up to dismount beside Brandeth. When Ames reached them he saw that the robber had been shot through the temple.

"Bill Ackers! He shore fooled me," said Ames, shaking his head. "If I hadn't pitched *quick* off that horse..."

"He's dead," said Heady, hoarsely.

"Reckon he is, an' so's his pard."

"Ames, you come awful close to bein' in the same fix," rejoined the Mormon. "My Gawd! but it all happened sudden!...Were you lookin' fer it?"

"I had a hunch."

Amos rode up within fifty paces and called out, "Ames, I hope you've nothin' ag'in' me?"

"Shore haven't, Amos. Come heah," replied Ames. "I didn't start this....Heady, step over an' see what Noggin's got on him."

Ames approached and got off. He was livid, and his eyes rolled, then fixed on the ghastly features of his employer.

"Search him," said Ames.

Brandeth had some gold and currency upon his person, a watch and knife, besides his gun.

"Amos, I reckon you'd better keep them."

Heady returned with Noggin's gun, watch, a leather wallet, a money-belt, a silver-mounted pipe. The Mormon's eyes glistened, as if he had a premonition of fortune.

"He was well heeled."

"So it looks. Let's see," returned Ames, and he opened the heavy money-belt. At each end of a long roll of double eagles lay a packet of greenbacks.

"Reckon it's an ill wind that blows nobody good," said Ames, handing the belt back to the gaping Mormon.

The wallet contained papers, which Ames placed in his pocket for future examination.

"Heady, keep that stuff, an' whatever else he's got."

"There ain't anymore 'cept his saddle. I sure want that," returned Heady.

"Amos, the little expedition has been busted up. What're you goin' to do?"

"If it's all the same to you, Ames, I'll take Brandeth's hoss an' go back to camp. I'll pack the outfit an' make a break fer Nevada."

"It's shore all the same to me," replied Ames. "Only I'd like to think you'll throw in with a straight outfit next time."

"So long, Ames," replied the cook, with one short, steady glance, then mounting his horse he rode across the space to gather up the bridle of Brandeth's horse, which he led at a brisk trot up the trail toward the canyon.

"Heady, I'm goin' to ride over to Morgan an' tell him aboot this," said Ames. "Do you want to go?"

"Yes, if you won't give me away."

"Will you go back to that nice wife an' two kids?"

"You bet I will."

"You'll be honest an' decent?" added Ames, sharply.

"Ames, I swear by the Prophets I will!" exclaimed

the Mormon. He was sweating hard and extremely agitated. "All I ever needed was a little money. To get out of debt an' start over!...An' there must be thousands in this money-belt."

"Shore is. An' you can keep it, I reckon, without any bad qualms. Money isn't much to me anymore."

"My Gawd!...I'll never forget you—Arizona Ames!"

CHAPTER
12

*T*HE summer storm broke while Ames and the Mormon gave the best burial available to the two robbers. And that was to deposit them in a deep crevice and cover them with heavy rocks. The Mormon went further and added enough rocks to form a monument.

"It ain't likely," he said, "but somebody livin' might want to see their graves."

Thunder burst with tremendous boom and crash, to roll over the desert, and rumble away weirdly into the canyons. Streaks of white lightning blazed out of the purple clouds. Veils of down-dropping rain streaked a belt of rosy sky in the east. They coalesced to form a gray pall that marched across the desert. Then it appeared the hot air that hung round Hurricane Ledge, as if lodged there, began to move and gather strength, to whip up the dust, to shriek down from the crags, to rage into a gale.

Before it Ames and the Mormon sped northward on the trail, their horses blown from trot to lope. The pall of rain never caught up with them. Soon the full fury of the freakish gale roared at their backs, and they were lost in a yellow cloud of dust.

They halted in the lee of a huge rock, and waited till the hurricane passed. It roared and whirled away. Mounting once more, the riders went on, and Ames looked back. Hurricane Ledge was draped in the gray pall; all to the south was dim and dark, whorled low clouds, dipping into the canyons; eastward gold and silver hues had displaced the angry reds, and through bright rimmed clouds the sun shone with the glory of dawn, illumining the livid and ridged desert, clearing away the deceitful shadows and revealing distance and sublimity.

For Ames the hours of that ride were short and the miles more and more replete with the wonder of Utah. It staggered him by its canyoned and clipped and walled vastness. Spots of green were rare and stood out like gems in boundless gray.

Late in the afternoon the Mormon led Ames through a rocky break into a valley that afforded soothing relief to his seared eyes. It was a triangular oasis walled in by red bluffs. Squares of rich green alfalfa seemed to leap up alive into the quivering air; orchards and vineyards bloomed; and a grove of stately cottonwoods surrounded a stone house.

They rode on into the shade. The grounds round the house were bare and clean except where grass and willow lined the irrigation ditch. The leaves of the cottonwoods rustled; birds sang sweetly; burros and turkeys and calves had the run of the place. The stone walks, the fences, the sheds, the gray old porch, all seemed as aged as the cottonwoods.

Heady came out with a striking gray-haired man who stood erect and whose gray eyes still held fire.

"Ames, this is Mr. Morgan," announced Heady.

"Shore glad to meet you, sir," said Ames, extending his hand.

"It seems I have reason to be glad to welcome you," replied Mr. Morgan, meeting Ames' grip. "Come have a seat on the porch." He led Ames up the stone steps, still holding his hand, and bending those kind, searching gray eyes upon his countenance. "My daughter will welcome you, too....Don't be backward, lass. Come out. He's a very mild-looking Gentile."

Ames turned at the sound of a light step. A tall girl came out into the light, a wholesome, blooming, rosy-cheeked young woman, whose large gray eyes met Ames' with fearless interest.

"Lespeth, this is the gentleman who has served us well. Ames, a rider from Arizona....This is my daughter Lespeth."

"I'm happy to meet Mr. Ames," she said, and gave him her hand.

"Miss, the pleasure's shore mine," replied Ames, somewhat embarrassed. Morgan slid forward an old rocking-chair, which he placed for Ames.

"Sit down, and you, too, Heady," he invited, as he seated himself on a bench. "Lespeth, fetch out a chair. Tell Mrs. Clegg we'll have company for supper. ...Ames, you look dusty and worn. Let me have the straight of this extraordinary claim Heady made. Then you can clean up and make yourself comfortable."

"What did Heady tell you?" queried Ames, laying his sombrero and gloves on the floor.

The girl came out with a chair, which she placed before Ames. Then she stood a moment, hands on the back of it, with unconscious smile as she gazed down upon him. Ames became aware that she was a magnificent creature.

"That he'd fallen in with thieves, who had forced him to act as guide for them, and but for your timely intervention I would have been robbed again, and perhaps killed, while Lespeth would have been at the mercy of a lecherous villain."

Ames briefly related, with little reference to Heady, the circumstances of his meeting with Brandeth and Noggin, his suspicion as to their character and how that was verified by what he heard, the plot as defined by Brandeth, and then the disagreement between the two men, the ride up out of the canyon, and lastly the fight.

"Dead!—They're dead?" asked the Mormon, aghast. Manifestly Heady had not revealed that.

"Shore they're dead," replied Ames, grimly. "You gather, of course, that I led Brandeth to believe I'd throw in with him an' help rob you. But Noggin saw through me—knew I was lyin'. Well, when it came to the pinch I had to do some tall figurin'. Noggin swore I wouldn't go with them an' I admitted it. Brandeth was so surprised an' sore that he made a grab for my bridle. He'd been keen to get my horse, an' when he told me to get off, that was what he was up to. But Noggin shot him. I threw myself off my horse just as Noggin shot at *me*. When I hit the ground I was behind my horse. That saved me. For when Cappy jumped I took a shot at Noggin. His horse threw him. But he bounced up like a rooster an' was just as swift with his gun—when I got him.... That's all. It shore was a close shave for me. Noggin fooled me. He was all cold nerve an' swift on the draw. Whew! If it had been an even break, I believe he might have killed me."

"Thank God he didn't!" exclaimed the Mormon, fervently. "The unrighteous villain! ...Ames, you are a brave, resourceful young man. I am grateful. You are not the first Gentile who has befriended me, and therefore I have reverence for your creed."

Ames took this coolly enough, but when he glanced up at Lespeth his serenity went into eclipse. The rosy face had become pale; the great gray eyes dark with horror; her red lips parted, and her body shook in a tide of emotion.

"Noggin had this wallet on him," went on Ames, producing it. "I haven't looked at his papers yet. But, by the way, it seems his real name was Bill Ackers."

"Bill Ackers? Oh no, impossible!" ejaculated Morgan, with uplifted hands of protest. "I know Ackers. Have sold stock to him. He had paid court to Lespeth. Isn't it true, Lespeth?"

"Yes, but not with my consent," she replied, low-voiced.

"Ames, I looked with favor on his suit once," explained Morgan. "He was well off and wanted to go into business with me. And Lespeth seemed not to want to marry any of the many Mormons who have ridden here.... But this Noggin could not have been Bill Ackers."

"Describe him," said Lespeth.

"Well, he was not a big man an' near forty, I'd say," replied Ames, reflectively. "He had a thin smooth face, not bad-lookin', except for his eyes, which were small an' sharp, like a ferret's."

Morgan gazed incredulously at his daughter.

"Father, he has described Ackers perfectly," Lespeth cried. "Ferret eyes! They used to look through me.... But could this blood-thirsty Noggin be Bill Ackers?"

"I can't believe it, lass," replied her father, sadly.

"Well, I've run across stranger things," said Ames. "Let's look at his papers."

Indisputable evidence was forthcoming that Noggin had not lied when he had assured Brandeth that he was Bill Ackers. His papers contained only the name which he had claimed was his.

"Heah we are," continued Ames, with an air of finality. "Reckon he sailed under many handles, but this must be his right name. Bill Ackers."

"I never trusted him," broke out the girl, with intense relief.

"Hope you wasn't sweet on him," Ames teased her. "I'd shore hate to make you unhappy."

"Sweet on him?—I was not," she declared, in a tone that matched her face. Perhaps Ames' glance, more than his words, had been responsible for her blush.

"Mr. Morgan, did he owe you any money?" asked Ames.

"No. But I owed him. Soon I would have paid

it—though that would have left me poor."

"Ahuh. Well, the debt is canceled," rejoined Ames, rising. "An' now if you good folks will excuse me I'd like to wash up."

"Yes, indeed," responded Morgan, heartily. "You must excuse our neglect in forgetting that. Heady, you take care of Mr. Ames. You may use the log cabin there. We always keep it ready. I will have your horses looked after."

As Heady led Ames away toward a snug little cabin under the cottonwoods he whispered:

"Did you see them big hungry eyes?"

"Hungry eyes! Whose, man?" asked Ames, in surprise.

"Lespeth's. They just ate you up."

"See heah, Heady. You're shore named appropriate," reproved Ames, though he felt himself tingle. "All that money has gone to your haid."

"No. I'm as cool as a cucumber. I've knowed Lespeth for years. An' I've seen them hungry eyes look at a good many men, but you're the first one they ever swallared."

"Gosh! Who'd ever take you for a sentimental cuss?" retorted Ames.

"But don't you think she's beautiful?"

"Hardly. Nor pretty, either....She's more than both. She's a goddess, if I know what one is."

The extravagant compliment brought a glow to the Mormon's sallow face. He seemed a changed man. His grimy hands shook as he opened the door of the little cabin. Ames peeped into a clean, tidy room, with two beds on which lay white spreads. Chair, table, bureau, all homemade furniture, as well as an open fireplace, reminded Ames of home.

"I forgot my saddle-bag," he said, and when Heady ran back to fetch it he sat down on a rustic bench in the shade of a giant cottonwood. An arm of the irrigation ditch ran by the cabin, making soft, restful music. What sweetness and peace here! Ames had not felt surrounded by such atmosphere for many years. Then the Mormon came trudging back with Ames' bag.

The next half hour the men spent in making themselves fit to sit at table with white folk, as Heady put it. When Ames resumed his seat outside the sun was setting gold over the western wall. All about him the golden light merged with the green. The water murmured, the bees buzzed. A burro brayed off in the background. Ames heaved a great sigh of relief at the thought that he had played some part in preserving the sweetness and tranquility of this place for these good Mormons.

Heady came out, beaming and shining, though there were sundry signs of his awkwardness with a razor.

"Ames, I'll rest here today, an' tomorrer ride home hell-bent fer election. I want to go down on my knees to my wife an' tell her about the cowboy who got me out of the worst fix of my life."

"Fine. But don't lay it on too thick aboot me," said Ames.

"Say, Ames, if you'll excuse me—are you really a cowboy?"

"Shore. Just a grub-line-ridin' cowpuncher who cain't hold a job."

"Arizona Ames, I'll take your word fer it. But if

you ain't a son-of-a-gun in spurs I miss my guess....
I swore to you I'd go straight. An' thet's somethin'.
I'll make up with the wife, pay my debts an' tithes,
an' go back to honest ranchin'. I'll be rich, Ames. I
jest took another peek at this money. I'll be rich. But
I'll take a drink damn good an' seldom, an' I'll be
savin' an' careful. You can bet your life no use of
Noggin's money could be better'n what it'll do fer me
an' mine."

"Now you're talkin'," drawled Ames.

"So much fer me. What'll you do?"

"I'll stay heah a day or so, an' then ride on. Shore
will look you up in St. George, to see the wife an'
kids."

"I'd like thet heaps. Then she'll believe I haven't
robbed a bank or somethin'. But, Ames, I'd hang here
fer a spell. It's pretty. No doubt you could give the
old man some hunches about hosses. He'll want to
give you a job. An' you could do worse, if it's true
you're a grub-line-ridin' cowpuncher."

"True as gospel, Heady."

"Then stay awhile, Ames—if only to give Lespeth what she needs."

Ames' leisurely composure vanished in a quick
start and a sharp glance at his companion.

"What?" he shot at Heady.

"Don't bite my head off. I don't mean nothin'
bad. Lespeth is a good girl, clean an' fine, more dutiful
than most Mormon girls still unmarried. An' she's not
too religious. Mebbe thet's why she ain't married.
Mormon cowboys, wranglers, ranchers, preachers,
an' elders, an' one bishop I know of, have come here
after her. All solemn an' slow an' full of church in

their wooin'. There's been some Gentiles, too, like Noggin, an' wanderin' fellars. But none of them ever struck Lespeth right. A few times the old man has tried to get her married—like in Noggin's case—but it always fell through."

"Ahuh. Well, if she's so wonderful as you say, what's this she needs?"

"Lespeth needs to be made love to."

Ames stared at the man as if he had not heard aright.

"Mormon girls like Lespeth don't get any love-makin' *before* they're married. An' a lot of it *after*. Well, I'm a Mormon....But there's a girl who's jest dyin' to be made up to. Talked soft an' sweet to an' patted an' kissed an' hugged!"

"Wal, I'll be dog-goned!" ejaculated Ames, red in the face, as much from consciousness of his own sudden thrilling rush of blood, as shame at the brazen Mormon who could propose such a thing.

"You're a queer cowboy, *if* you are a Gentile," went on Heady. "Can't you see what I'm tellin' you is so?"

"Reckon I cain't. But, by gosh! I can see you're a mushy cuss who hasn't any respect for good women."

"Aw, go 'long," laughed the Mormon. "Even if you did get tolerable thick with Lespeth you'd be doin' her a favor. But all I mean is, if you don't want to stay here an' make a go of it—an' you could do worse, my friend—why, stay long enough to love her a little."

"Lord! ... You take my breath."

"Not me. It's thought of Lespeth thet does thet."

"Heady, if I'd ever been a fellow to make up to girls—an' I never had a chance—I reckon I couldn't make up to Lespeth unless I meant it serious."

"All the better. Then be serious. Marry her!—I'll let you in on this much of the secret, because I trust you, Ames....Lespeth's mother was a Gentile. But she doesn't know it."

"Say, man, you're figurin' me in deep. An' it's all nonsense. That girl couldn't see me with a spyglass. I'm no more than another wanderin' cowboy."

"All right. Have it your way," replied the Mormon, resignedly. "I was only givin' you a hunch. You could rest right here, my wanderin' cowboy, all your life, an' with thet girl it's sure a soft place to light."

"Too good for me, Heady. Thanks all the same."

"Arizona, I figger from your talk thet you never had a sweetheart. But didn't you never love no one? No woman?"

"Shore. My twin sister. Her name was Nesta. She looked like a gold columbine as much as this Lespeth looks like a rose," replied Ames, and he gazed away over the green fields, out over the desert and the darkening walls, without seeing them.

"Twin sister? She must have been a beauty.... An' I reckon you ruined yourself fer her!...All right, take it or leave it. But I'm wonderin' at you. How any fellar who could have Lespeth in his arms an' wouldn't take her—I jest can't understand."

Ames sustained what seemed a strange, vague knocking at his heart, as if life were clamoring at a closed door he had never known was there.

A mellow bell rang. Then a voice that seemed

as sweet gayly called, "Come to supper, Arizona Ames!"

Heady laughed cheerfully. "See, she doesn't even think of me. Come on, you Arizona Gentile, an' take your medicine."

Ames felt like a lamb being led to slaughter, which was something he certainly attributed to this loquacious Mormon. As they neared the house he saw that the supper table had been set upon the porch, and that Lespeth had changed her plain linsey dress to a white one, which even at a distance, transformed her incredibly.

"Crawl, you Arizona iceberg," whispered Heady, as they reached the steps.

Morgan met them, courteous and dignified, with the air of one who considered hospitality a matter of the spirit. Lespeth stood by his side. Her golden head reached to his shoulder. Little trace of shock lingered on her face; she now seemed shy, fascinated, eager, yet unable to meet Ames' look.

Ames remembered to hold a chair for her, but when they were all seated it took a kick from Heady to acquaint him with the fact that the venerable head of Lespeth's father was bent. He asked a blessing that sounded beautiful to Ames. And while he supplicated for this stranger within his gates, Ames watched the girl, whose face was lowered. It seemed to have more than mere beauty—fair, strong, resolute, with a suggestion of austerity that required the fire of eyes and smile of lips to hide its loneliness.

"I would not have recognized you, Arizona Ames," she said, looking up.

He had not been aware that the blessing had

been concluded. And no doubt she had been prepared with that pretty speech before she raised her head, but certainly not prepared for Ames' absorbed gaze. Her confusion added to her simplicity and charm.

"Shore you're wonderful changed yourself," he replied.

A pleasant-faced woman brought in the food.

The ordeal of the meal began, and it was almost beyond Ames. Here he sat a starved beggar at a feast, and he desired to watch Lespeth and at the same time appear well to her.

"Ames, is this your first visit to Utah?" asked Morgan.

"Yes, an' I happened to come by accident."

"Indeed it was a fortunate one for Lespeth and me. How did it come about?"

"Well, I cain't stick at one job any length of time. I'm always ridin' on. An' I was in Williams, where some boy told me to cross the Canyon."

"Our Lord works in strange ways. To think of a boy's chance remark directing you to us! To think of the terrible Colorado River! I have always believed things happen for some definite reason. Back of all is the Divine Mind."

"Mr. Ames, you swam your horse across the Colorado?" asked Lespeth, her eyes wide.

"He swam an' I held to his tail."

"Oh, how wonderful!—Father, you remember the Stuart boys crossed at the Shinumo. Jack told me about it once."

"I reckon the danger wasn't really as great as it looked. An' I shore have a horse."

"He's splendid. I love horses, Mr. Ames.... Would you let me ride him?"

"Shore I'd be delighted—that is, if you can ride him."

"If I *can!*—Mr. Ames, I can ride any horse in Utah," she retorted, with spirit.

"Wild or broke?" drawled Ames.

"Well, I draw the line at wild horses."

"Ames, I've been a horse raiser and dealer all my life," said Morgan. "I knew Bostil, of Bostil's Ford, probably the greatest of Utah horse-breeders. He was wont to say his daughter Lucy had been born on a horse. I can almost claim that for Lespeth."

"Bostil's Ford. Where'd I heah that name?"

"Some old horseman likely spoke of it. The ford is gone these many years.... You like horses, Ames?"

"Reckon I do. Much better than cattle."

"How would you like to see how long you can hold a job with me?" queried Morgan, directly.

"I—well—thank you, Mr. Morgan. I—I'll think it over," replied Ames, in embarrassment. "But shore I'm likely a hard proposition. I cain't keep out of fights."

"Ames, I know men. You don't strike me as a drinkin', quarrelsome rider."

"Shore I'm not either," said Ames, quickly, and he looked straight at Lespeth. "But I'm always gettin' mixed up in other fellows' troubles. I just cain't keep out of things."

"Mr. Morgan," interposed Heady, "Ames should have said takin' up other peoples' burdens."

"You see, Heady would make you a Christian whether you will have it or not.... Ames, I'd like to ask a blunt question, if you will permit me?"

"Shore you can ask me anythin'," replied Ames, with a smile. But inwardly he quaked.

"Are you a fugitive from justice?" asked the Mormon, gravely.

Ames met that kind, penetrating regard with a level glance and a clean conscience.

"No, I'm not. Years ago I shot a man to save my sister. He had relatives. An' this I should tell you happened in the Tonto Basin, where feuds are the rule. Then, not so long ago, I took a cowboy's petty thievin' upon my shoulders. He was to marry the daughter of a rancher he stole from. She loved him, an' I thought she might make a man of him. So I rode away.... That is the black mark on my name, Mr. Morgan."

Ames had never told so much to any man, but he wanted this fine old Mormon to know he had a clear conscience. How much the girl influenced him in this confession he found it hard to define. He had not meant to make of himself a hero, but he instantly feared that in Lespeth's case he had done so. Solid ground seemed slipping from under his feet.

"Thank you, Ames," returned the Mormon. "Please recall that I offered you a job before I asked you the personal question. And what you have told me only adds to my interest in you and my desire to have you work for me.... Come, let us go out before the light fades. I want to show you my alfalfa-fields."

They walked through the orchards and along the fields with the afterglow of sunset reflected from the lofty eastern wall of the valley. The ranch was a rich fertile spot in the desert. Morgan's likening it to a "milk-and-honey land" seemed felicitous.

In the twilight on the return, Ames found himself delivered to Lespeth. It was like a dream, that walk in the gathering dusk, under the shadow of the towering walls, with drowsy summer evening trilling to the melody of innumerable frogs. They walked under the cottonwoods, and it was the girl who talked—of how she loved the ranch, the horses, life in this lonely southern Utah; then of years when her father had been prosperous and she had attended school in Salt Lake City; and lastly of her father's friendship and business relations with Gentiles.

Night fell and the round golden moon soared above the wall, silvering the dark desert. An overwhelming sense of the peace and beauty of this lonely valley flooded Ames. What a haven of rest for a tired and unhappy cowboy! But he did not deserve that, or at least the bewildering possibility which did not now seem remote. All the numberless nights of his watching and riding on the ranges plunged back upon him, as if to crowd upon him the difference between them and moonlit nights like this with the wide-eyed Lespeth.

They were left alone on the porch and Ames realized he was too silent, too unresponsive to this glorious night. And this girl of Utah.

"You spoke of a sister," said Lespeth, softly. "What was her name?"

"Nesta. We were twins."

"What a sweet name! Nesta. Tell me about her."

In that hour, after the strenuous day for body and mind, Ames seemed impelled to tell that story as it lived in his heart. The girl's interest tugged at the gates of his reserve.

Brooding mystery lay like a mantle over the valley. The fragrance of verdant fields, the music of murmuring stream, the dreaming trill of frogs, the splendor of moon-blanched walls—these were not new to Ames, but this responsive girl was, this Mormon who could ride like a cowboy, to whom hard work was natural and right. He found himself telling Nesta's story. Lespeth's eyes turned dark in the moonlight, her strong hands grasped Ames', her breast rose and fell.

"You will go back some day to see Nesta and that boy named after you? Oh, you will go back?" she pleaded.

"Yes, some day, an' seein' you makes me wish it could be soon."

"Am *I* like Nesta?"

"You shore are, somehow."

Ames suddenly realized that he had a tremendous longing to take Lespeth in his arms. All at once there seemed a great aching void that she could fill. The temptation was almost overwhelming with its astoundingly fierce sweetness, its shame and its regret. What would she do? Struggle, protest, and then perhaps she would cease resisting and she would.... He dared not listen to his insidious imagination.

"Father likes you," Lespeth was saying.

"Shore seems so. I'm glad. I know I like him," returned Ames.

"Will you stay and work for him?"

"It'd be fine, but it'd hardly be fair. I shore cain't stay long anywhere, an'—"

"But you might stay long—here?" she went on.

"Shore I might—at that," said Ames, helplessly.

"We have several boys, but no rider now. Father needs one."

"So I reckoned. I—I'd like to, but—"

"Arizona, I will ride with you."

He stared at her in the light of the moon. He felt as if the very fiber of his being dissolved in water.

"We shall race. I on your horse. You on mine. ...Oh, what a race that will be!"

"Girl, you—don't know what you ask," he replied, almost roughly.

"I do know—and I do ask."

"But I am only a wanderin' cowboy," he protested. "I have nothin' except a horse—an' this blood-stained gun. You're a Mormon. Shore I've no religion, but your people would never accept me."

"You are a man. Father and I will accept you."

Ames looked sadly down upon the dreamy face. He could never hide the truth.

"Shore I'd only fetch you more trouble."

"Stay, Arizona!" she whispered.

That seemed the moment for which all the terrible journey across the canyon had been undertaken, and the fatal crisis under Hurricane Ledge. Something rose up in him, out of the long past, it seemed, to prop his failing manhood.

"Lespeth, I'm only human. An' I'd fall in love with you."

"Would that be so terrible?"

"For me, an' shore for you. Because you've a longin' for you know not what. Even if you overlooked the Mormon barrier it would yet be bad. . . . Like as not one of the enemies I've made would cross my trail again....Always that step on my trail, Lespeth! It would be disgrace for one of your creed....No, lass, I'd better leave in the mawnin'."

"But—if I am like Nesta?"

That sweet, almost insurmountable appeal rang in Ames' sleepless ears all night, mingling with the tinkle of the running water and the rustle of the leaves, rang still in the soft dark dawn when he rode away like a guilty man, torn by doubts, sustained only by the conviction that he was doing what was right.

CHAPTER
13

A*UTUMN* burned crimson and gold and purple in the valley of the Troublesome.

The noisy, quarrelsome stream might have had a quiet birth somewhere up in the Flat Tops of Colorado, but when it emerged from the rocks to wind its swift course down between the great grassy timberless hills, it fretted here and roared there, tarried surlily in a bend only to rush on, jealous of time, and pour its amber current over a succession of low falls, step by step, petulant and reluctant, at last to race in a long frothy incline by the only habitation of the valley—Halstead's ranch—and thunder its wrath into the dark green gorge below.

Forest fire in bygone years had denuded these numberless slopes, some of which rolled up to the dignity of mountains. No green trees were left on the heights, but in patches branchless bare poles, sharp as masts, some charred black and others bleached white, stood silent, ghastly, mute monuments to the archenemy of the woodland. Everywhere, on all the slopes, fallen timber lay in windrows, thick as fence pickets, up to the scattered groves of aspens, saplings grown since the fire, and now shining exquisitely gold and white in the sunlight. Of late years grass had sprung between the fallen trees.

And since Esther Halstead had left school in Denver, to take her mother's place in Halstead's household, each succeeding year had added more grass to the burned slopes; and amber moss and scarlet vines, and the beautiful blue lupine, and such amazing and glorious beds of purple asters and Indian paintbrush and columbines that never bloomed so profusely anywhere else on earth.

So Esther thought, as she feasted her eyes upon the autumn hills. Winter was a long, cold, shut-in season at that altitude, and though Esther thrilled to see the lines of elk troop down the snowy white slopes and the mountain sheep come to the garden with the deer, she did not love the Colorado winter. Spring was raw, wet, windy, muddy—a trying time for new ranchers in a new country. Summer was wonderful, but fall a time of enchantment.

Esther needed some compensations for the trials and hardships of this lonely life. She had been born and brought up in Missouri, had attended school there from six years of age until twelve, when, owing to the failing health of her mother, she had journeyed with her family across the plains to Denver, where they lived awhile and she went to school again. Then John Halstead had adventured into the wild northwest corner of Colorado, first lured by the gold-fields at Yampa. Later he had wisely settled down to learn the less glamorous but more stable value of the soil.

At fifteen Esther had come to Troublesome to take charge of the children and otherwise, as best she could, to make up to them and her father for their mutual loss. She was now nineteen, and not the eldest, for Fred was two years her senior. He scarcely counted, however, as far as the manifold tasks were concerned, though when he was at home he did keep the household supplied with fresh meat. Fred had reacted disappointingly to ranch life, which had been his father's hope for him. He had fallen into questionable habits with young men of Yampa, the mining town a day's round journey from Troublesome. Then there were Ronald, aged six, and Brown, a year older, and their sister Gertrude, who was nine, all of whom Esther had to try to control and teach. Her great difficulty lay in restraining them from running wild, a task which required a never-ceasing vigilance and restraint. These children were doing their best to revert to the wild, something Fred had already succumbed to, and to which Esther herself had strange secret leanings.

In winter-time she managed to make them study and learn. But the other seasons were blank so far as education was concerned, unless contact with wild nature held some elements of education. Ronald was a born hunter, Brown had a passion to fish, and Gertrude loved the wild flowers, of which there were a hundred varieties at Troublesome.

The circumstances of the Halsteads were still comfortable, though of late Esther had reason to be concerned. They had a camp cook, Joe Cabel, a most excellent cook, a man with the kindest of hearts, the most amiable of dispositions, and a vast sense of humor. But he had one glaring fault. He could not distinguish between profanity and the ordinary use of words. From him the children were beginning to learn the most terrible language, which was Esther's despair. At present Halstead employed a teamster, a farmer, and two riders; and he was wont to say that he accomplished more work than all of them.

The ranch house stood on a bench above Troublesome Creek, and consisted of repaired and enlarged log cabins which had been erected by trappers, and which Halstead had ingeniously connected. The unit provided simple and crude quarters, but ample for all, and comfortable without any luxuries, unless clear ice-cold water running through the house could be so designated.

Early September had brought frost, at least high up on the slopes, which always appeared so close to Esther until she attempted to climb them. When she half closed her eyes these hills were marvelously colored. She had to peer with wide searching eyes to see the ghastliness of them anymore. Some day, when all the bare spear-like poles were down, and the aspens thickened, they would begin to revert to their original beauty. Esther had learned that nothing in nature was originally ugly, and after it had been despoiled by man, would soon go back to beauty.

From Esther's stand on the grassy bench, somewhat below the house, and from which perch she could keep track of the children, she had a never-palling view of miles up Troublesome Valley. At this season it resembled a marvelous painting. The troubled creek came babbling down between rocky, willowy banks that ranged off level across the valley floor, and then sloped up, to swell, to lift in vast mounds of gray, of green, of blue and red and lavender, marred ever by the black fallen timber, and on the crests fringed by the ghastly poles, that stood like naked masts of naked ships up into the sky. In the far distance these hills were mountains, yet appeared only foothills to the dark ragged peaks higher up.

Downstream there was only a half mile of V-shaped valley, which terminated in the black gorge whence, even at this distance, the Troublesome growled and rumbled in angry thunder at its confinement.

Ronald was running around with the dogs, chasing an unlucky rabbit, while Brown was fishing. Troublesome Creek was full of big trout, many of which Brown had hooked, only to lose. His father occasionally hooked one for him and did battle with it until Brown could manage to land it, and often Joe Cabel would render like assistance. But Brown had no love for this kind of fishing. He had ambition to cut his pole, rig his line and hook, find his bait, raise his trout, hook and catch him all alone without any help. This ambition, like most ambitions, had wrought havoc. Brown had always a goodly supply of fishing-poles, but he could not keep himself supplied with lines and hooks.

This morning, however, he had fished for hours

without any luck. Up to a certain limit he was amazingly patient for a lad of seven. Lunch meant nothing in his young life, wherefore Esther feared to bring wrath down upon her head by calling him.

Presently he looked up at Esther, a freckled-faced, dirty, wet, tousled imp if there ever was one.

"Aw, hell, Ess, there ain't no trout," he yelled.

Esther saw no sense in screeching at Brown, but she made motions which signified that he was again sullying his lips. Brown grinned back in honest contrition. And just at this instant, unfortunately for Esther, Brown had a terrific strike from a trout, which, catching him unawares, jerked him off the slippery stone. Valiantly Brown bent the pole and floundered to recover his equilibrium, but he went down with a great splash.

Esther suffered no alarm on the score of danger. Her small brother was a second cousin to a fish. But her heart leaped to her throat for fear she might in some way be held responsible for this catastrophe. Brown waded out, a bedraggled figure, and as he came up the bank, Esther, in dismay, discovered that his fishing-line was gone. It had broken off at the tip.

Water dripped off Brown. Besides the wet blotches on his face, and the freckles, there was a green slime from the brook. His hazel eyes were beautifully full of fire.

"———luck, anyhow, Ess. *You* made me lose thet fish. I wouldn't 'a' cared, but he took my hook, sinker, line!"

Esther was horrified in several degrees, particularly at this newer and more stunning explosion of profanity. What on earth could she do with such a child? He must be punished. And Joe Cabel must be discharged. Then Esther despaired at the futility of the first exigency and the impossibility of the second.

"Say, Ess, look! Who's comin'?" asked Brown, pointing up the creek. "Gee! Is he drunk or suthin'?"

Esther espied a tall man leading a horse. He appeared to be staggering along very slowly. Her first impulse was to run into the house and call Joe, for rough characters were not infrequent in that country. Her father never permitted her to ride far alone. But on second glance Esther decided the stranger was not drunk, but lame and almost exhausted. The horse, too, showed signs of extreme fatigue.

She thought better of another impulse—to go forward to meet him, though the longer she watched him the more restraint she needed. He approached so slowly that she had ample time for impressions, that gradually grew from curiosity and surprise, to wonder and concern, and at last to thrilling interest. He was the finest-looking man she had ever seen, obviously a cowboy, or most certainly a rider. Tall, lithe, booted, spurred, belted, with gun swinging low, gray-clad, his head drooping, with face hidden under a wide sombrero that had once been white, he certainly excited Esther Halstead.

Evidently he had espied her, because when he drew near he took off his sombrero before he raised his head. When he looked up Esther sustained a shock. Fair hair, almost silver in color, lay dishevelled and wet on a high, white brow, lined with pain, and from under which piercing blue eyes flashed upon Esther. The lower part of his face was bearded, drawn, haggard, and begrimed by sweat and dust.

"Howdy, miss! Have I—made—Halstead's ranch?" he asked, in low, husky tones.

"Yes, sir," replied Esther.

"I reckoned so. But—any ranch—would have—done me." Dropping the bridle, he moved to a big flat stone and sat down as if he could stand no longer. "I don't care—so much aboot myself—but Cappy heah—I was shore sorry for him."

The horse he indicated, a magnificent chestnut, no longer young, stood motionless, his noble head bent, his gaunt lathered sides moving in slow heaves.

"You have come far," said Esther, hurriedly. "Are you crippled or ill?"

"No, miss; we're just—tuckered out," he replied, with a long breath, and he leaned his face upon his hands. His sombrero lay on the ground. Esther's eyes made inventory of the long silver spurs, of old Spanish design, the black leather gun-sheath upon which shone a worn letter A in silver, and then a bone-handled gun, which, though she was accustomed to armed men, gave her a shiver. The man's broad shoulders heaved slowly and painfully.

"Miss, excuse me—a minute. Shore I've not—forgotten my manners. . . . I'm just all in," he gasped.

"I need to be excused, not you," replied Esther, quickly. "I'm forgetting to ask you in—and if anything ails you—"

"Thanks, miss. I'm not hurt—an' nothin' ails me—except I'm worn out.—Starved, too, I reckon, though I shore don't feel hungry."

"Have you come far without food?" asked Esther.

"Well, I don't know just how long—or how far," he replied. "But it was across the Flat Tops."

"Oh, how dreadful! Why, that is a great mountain range."

"It shore is. Up on top I met a trapper—stayed with him one night," returned the stranger. "He told me how to hit the Troublesome—an' follow down to Halstead's ranch. But I got on the wrong trail."

At this juncture Esther's little brother appeared, and curiosity getting the better of his shyness, he moved round in front of the man to ask, "Mister, are you hurted?"

"Hello, there, youngster! I didn't see you. . . . No, I'm not hurted."

"Gee! you look orful tired," went on Brown, sympathetically.

"I shore am."

"Did you come down the crick?"

"Yes, all the way, from the very haid."

"Did you see any big trout?"

"You bet I did, sonny. Far up, though, in the deep still pools."

"How big?"

"Long as my arm. You must be a fisherman. Say, did you fall in?"

"Nope. I was fishin'—an' Ess, here—she's my sister—she called me—an' I was lookin' up when a whale of a trout hooked himself an' pulled me in— the————!"

"Brown!" burst out Esther. "You're a disgrace."

The man lifted his haggard face, stared, and then laughed heartily.

"Sonny, shore that's strong talk."

"It's unpardonable," interposed Esther, ashamed and angry. "We have a cook whose every word is profane. And my little brothers, especially Brown here, have been utterly ruined."

"Well, I reckon it won't hurt them bad," replied the stranger, with a drawl pleasant to Esther's ears. "So you have a cook who cusses?"

"Terribly. We have had many cooks. It's hard to keep one here on the Troublesome. This one is fine— the jolliest, nicest man! But he cant' keep from cursing every time he opens his mouth. But father won't let him go and I have to put up with him."

"An' he cain't keep from cussin'? Now I shore wonder. Is this heah cook's name Joe Cabel?"

"It is. Do you know Joe?" burst out Esther, amazed and somehow glad.

"I reckon—a little," he said, with a smile that softened the piercing blue fire of his eyes. "Miss, will you be so kind as to ask Joe—to come heah."

"Indeed I will!" replied Esther, cordially. "But come in now with me. Joe would surely fetch you in."

"I'm sorry. I cain't make it. My legs are daid."

"I will help you. Come, lean on me," rejoined Esther, impulsively. "I'm strong as a horse, father says."

He regarded her attentively, as if he had scarcely seen her before.

"You're shore kind, miss. But—"

"I'll call Joe," interrupted Esther, hastily. "Who shall I tell him you are?"

The stranger studied over that query a moment, as if it had awakened latent considerations. Presently he replied, "Tell him an old friend—Arizona Ames."

"Arizona Ames?" echoed Esther, blankly.

"Yes, Arizona Ames, miss, I'm tolerable sorry to have to tell you," he replied. And as Esther turned away she heard him go on to himself, "This heah West used to be big, but shore no more!"

She hurried to the house, and running round the long corner of the kitchen extension she called: "Joe!—Joe!"

Esther rushed into the clean light kitchen, which had taken on these desirable qualities only since Joe's advent, but he was not there. She heard him whistling, however, in the store cabin, which was adjacent, and she ran to the door.

"Joe, don't you hear me yelling?"

The cook was a little man, past middle age, with a cadaverous solemn face, huge nose, and eyes like the faithful brown ones of a dog. He wore a white cap with a black rim, and an apron.

"Wal, now, Miss Esther, what the hell you-all so flushed an' rarin' about?" he queried, with a smile that engulfed her.

"Joe, there's a stranger just come—down the Troublesome," said Esther, breathlessly. "He's worn out—had to sit down. Oh, he must have had—an awful ride. Over the Flat Tops!—His horse, too, poor thing, is ready to drop. Come out, Joe. He says he knows you."

"Wal, thet's nothin' much fer you to get such red cheeks about," replied Joe, calmly. "There's a hell of a lot of fellars know me. I've fed about a million."

"But this man's different. Come, Joe. Hurry!"

"Wal, now, Esther Halstead! When did I ever see you hurry on any man's account? Different, is he?"

queried the cook, as he sat there with his lap full of cans. He was not in the least curious about the visitor, that was most irritatingly evident to Esther.

"He's weak. He can't walk. You must help him in."

"Miss Esther, is this galoot who's upset you a young fellar?" demanded Joe.

"No, not very. Joe, he's an old friend of yours. Arizona Ames."

"Who?"

"Arizona Ames. He's a rider—a wonderful-look-ing—"

"*Arizona Ames!*" Joe leaped up, scattering the cans with a metallic clatter all over the storeroom.

"Joe, do you know him?" asked Esther, eagerly.

"Know Arizona Ames?————! I'd have been bone dust long ago but for that————!"

Then he darted out, his apron flying, and sped round the cabin. Esther started to run, but presently reminded herself that it did not seem imperative for her to use indecorous haste. Nevertheless, her intense interest could not be thus checked. Presently she came upon Brown leading the visitor's horse, and Joe half supporting him down the path. What struck Esther most vividly then was the expression on Joe Cabel's face. It halted Esther. The ugliest man in the world had suddenly become beautiful. But his language! She was about to clap her hands over her ears when the cook changed to rationality.

"Miss Esther, I'll take him to my cabin. An' Brown's leading his hoss to the barn."

"All right, Joe. If you need anything, tell me. Perhaps I had better go with Brown to the barn."

They passed on, with Ames leaning heavily upon Joe, who was roaring: "My Gawd! to think it's really you, Arizona Ames! You long-legged, iron-jawed, fire-eatin', cow-punchin'————! What you need is a—drink an' I'll have one with you, by the————! Aw, the old cow camp in the Superstitions! Cactus, rattlesnakes, an' whisky! Them was the days!"

Esther was relieved when the verbose cook had gone out of earshot. Then she followed, and when they cut off to go to Joe's cabin she hurried on to join Brown. The lad would not relinquish the bridle to her, but at the barn he had perforce to turn the horse over to her. The teamster, Jed, would of course be absent, as he had driven her father to Yampa. But Smith, who looked after the farming on the ranch, might be available, and she sent her brother to call him.

Meanwhile she patted the horse and rubbed his nose and talked to him, discovering in the performance that he was neither shy nor mean. His eyes were tired.

Brown came running back: "Ess, that———farmer ain't anywhere!"

"If you dare to swear once more in my presence I—I'll lick you!" burst out Esther, goaded to desperation.

"Aw, Ess, I don't know when I swear—honest to Gawd."

"Get some hay down. We'll take care of Cappy. ...He called him that. Anyone could see he loves the horse."

Esther knew how to go about this sort of work because she often took care of her own horse. She led Cappy into a stall, gave him water sparingly, and likewise grain, and then she combed and brushed him, finding infinite satisfaction in the task. Finally she spread hay for a soft bed and barred him in.

"Come, Brown. You must change to dry clothes. And wash, too, you dirty boy."

"Ess, you ain't so orful clean yourself this minnit. Funny you rubbin' down thet horse. Fred would have a fit. You'd see him in—. Aw, you'd die before you'd do it for him."

"Don't you dare tell Fred," warned Esther.

"All right, Ess, if you give me two bits. You owe it to me, anyhow, fer losing my hook an' line.... Gee! I wish dad would get home today. He promised to fetch some."

Upon their return to the ranch house, they discovered Ronald carrying a rabbit by the ears.

"Look what I ketched," he cried, in glee, holding up his prize.

Ronald was dark and small, a quiet, solitary boy, easier than Brown to control, but as much of a responsibility because of his habit of staying away. Several half-grown, long-eared hounds hung at his heels. He and Brown fell into one of their endless arguments.

Esther entered the living-room, which was the newest and most comfortable of the many apartments of the divided ranch house. Her own room, which she shared with her sister Gertrude, opened from the living-room, and had been a small cabin in itself, into which two windows had been built. It had a rude fireplace, upon the yellow stones of which a trapper had once kept count of his beaver hides.

Esther had played carpenter, mason, decorator, and what not in her neverending efforts to make this room livable.

Gertrude, a dark, pretty child, growing like a weed, bent over the sewing she had been commissioned to do. Seldom, indeed, did Esther and her sister ever have any clothes save those they themselves made. They also manufactured garments for the boys. Gertrude hated to sew, and that was why she scornfully ignored Esther, who told about the strange visitor. So Esther, while removing dust and stains, communed with herself. Something very much out of the ordinary had happened, most unaccountably accelerating her pulse.

It was not because she did not want to, that she did not see Joe until dinner time. Then he presented quite a puzzle to Esther. Joe was nothing if not loquacious, and he had a reputation for story-telling. But he vouchsafed not a word about this stranger, Arizona Ames.

"How's your friend, Joe?" she asked, finally.

"He's dead to the world," replied the cook. "I made him a hot toddy an' almost before I could get his boots off he was asleep. I just peeped in on him. Like a stone! Reckon he'll sleep all day an' all night, an' mebbe then some. Last thing he said was to ask about his hoss. Reckon you turned the hoss over to Smith."

"No. We couldn't find him. But I took care of Mr. Ames' horse. Brown helped me."

"Wal, why didn't you wait an' tell me," protested Joe, perturbed. "Thet was imposin' on you."

"Not at all. I can take care of a horse, Joe. Goodness! don't I do it often enough? ... Who is this man, Joe?"

"Wal, you heard his name, didn't you?" returned the cook, rather evasively, Esther thought. "He's a range-rider."

"Where is he from? Arizona?"

"They call him Arizona, but he's from all over."

"An old friend of yours?"

"Wal, I knowed him in New Mexico. We worked for the same cow outfit. Reckon thet's five years ago, almost. Time sure flies."

"You told me you'd have been bone dust but for Arizona Ames," declared Esther, bluntly, vaguely disappointed in Joe.

"Wal, I sure was excited, Miss Esther," returned Joe, coolly. "Mebbe I was makin' too much of a little service Ames wouldn't like remembered."

Esther realized, to her disappointment, that Cabel was not going to tell her one of his fascinating stories, in which this rider Ames was to figure largely. A subtle change, which Esther felt rather than saw, had come over Joe. She had not known him like this. Esther took one intuitive glance at his impassive face and then went on with her dinner, without asking another question. But his reticence had only augmented her curiosity. The children, squabbling over the rabbit, which the cook had served for dinner, bothered Esther so that she could not think connectedly.

But afterward when she was alone she returned to the subject and went over the few details singly and ponderingly.

She did not need to be told that this Arizona

Ames was somebody out of the ordinary. She had
seen him, heard him. Recalling Joe's indifference to
a visitor, even though in need of assistance, and then
the remarkable change a mere name could produce,
Esther reasoned that she had been perfectly justified
in conceiving some extraordinary past relation between the cook and this rider. What a light had il-
lumined Joe's face! Then his rushing out, and his loud
wild talk as he helped Ames toward the cabin! Superstitions! That must have been a name for mountains of which Esther had vaguely heard. Cactus,
rattlesnakes, and whisky! Them was the days! . . . Esther made a reservation that probably these remembered days had not been very respectable. Lastly, all
of a sudden, Joe had intrenched himself behind a
reserve that he had endeavored to make casual. But
Esther was not deceived.

Joe Cabel had been a source of comfort and help,
and Esther's regard for him had steadily grown since
his arrival at Troublesome. Thinking of that, she recalled with surprise how his coming had not been
greatly dissimilar to that of this Arizona Ames. No
one at Troublesome had ever heard of Joe Cabel.
And after two years no one knew any more about
him than he had chosen to tell, which, despite his
innumerable yarns of adventure and humor, was next
to nothing.

But he had been a tower of strength for Esther
to lean upon. She dated the beginning of her reconciliation to Troublesome to this man's coming. It
was astonishing to realize. What had he not done for
her? Halstead, her father, was always away, either
out on the range to return dead tired, or on a trip to

Yampa or Craig or Denver. Fred had gradually drifted to the shiftless ways of the backwoods men, if not worse. The several riders Halstead employed on and off had been eager, willing, capable, in many ways, but Esther had soon learned she dare not be alone with any one of them. It was Joe Cabel who had taken the cooking burden off her hands, and who had made easy or bearable the thousand and one other duties. Particularly when accidents happened to the children, and when they fell ill, more or less regular occurrences, Cabel had saved Esther from going frantic.

"How silly of me—to be hurt—or angry with Joe!" she mused. "I don't believe I ever appreciated him until—this—this Arizona Ames dropped out of the sky.... What's the matter with me, anyhow?"

CHAPTER

14

*T*HE boys, Ronald and Brown, slept in a loft, to which they had access by way of a ladder on the back porch. This airy chamber was isolated from the rest of the house, but it looked down upon the righthand window of Esther's room. The last thing the boys did was to call to Esther, who always left her window open at night. Ronald and Brown were wonderfully brave in the daylight, but when darkness came their courage oozed somewhat. The Halsteads, like all mountain folk, went to bed early. But on this night the two boys were later than usual.

While Esther sat trying to read, aware that the air had a decided touch of fall, she heard a noise outside. Perhaps the stranger, Ames, had made her nervous. At any rate, she could not get her mind off him.

She peeped out of the window, to do which she had to stand on tiptoe. The night was starry, but there was gloom under the roof of the back porch. She heard a rustling sound. In that wild country it was nothing for foxes, skunks, coyotes, bears, and lions to visit the ranch at night. Usually the dogs gave the alarm.

"Aw, it's a—ole skunk!" burst out a voice unmistakably Brown's.

"————!" was Ronald's reply.

Esther, as always, instinctively clapped her hands to her ears. Then she removed them. Presently, as her eyes grew accustomed to the darkness, she made out one of the boys halfway up the ladder. Evidently the other was already in the loft.

"Cummon down an' help me chase the————," said Brown.

"Ha! Like the old lady who keeps tavern out West I will," replied Ronald.

" 'Fraid cat!"

"————!"

"Tomorrer I'll lick you fer thet, you————!"

"You can sleep down there, you————."

"I'm a-comin' up—soon as I pulverize this— animal."

Brown dropped down to the porch and disappeared. Esther heard him calling names and throwing rocks. Suddenly he let out a half-suppressed yell and came bounding back to the ladder.

"Ronnie, she's a-chasin' me! Lemme up!"

"By gum! I can't see her but I can smell her," declared Ronald.

"If I only had a gun! The———!"

Esther had a forced knowledge of profanity, owing to close contact with her father and Fred, and especially Joe Cabel, and she knew that the language the boys were using had no significance whatever to them. But she could not stand anymore.

"Boys, stop cursing this minute," she burst out, in a terrible voice.

A silence ensued. The boys were as quiet as mice.

"Oh, I saw you and heard you," continued Esther.

"Ess, you better pull your nose in thet winder if you don't want it all skunked up," advised Brown, while Ronald tittered gleefully.

Esther availed herself somewhat hastily of this advice. Past experience had educated her.

"Where have you boys been so late?" she demanded.

"Where'd you s'pose?"

"Course we been in bed, Ess."

"Don't lie to me."

"Aw, we ain't lyin'. The ole skunk woke us up."

"Boys, I shall tell father," warned Esther, reverting to the last resource. This threat invariably moved the boys.

"Aw, Ess, please, don't," begged Brown.

"It wasn't me, Esther. It was Brown," said Ronald.

"Don't blame things on each other. Tell me," added Esther, more forcibly, knowing now that something unusual indeed was afoot.

"You won't give us away?"

"Cross your heart you won't tell, Ess?"

"I'll make no promises till I know. You rascals. What have you been up to?"

"We been stealin' grub fer Fred."

"Fred!—Stealing grub!—What for? And where's Fred?"

"Ess, it wasn't fer Fred. Two men fetched Fred home. An' they made us steal some grub."

"Where are they?"

"Down at the barn."

"Fred was drunk?"

"I don't know, Ess. It was 'most dark. Fred didn't say nothin'. He just fell down on the hay. Then the two fellars made us slip into the kitchen."

"Well, go to bed now. I promise not to tell on you," replied Esther. She partly closed the window, barring it on the inside, and extinguished the lamp. Not until she was snug under the blankets beside Gertrude did she feel at ease, and then she had no great liking for the fact that there were unknown men down at the barn with Fred.

This was the second time that had happened. If their father should discover it! Fred was becoming a serious problem. Esther had lost patience with him and now began to suffer apprehensions. She had refused to give credence to various rumors about the company Fred kept. Evidently these would have to be faced, as well as other matters that seemed working to a climax for the Halsteads. When Esther at last dropped off to sleep her pillow was wet with tears.

Esther awoke with a feeling new to her and one pretty disheartening. She was sorry another day had dawned. How ridiculous and little of her! But she could not deny it. And she lay there a long while, thinking.

She heard the boys talking and snickering, and then their noisy descent of the ladder. Gertrude crawled over her, got out of bed and dressed, making fun of her laziness. Still she lay there, reluctant to get up and meet the unknown that seemed to portend catastrophe this day.

It drove her presently, and she arose conscious that her fighting spirit was not in the ascendant. It struck Esther suddenly, while dressing, that she was paying some attention to her appearance. She knew she was pretty and on occasion she took pride in her rippling brown hair with its streaks of chestnut, her large brown eyes and red lips. But what occasion was this? She gravely contemplated herself in the mirror. She was pleased with the image she saw, but displeased that her hair did not suit her this morning, nor the bit of red ribbon, nor the blouse, that was certainly not an everyday one. Esther was nothing if not honest. Each time a young man, stranger or otherwise, happened to drop in at Troublesome the event had affected her singularly. What was that eager, haunting light in her eyes? She was looking, hoping, hunting for something. Still, it had never been quite so pronounced as this time, and when she realized it an angry blush suffused her cheeks.

She arrived late at breakfast. The children had eaten and gone. To her surprise Fred was there, and he greeted her with more than his usual warmth. Esther's heart governed her head now as always. Fred had shaved himself that morning and he wore a new shirt and tie. His tanned face appeared a little thin and strained. Fred's good looks had always militated against his demerits.

Joe came in with Esther's breakfast.

"Mornin', Miss Esther. You're a lady of leisure, I see, an' like Fred here, all shiny an' pretty," he said.

"Good morning, Joe," replied Esther, shortly, and began to eat, wondering at Joe's tone and what Fred was going to say.

"Joe tells me a stranger rode in yesterday," began Fred, when the cook had gone out. "Some fellow he used to work with. Arizona somethin' or other."

"Yes. Arizona Ames."

"Who is he?"

"I don't know. Ask Joe?"

"Sure I did. But he's grumpy. Hasn't cussed once this mornin'. . . . What's this Ames like?"

"He's a rider—no longer a boy. He could hardly walk. And he was so—so travel worn, so grimy and bearded, that I couldn't tell what he might look like."

"Queer. Don't like it. I was tellin' Joe that he'd better have this rider go on ridin'."

"Why, Fred!" retorted Esther, indignantly. "Have you no more sense of hospitality than that? The man was crippled. And he looked starved."

"Sure. *You'd* take any rider in," returned Fred, with sarcasm. "But I don't know this Arizona Ames."

"You haven't much to say about what goes on at Halstead ranch," said Esther, likewise sarcastically. And when the cook came in at that juncture she addressed him. "Joe, please do not allow Fred's attitude toward strangers to influence you. Please treat Mr. Ames the same as if this was your house."

"Thanks, Miss Esther. It'd sure gone against the

grain to have hurt the feelin's of my friend," replied Cabel, simply. But the glance he gave Fred furnished Esther more food for reflection.

Evidently Fred struggled against feelings of which he was ashamed. For one thing, he certainly bit his lip to hold in a quick retort.

"Fred, where are the riders who fetched you home?" asked Esther.

"Who told you?" he demanded.

"Never mind. I know."

"I'll skin those kids alive."

"If you lay a hand on them I'll give you away to father. They fetched you home drunk.... This is the second time!"

"Aw, hell!" ejaculated her brother, hotly, as he arose with the manner of one who saw the uselessness of subterfuge. "Come outside where that owl-eyed cook can't hear." And he stalked out, leaving Esther convinced that one of her premonitions had been correct.

Esther called after her brother that he could wait until she finished her breakfast, which she certainly did not hurry. Meanwhile Joe returned, this time with the old fond smile for her, and anxious solicitude added.

"Miss Esther, I sure never was a squealer, but I reckon I've got to tell you somethin' or bust."

"Joe, maybe I can spare you. Listen," replied Esther, hurriedly. "Fred came home drunk last night. Two men fetched him back. He couldn't walk. Is that what you mean?"

"Wal, no. Thet ain't so bad. It's who them fellars *was*," returned Joe, seriously. "I was down the trail and seen them ride in. Didn't come by the road. They were holdin' Fred on his hoss. I ducked into the brush an' let them pass."

"Well, who were they?" queried Esther, sharply, as he halted, loth to continue.

"One was Barsh Hensler. I've seen the other fellar in Yampa, but don't know his name."

"Barsh Hensler! Why, Joe, hasn't his name been connected with those cattle-thieves whom father hates so?"

"Sure has. Hensler lives in Yampa. He's got a bad name, an' it's hinted he belongs to Clive Bannard's outfit."

"And Fred is associating with them—or at least some of them?—How dreadful!"

"Wal, don't be upset, Miss Esther," went on Cabel, calmly. "Fred ain't bad at heart. He's easy-goin' an' when he drinks his brain gets addled. He sure can't stand liquor. Wal, he likes to play cards an' strut around Bosomer's saloon in Yampa. Naturally he falls in bad company. I'm afraid your dad hasn't handled him proper. Anyway, I reckon it's through this thet Barsh Hensler has got hold of Fred."

"Oh, Joe, what shall we do?" asked Esther, almost in distress.

"Wal, I'll talk it over with Ames. Queer thet he should drop in on Troublesome jest now," replied Cabel, his deep, cavernous eyes gleaming.

"I don't know that I like the idea of your talking it over with a stranger.... But why does it seem queer to you—that Mr. Ames should drop in on Troublesome just now?"

"Things are comin' to a sad pass here, Miss Esther," said Joe. "An' it's queer because Arizona Ames is the man to straighten them out."

"Oh, indeed! Why is he—particularly?" queried Esther, her curiosity augmenting.

"Wal, no use to tell you unless I can get him to stay. An' I'm afraid thet jest ain't possible."

"Why impossible?—Perhaps father might give this—this rider a job," rejoined Esther, and marveled at the thrill the thought gave her.

"You bet he would—if I tell him who Ames is. I'll do it, too, if Ames will let me."

"Joe, you excite me!—Tell father anyhow, without asking Mr. Ames,"

"Wal, thet's not a bad idee," said Cabel, pleased with Esther. "But it's jest a hundred to one Ames will ride away soon as he is fit to travel."

"What would be his hurry?" asked Esther, resentfully. "Are we such—terrible people?"

"Wal, if you must know, the only thing Arizona Ames ever run from was a pretty girl."

"Joe!—Meaning I'm the pretty girl?" exclaimed Esther, with a merry laugh. Nevertheless her cheeks grew hot.

"I sure do."

"But I am not so pretty," retorted Esther.

"Lord! girl, you sure are, all the time an' any time. An' when you're dressed up in white, like thet night here once, my—! Beg pardon, I'm forgettin' my tongue."

"Yes, Joe, you are, rather," she rejoined, demurely. "So this wonderful Arizona Ames is likely to run away from me? What's the matter with him, Joe? Is he a woman-hater?"

"No, I reckon Arizona wouldn't hate anyone, much less a nice girl."

"He didn't strike me as a bashful rider. How old is he, Joe?"

"Ames? Wal, I don't know. But he's young, compared to me."

"I saw his hair was silver, over his temples. He looked old, Joe."

"Wal, he's sure old in the life of the ranges, Miss Esther. But Arizona can't be much over thirty, if he's thet."

"Oh, come now, Joe. Be reasonable."

"I'm tellin' you straight, Miss Esther," replied Joe. "An' I'm talkin' too much."

"Joe!—See here. You're not going to run from me like that," cried Esther, seizing Joe's sleeve as he started to leave. She rose from the table. "Please don't go. . . . Joe, you've been my very good friend. I'd never have stood it all but for your help and kindness."

"Is thet so, Miss Esther?" he queried, amazed and delighted.

"It is, indeed. I've never realized how much I appreciate you, until lately."

"Wal, now, I reckon no one could make me no happier than tellin' me thet."

"Then don't freeze up again, like you did last night and just now. No matter what the reason is! Shake hands on it, Joe. I've a hunch I'm going to need you more than ever."

Joe was so overcome that even his profane tongue failed him, but he squeezed Esther's hand so hard it was numb. She smiled ruefully, holding it up, then she ran out to find Fred.

He was waiting, his brow like a thundercloud.

"'Pears to me you talk a lot to that cook," he growled.

"Yes, I do. He's more of a big brother than you are, Fred Halstead."

That made him wince, and then flush. "Sister, you sure have a knife-edge tongue."

"Fred, I'm in no mood for you, if you're in a temper. I'm too disgusted."

"The kids told you about me bein' fetched home drunk?" he queried.

"Yes. But they didn't know you were drunk."

"Well, the fact is, I wasn't. But I had been an' I was tuckered out.—Esther, I've got to have some money."

Esther laughed at him. "You don't say."

"Have you got any? I mean of your own."

"Yes, a little, and I'm going to keep it, Fred Halstead. You'll never get another dollar from me to drink and gamble with."

"I need this to pay a debt. I owe money, Esther, an' I've *got* to pay it."

"To those men who fetched you here last night?"

"Yes, to one of them."

"What's his name?"

"Never mind who he is. But he's waitin' out there."

"You're ashamed to tell me, Fred Halstead."

"What's the difference to you?" he demanded, dragging a shaking hand through his hair.

"Will you trust me with his name?"

"No, I won't. You'd tell dad."

"Fred, if you ever had a chance to get the money, it's gone now. How many times have I helped you and kept your secrets. You're ungrateful....But you needn't confess. I don't blame you for being ashamed. I know whom you've lost money to."

"Shut up, then, if you do," he flashed.

"Barsh Hen—!" Suddenly Fred clapped a hand over Esther's mouth and dragged her into the living-room. Amazed and furious, Esther freed herself.

"How dare you, Fred Halstead!" she cried, hotly.

"There was a man—right behind you," panted her brother.

"What! Right behind me?" ejaculated Esther.

"Yes, a stranger, a tall fellow with eyes like daggers. I didn't see him. He must have come up close—or he'd been there all the time. He *heard* you, Esther. I know it. I could tell by his look. Damn the luck! I told you to shut up."

"It serves you right," replied Esther, thoughtfully.

"He must have been that stranger Joe took in," fumed Fred. "What was his name? Ames somethin'?"

"I didn't see him," replied Esther, coolly. "Go out and satisfy yourself."

"But, Esther, you'll give me the money?" he implored.

"How much?" she asked.

"Three hundred dollars."

"Good heavens!....I wouldn't if I had it," replied Esther, and retreating into her room she closed the door. There she sat down on her bed in a brown study, which was as much of an effort to analyze her own feelings as to forget Fred and his troubles. After a while she returned to the living-room to find Gertrude there alone.

"Gertie, did you see Fred?"

"Yes, a little while ago. He was sittin' out there with his head in his hands. I asked him if he was still in love with Biny Wood. He roared at me an' stamped off."

"Good for you! I didn't think of that," replied Esther, unable to resist a giggle. "Sis, did you see anyone else?"

"Ahuh. A tall fellow in cowboy boots. He's gone down to the creek with Brown. Joe went down, too, right after."

"He has," cried Esther, eagerly, and she ran to look out of the window. From there only a bit of the creek was visible, so she went out on the porch. She caught no glimpse of the stranger, but as she turned to look down the lane she was amazed and delighted to see her father's familiar stalwart figure striding up. She ran to meet him, but at closer sight of his face her delight changed to concern. Once only had she ever seen his fine dark face and eyes betray such trouble, and that time had been at her mother's death.

"Father! Back in the morning? Oh, I'm glad!" she cried.

"Hello, daughter!" he replied, heartily kissing her, and relinquished to her one of the armloads of packages he was carrying. "For you and the kids.... Well, bless you! It's good to see *you*, anyway."

His emphasis on the pronoun did not fail to arrest Esther, who mutely followed him in. Fred had been her father's favorite, and this could mean nothing but that Fred had hurt him again and no doubt gravely.

"Hello, Gertie!" Halstead greeted his younger daughter, as he spilled his other armload and took Gertrude in its place. He gave her a great hug, lifting her from the floor, stifling her gleeful cries and queries. "Yes, I fetched the candy. Esther has it.... Where are the boys?"

"I think down at the creek," replied Esther. "Shall I go call them?"

"No hurry. My, what rosy cheeks you have! Well, I hate to chase them away."

"Father, you've bad news?"

"What'd you expect?" he queried, with mock jocularity. "We live on Troublesome, don't we?... Never mind, Esther. We'll lick it yet."

"But tell me, Father," said Esther, earnestly. "Surely I'm old enough now to hear all your troubles and share them."

"Well! Listen to my nineteen-year-old!" he returned, gayly. "Put these parcels away. They're marked, Gertie. Hide your own and don't dig into the boys'. I declare, I bought all the fishing hooks and lines in Yampa. Tell Joe the wagon is full of supplies. Jed will help him up with them. Have the cowboys been in?"

"No. Not since you left."

"Well, that's one comfort. Did Fred come home?"

"Yes, last night."

"Was he drunk?" asked the father, bitterly.

"He said he—had been," replied Esther, reluctantly. Then she added, loyally, "He was all right this morning."

Without more comment her father opened the door of his room, which was to the left of the fireplace, and went in. Esther assorted the numerous parcels, some of which she opened, and carried their precious contents to her room. Her father never had been close, but when had he ever, since they had lived in the West, bought so generously? It worried Esther. She carried other parcels to the kitchen, where she encountered the teamster, Jed, packing in supplies.

"Whar's thet air cook?" queried Jed.

"He went off up the creek with the boys. Get Smith to help you, Jed."

"Don't need none, miss. I was just wantin' to give Joe his terbaccer. I'm leavin' it hyar, with you as my witness."

"I'll guarantee its delivery, Jed," replied Esther, laughing. "How were things in Yampa?"

"Not slow fer onct," said Jed, with a guffaw. "Too swift fer this gennelman."

"Swift. You mean fights?"

"A couple, fair to middlin'. But I was meanin' the play at Bosomer's. I like to have a little fly. But I didn't set in nothin'. Clive Bannard an' his gang was in town, flush with money."

"Lucky for you then, Jed," replied Esther. She went back to her room, and assiduously applied herself to sewing that had waited for necessities from Yampa. But her mind was as active as her fingers, and she had a sensitive ear for what went on in the living-room. She heard Gertrude say to the boys:

"Here's your candy. An', Ronnie, dad's got a little gun for you when you stop swearin'."

"Aw, hell! thet's wuss than no gun atall!" wailed Ronnie.

"An', Brown, here's a grand lot of trash."

"Trash! Wot is it?"

"It says, 'Brown's fishin' hooks an' lines.'"

"*Trash!*———*! Whoopee!* Gimme thet, woman! ...Cummon, Ronnie, grab your oufit an' let's go show Arizonie."

"But, Brown, wot's candy? I got my gun, only I ain't got it. An' there you are with a million dollars' wuth of fishin' stuff."

"Cummon. You're showin' a streak of yaller. Arizonie will get thet gun fer you. Can't you tell? He'll get it. I hope to die if he doesn't."

They ran out to the shrill laughter of the little sister, who then communed with herself. "Gee! this Arizonie must be a fairy!"

Esther whispered to herself: "Gee! Arizonie?— Well, I declare!" And there followed a slow swelling beat of her heart. He might be the rider she had dreamed of. But, no, he was too old. And that vague hint of Joe's! Yet the fascination grew. It was revealed to Esther that she had been fascinated by every rider of the last few years—for a few dreamy moments, before she saw them. She had seen Arizona Ames, a weary, bent, ashen-faced man of uncertain age, yet the illusion still persisted. She must go out presently to meet him, and have it dispelled.

Other things happened that long morning. Esther heard Halstead's riders go by, following which a long colloquy took place in her father's office. She heard their voices, sometimes loud and again low, but the words never distinguishable. She did not need to catch the content, however, for her father's tones were fraught with trouble. Esther sighed. Did they not live on the Troublesome? At the moment she almost hated it. But never long could she feel resentment for the rushing stream and the colorful hills.

At length Gertrude ran in to tell her they had rung the dinner bell twice. Then Esther hastily put her work upon the bed, and tarried a moment before the mirror, at once abandoning whatever vain impulse had actuated her. When she went out through the living-room and down the porch toward the dining-room she had a flitting wild idea that she was walking to her doom. But she strolled in, cool, casual, humming a tune. Only the family sat at the table, and there was a sudden drop of her unaccountable sense of buoyancy and expectation.

"Where is Mr. Ames?" asked Esther, seating herself as Joe entered.

"Wal, Miss Esther, he excused himself this time, sayin' he'd wait for me an' the riders," replied Cabel, and he gave Esther a deliberate knowing wink. A hot tingle shot up into Esther's cheeks. What did the fool mean?

"Father, have you met Mr. Ames?" she inquired, presently.

"No, daughter. I had a set-to with your brother. After that Stevens and Mecklin."

"Cheer up, Daddy," replied Esther, incomprehensibly gay all of a sudden. Seldom, indeed, did she ever revert to the more childish epithet. "If things have to get worse to turn better, maybe this is the day."

"Well!" ejaculated Halstead, giving her a surprised and grateful look.

Presently he finished his dinner, and rising called to Joe, "Fetch your friend in to see me when you're through."

During the meal, at least while Esther had sat with them, Fred had not spoken a word or lifted his eyes from his plate, even though the excited boys had plied him to give attention to their gifts. Finally Esther was left alone with Fred and she took advantage of the opportunity to ask, "What's up between you and father?"

"Same old thing," he replied, gloomily.

"No, it isn't. You can't fool me. Does he know about your debt to—"

Fred made a warning sign toward the open door of the kitchen. Then he got up and slouched out. Esther followed.

"If dad does know, he never let on. But he sure gave me a rakin' over the coals," continued her brother.

"Did you see this Barsh Hensler this morning?" asked Esther.

"Yes. Down the creek trail. He raised hell with me. Threatened to....Well, never mind that."

"It's a gambling debt?"

"Sure. What else? And the worst of it is he's a crooked gambler. I knew it. But when I get a few drinks, I think I'm the slickest fellow in the world."

"Fred, you show a faint glimmering of intelligence," replied Esther, dryly.

"I know what you think of me, Esther," he rejoined, thickly, and left her.

Somehow from that Esther extracted a grain of comfort, if not actual hope. Fred had not grown wholly callous. He might be reclaimed, but she had not the slightest idea how to go about it.

Esther went to her room, and quite without intent left the door slightly open. Presently she heard her father and Fred come in.

"But, Dad, it was rotten of you to—to rake me before the cowboys, and especially that stranger, Ames," Fred was expostulating, poignantly.

"What do I care for them?" rejoined Halstead, coldly. "You don't care for my feelings, let alone other and more important things."

"My word! I never had a man look through me like he did. I felt like—like a toad."

"No wonder. You've quite a little reason," said his father, with sarcasm.

"Dad, will you let me stay while you're having this talk?" queried Fred.

"It wouldn't interest you."

"But I heard Joe tell that man Ames you were facing ruin."

"That's why it wouldn't interest you. There won't be any cards or drinks or saloon gossip or shady stories."

"Dad!" cried Fred, miserably.

"Get out."

"But I—I might be of some—use. I—I know— I've heard things—"

"Fred, it's too late for you to help me. Please

oblige me by leaving me to talk over my misfortunes with *men*."

Fred's dragging steps from the living-room were eloquent testimony of the state of his mind. Esther's heart ached for him. There seemed some little extenuating circumstance in Fred's favor. He had been brought young and raw into this wild country, and had not been able to resist its bad elements.

While Esther was cogitating over the perplexing questions, Joe came hurriedly into the living-room.

"Boss, I just run in ahead of time to ask you somethin'," he said.

"Fire away, Joe," returned Halstead.

"I sure don't want to make any mistakes in a delicate family matter like this," went on Cabel, earnestly. "The thing is now—do you trust me well enough to want me in on it?"

"Why, yes, I do, Joe. You've been a help. If I'd listened to you—"

He did not conclude the sentence.

"Much obliged, boss. Wal, then, if you trust me you'll take my word for Arizona Ames."

"I would take your word for him or anyone."

"Fine. Then I'll fetch Ames in. That's what I wanted to ask. I'm sure relieved an' glad. For Ames is goin' to hurt. He'll cut right to the roots of this sore spot at Troublesome."

"Well! Who is this Arizona Ames, Joe?" queried Halstead, gruffly.

"Sure it'd take too long to tell. But he's the damndest fellow I ever knew on the ranges. An' thet's sayin' a great deal, boss."

"What do you mean? Damndest fellow—that's

no recommendation," returned Halstead, irritably.

"Halstead, if you was a born Westerner or had lived long enough out here you'd know what I mean. But, to put it blunt—if you can get Ames to stay here your troubles will be over pronto."

"Impossible! How could any one man do that?"

"I'm tellin' you. I know."

"But, Joe, I'm poor, almost ruined. Even if there were such a man, I couldn't pay him."

"Hell! Who's talkin' about pay?" retorted Cabel, in a tone Esther had never heard. "I reckon Ames wouldn't even take a rider's wages from you, at least now."

"Joe, you've made me see many times how little I know about the West and Western men. I certainly can't—what do you call it?—savvy?—savvy such a man as Ames. I don't savvy you, either."

"Listen. You don't need to, this minute. Take my word for Ames. He's clean an' fine as gold. He's ridden the ranges now for thirteen or fourteen years, an' he's forgotten more about cattle than these Colorado two-bit ranchers ever knew. Years ago he was one of the greatest cowboys thet I ever seen fork a hoss. But his qualifications to straighten your troubles are more than these. You are bein' robbed by low-down cattle-thieves who wouldn't dare show their tracks on a real range. An' my friend Arizona Ames is sure the man to fix them hombres."

"Why is he? What'll *he* do?" asked Halstead, sharply.

"Boss, if you tell Ames what you're up against here on the Troublesome he'll *stay*. An', my Gawd! I wish I could convince you what thet'll mean. Why, it's no less than an act of Providence thet he got lost up on the Flat Tops an', wanderin' round, struck the Troublesome an' ended up here. He loves kids an' has taken a shine to Ronnie an' Brown already. I'm bound to admit, though, thet Miss Esther is a stumblin'-block—in fact, the only one. Ames is a shy, queer man where women are concerned. An' if there ever was a prettier an' sweeter girl than Miss Esther I never seen her. But, boss, if you make your story strong enough, sayin' your son has gone to the bad, an' thet you're afraid you might get shot an' leave Miss Esther alone to fight this Troublesome hell— why, I reckon Ames just won't be able to ride away."

"Joe, you're not so shy, but you're a queer man yourself," remarked Halstead, with a laugh. "But I like your talk—your interest in me and my family. I'll take your advice this time. My story will be strong enough. I don't need to enlarge on the truth, as you'll see."

"Good! Then Ames will *stay*. Then, boss, if Clive Bannard an' thet Barsh Hensler steal as much as an unbranded calf—wal, it'll be all day with them."

"It will. And how?"

"Ames will kill them. He sure is bad medicine. But I don't want you to get a wrong impression of my friend. Any day you might meet a traveler in Yampa or a line-ridin' cowpuncher who'd tell you Arizona Ames is one of these notorious gun-men. It's not true. He's a little handy with a gun—I reckon, an' he's killed a half dozen fellars thet I know of. But don't get any wrong idee of him."

"Cabel, you astonish me!" ejaculated Halstead.

"Wal, I've only begun, then. Now listen. This

mornin' Ames went down the creek with the kids. An' while they fished he walked around a bit to stretch his sore legs. He seen two riders on the trail, an' your son Fred meet them. Wal, things don't strike Ames queer unless they *are* queer. Fred sure didn't want anyone to see him with these riders. An' for thet reason Ames slipped up close to get a peek at them. An' he described them to me....Boss, one of them was Barsh Hensler."

"I guessed it before you told me. Go on," replied Halstead, harshly.

"Wal, thet's all of thet. But I reckon Ames had some kind of a hunch about Fred. Anyway, I seen him lookin' the boy over most damn sharp. Next, when your riders, Stevens an' Mecklin, came in the kitchen Ames was there with me. They're eatin' dinner now, but this was earlier, I reckon, just after they'd had the row with you. They were excited, an' sure they talked. I never had any use for Mecklin. He couldn't look you in the eye. An' I'll gamble now there was a reason for it. Wal, to them Ames was only another rider goin' through an' one who'd talk, to you perhaps, an' sure in town, an' they had some things they wanted spread. After they'd gone Ames said: 'Joe, this cowboy, Mecklin, is crooked. Didn't you know it?' An' I said I'd just about come to thet conclusion."

"Mecklin! Is it possible? Yet he was always evasive—never satisfactory....And what about Stevens?"

"Wal, he's a harder proposition. Ames thought he was either deep or honest....Now, boss, I'll run back, an' fetch them all over soon. Reckon for the present it'd be better for you to keep mum about what I've told you."

"All right, Joe. Mum's the word. But hurry back."

Cabel hurried out, and Halstead, after a moment, stamped into his room. Esther closed her door and lay down on her bed in a tumult. It took stern effort of will to subdue her emotion so that she could think instead of feel, and then at intervals she lapsed back again. Her interest in this Arizona Ames had been rudely shocked into something she could not define. But her sentimentality, or whatever it had been, most surely had received a violent reverse. He had killed men. Esther shuddered. Had she ever before come in contact with any man who had shed blood? If so she had not been cognizant of it. Another of the vague little dreams dispelled! Regret mingled with relief. Her pondering fell solely upon the problem that concerned Fred and her father's dubious circumstances. But when Joe's strange and eloquent championing of this Arizona Ames returned to mind Esther grew bewildered. Yet this time a strong vibrating thrill, rather than a shudder, coursed through her. Was Joe drunk or over-excited or dishonest? Esther scouted each disloyal thought. She was discovering Joe. She believed his assertions, preposterous as they seemed.

"If this Arizona Ames stays, father's troubles will be over," whispered Esther to herself, as if that would aid conviction. She divined then that these troubles were not insurmountable to such men as Cabel and Ames. But they were Western. They knew how to deal with the hard knots of the range. Still, on reflection, it seemed no less marvelous, and dreadful, too, when she recalled Joe's terse explanation. Obviously, then, the wise course was to keep Ames at Troublesome, at any cost.

Esther found herself dealing with a possible side of the situation. Suppose this remarkable Ames, who was shy of women, did not think favorably of her father's proposition? That would be where she must come in. If Mr. Ames was afraid of a pretty girl, it might be because he feared he would fall in love with her. Very well! It would be a shame to sacrifice so wonderful a man on the altar of exigency. But would he sacrifice himself? She realized in the stark honesty of her heart that she was a firebrand ready for the spark. Pretty soon she knew she would fall in love with a clod, a dolt, anybody; and she ought to thank the Providence that Joe had spoken of, for dropping this range-riding Nemesis down into Troublesome Valley.

Esther's slumbering spirit roused into passion, and when she slipped off to bed to look at herself in the mirror she saw a woman with inscrutably dark and eloquent eyes.

"If dad fails, I'll make him stay!" she whisperingly promised the image she faced. "Then, oh dear! My troubles will begin."

She bathed her hot cheeks and brushed and rearranged her hair. Then she put on her most attractive dress, waiving the fact that it was not altogether suitable for afternoon wear.

CHAPTER

15

*I*T WAS just as well, Esther thought, that she had not a moment for reflection. She had scarcely satisfied herself as to her appearance, when she heard the men enter the living-room.

Her father was greeting them when Esther opened her door and stepped in. He halted in the midst of a word.

"Wal, now, Miss Esther!" exclaimed Joe, suddenly beaming upon her.

"Howdy, Joe!" replied Esther, coming forward with a smile. "Don't introduce your friend. We've already met."

Then she looked up as she extended her hand to Ames.

"How do you do, Mr. Ames?" she said, cordially,

wholly at ease on the surface. "I don't recognize you, but I'm sure you're Mr. Arizona Ames."

Indeed she did not recognize in this man the gray, dust-caked, and bearded rider of yesterday. His grip was firm and strong. She saw and felt the compelling power of singularly blue eyes, that only her late-mounting spirit would have enabled her to meet.

"Shore glad to meet you proper, Miss Halstead," he drawled in the cool, lazy accents of the Southerner. "An' if it's a compliment you're payin' me, I am returnin' it."

Shy! Whatever had Joe Cabel been dreaming of? This man seemed the serenest, the most unconscious of self of anyone Esther had ever met. Still, Joe had said that it was pretty women of whom Mr. Ames stood in awe and fear. Evidently he had not found her listed in this category.

"I must thank you, Mr. Ames, for I think I meant to be complimentary," continued Esther, with a smile. Then she went up to her father, who stood with an air of pride mixed with surprise and perplexity.

"Daughter, you look awful good, but this isn't a party," he said.

"I would go to a council of war just the same," she replied, enigmatically, and then she kissed him. "Father, from now on, when the little game of trouble comes up at Troublesome, I'm going to sit in."

"I savvy. Joe has been talking to you," said her father, resignedly.

"Joe has answered a few questions. Don't blame him. I'd soon have arrived at this decision without any help."

"You remind me of your mother," he rejoined. "You're grown up, Esther.... Well, well!—Joe, are those cowboys coming?"

"No. I sure insisted. But Mecklin wasn't keen about comin'. Said he'd made his report an' couldn't say no more an' no less. Stevens looked worried, but he stuck with him."

"Let's go in my room," said Halstead, and still holding Esther's hand he led the way into a large apartment that had been the interior of a whole cabin. It was plain, rude, yet livable. The chinks between the logs had been newly plastered up with clay; a smoldering fire burned on the wide yellow hearth.

"Have a seat, Ames," he went on. "And you, too, Joe, though I don't recollect ever seeing you sit down." He slid an old armchair round for Esther. "This was your grandmother's, as you know. It's about all I have left of the old home. She was a shrewd business-woman and I never saw the trouble that phased her. So it's most appropriate, daughter, that you have her chair while we initiate you as a lady director in the affairs of Troublesome Ranch. Too late, I fear!"

Halstead turned to his desk. "I can't talk unless I smoke. Ames, have a cigar?"

"Reckon I wouldn't know what to do with it," drawled the rider. "Sometimes, though, when I'm hungry or thirsty out on the range I'll smoke a cigarette, if I'm lucky enough to have one. Which I shore wasn't, comin' across the Flat Tops."

He stood to one side of the fireplace and he was

so tall that he leaned his elbow on the stone mantle. Esther had a momentary glimpse of his clean-cut profile, his tanned cheek, his lean square jaw. Then, as he turned, she quickly glanced down.

"Joe told me you rode in by way of the Troublesome," began Halstead, and with lighted cigar in hand he leaned back in his chair to look up with undisguised curiosity and interest at the rider.

"Reckon I walked most of the way down heah," replied Ames.

"Then you had more time and better chance to see my range. What do you think of it?"

"Is all this heah Troublesome Valley your range?"

"Yes, these burned-over slopes and the meadows along the creek. I own a thousand acres outright, and my territorial range-right takes in all this open valley."

"It's a big range in a big country. Are there any other ranchers near?"

"None. The closest is Jim Wood, over the ridge, ten miles and more. We've never seen a cow or steer of his on my side. Rough forest between."

"I reckon I never saw a finer range," said Ames, as if weighing his words.

"For what? Deer and elk—for hunters and fishermen like my kids are growing into; for Esther, who loves wild flowers?"

"I reckon it's pretty fine for them," replied the rider, with a slow understanding smile at Esther. "But I was speakin' for cattle."

"How do you make that out?" demanded Halstead, who evidently had expected Ames to share his opinion and damn the valley.

"It burned over four or five years ago an'—"

"Five," interrupted the rancher. "A year before I bought the ranch. Man named Bligh, who tried both sheep and cattle. Before that only trappers and prospectors ranged in here. Bligh was going to do well, but the fire ruined his chances. So I bought him out cheap."

"You were shore lucky. Bligh would have done well if he had only known enough. The fire made the range. I reckon the grass just came up good this year. It'll be many years before any timber growth gets hold again. An' you can check that."

"Humph! So I've got a good range instead of a poor one?"

"Shore fine. This heah Troublesome range will make you rich short of five years. An' in ten it'll double."

"Ames, if I wasn't looking at you and taking Cabel's word for your—your judgment, I'd laugh," burst out Halstead. "I'd laugh!"

"Shore. You can laugh, anyhow. I won't mind."

"I'll swear instead. . . . See here, Ames, I've lost two hundred head of cattle since the snow melted. They ate some poison weed, swelled up and died. Last year almost that many."

"Larkspur. You don't know how to handle it, an' you shore have hired some wise cowboys."

"Larkspur! What's that?"

"Father, I know," spoke up Esther, quickly. "It's one of the wild flowers I love so well."

"Correct, Miss Halstead," said Ames. "But it's

shore bad medicine for cattle....The fact is, Halstead, that larkspur is no longer any great menace to cattlemen. It used to be. But now we know what to do. Cattle eat this plant, which forms a gas inside them. Indigestion, I reckon. Anyway, they swell up an' if you don't stick them pronto an' relieve the gas pressure, they die."

"Stick them!" ejaculated Halstead, weakly.

"Shore. You take a long thin round instrument an' stick them. If they haven't gone too far they all recover. Then a few good riders could get rid the larkspur in a season or so."

"Larkspur! Ha! Ha! Ha!" roared Halstead. His face grew red. "Excuse me, Esther, while I go Joe one better." But he did not curse aloud, though it was evident that he indulged himself thoroughly. Then reaching for another cigar he added, "I'm a hell of a rancher!"

"Halstead, don't feel too bad aboot it," said Ames. "It's sort of new at that. An' this high Colorado country is long on larkspur an' short on cattlemen."

"Ames, you hit me right where Joe swore you would," went on Halstead, chewing at his cigar. "Maybe you can floor me again....I've lost at least half my cattle through thieves. Five hundred head this season. Over a hundred lately—the last week in fact, according to Mecklin. I can't stand that. Another raid will break me."

"I heahed your rider talkin' aboot it," drawled Ames, without the slightest trace of feeling, which lack marked such a contrast to Halstead's speech. "An' I gathered it wasn't work of rustlers."

"Rustlers!—Say, what's the difference between rustlers and cattle-thieves?"

"Reckon there's a lot. If it was the work of a rustler you might not find out soon who he was or how he operated. An' when you did corner him—well, you'd shore know it. But in the case of a low-down cattle-thief, why like as not he drinks aboot town with your cowpunchers—"

"Yes, and my own son!" interrupted Halstead, ringingly. "This thief's name is Clive Bannard, who hails from Eastern ranges, he says. And he has a right-hand man, Barsh Hensler, who lives in Yampa. How far they have actually corrupted Fred—that's my son—I don't know. But I've heard enough to distract me."

Esther leaned forward in her chair, laboring under excitement that made it almost impossible for her to keep silent. Ames moved his brown hand in slow deprecatory gesture.

"Halstead, I saw the boy this mawnin' talkin' to Hensler down by the trail. I told Joe aboot the one your son was arguin' with. An' shore that was Hensler. Then earlier this mawnin' I was out on the porch, sittin' in that little offset. I was watchin' Fred pacin' up an' down. He shore was a troubled lad. Miss Halstead came out, an' I shore heahed a lot not intended for my ears. That sort of thing happens to me often. Now I reckon heah's two an' two put together. Fred is a wild youngster, new to the West. He's been havin' a fling. An' he's overstepped himself. He's been gamblin'—it was money he wanted from his sister—an' no doubt through that he's been led into some shady deal. I've seen the like many an' many a time. But

Fred is honest at heart. He *might* go bad, if you all
went back on him, but at that I doubt it. Boys with
a background like his—such a mother as he must
have had—an' a sister like Miss Halstead heah—they
seldom go to hell. All Fred needs is to have this raw
tenderfoot stuff scared out of him. It's a good bet Joe
heah will side with me. How aboot it, Joe?"

"I'm sidin' with you, Arizona, all ways for Sunday," returned Cabel, and though he addressed Ames
he looked at Esther.

"By Heaven! Ames, you're dragging me out of
the depths by the hair!" exclaimed Halstead, fervently.

Esther arose impetuously. "Mr. Ames, you—you
do the same for me.... But, oh, don't raise me up—
only to let me sink back again!"

In her earnestness she forgot both the natural
tumult within her breast and the resolve to which
her extremity had driven her. How sad his face—
lined under its dark smoothness! She felt herself
being drawn into the unfathomable blue gulfs of his
gaze.

"Shore you folks are new to these heah little
matters of the range," he replied, simply. "But I just
cain't see anythin' troublesome heah. Shore Joe has
taught those wonderful kids a lot of cuss words—"

"Arizona, I didn't teach them," protested Cabel.

"But if you strangle him I reckon they'll soon
forget," went on Ames, as if he had not been interrupted. "Ronnie doesn't swear so bad at that. An'
he'd get over it pronto if Brown would quit."

"Will you stay and help us with them, Mr. Ames?"
asked Esther, with a sweet directness that was ab-

solutely involuntary, and foreign to the deceitful allurement she had planned.

"Ho! Ho!" boomed Halstead, banging his desk with a huge fist. His hair stood up. "Ames, next thing you'll be waving aside this cattle-thief burden of mine!"

"Shore; it's less than the larkspur," returned Ames, with his inimitable drawl.

Halstead leaped up, his hand in a snatching gesture, as if here was hope and life to be caught if he were quick enough. He approached Ames, faced him impressively.

"Ames, I said once you hit me deep. I say so again. I'm failing here at Troublesome. Failing where there is big opportunity. I just didn't know. Lately I've been sick about it all. My son was no good, it seemed. And I might die or be shot by some of this riff-raff. What would become of Esther and Gertie—and the kids? They've come to love it here. They'd lose all and have to go—God only knows where. But if I had a man like you—who might straighten Fred up and look after the girls and the youngsters—why, if the worst should happen to me, I'd not turn over in my grave....Suppose you stay on at Troublesome!"

"Shore you're makin' out the worst. I'll be only too glad to stop at Yampa on my way—an' pay my respects to Bannard an' Hensler....But then, an' now you're haided right, why you don't need me. Joe heah—"

"Pard," interposed Cabel, who had also left his seat, "it looks like a hunch to me. Not for nothin' did you get lost on the Flat Tops an' then wander down here to the Troublesome. I just told Miss Esther thet it was an act of Providence. An' before thet I told Halstead if he could get you to stay his troubles were over."

"Joe, you're shore double-crossin' an old friend who you owe somethin'," said Ames, darkly.

"Sure, Arizona, I know I am," went on Joe, swallowing hard. Esther wondered in her tensity why it was so difficult and reprehensible for him to ask Ames that. "But there's another side to this. Troublesome needs you. I reckon you just dropped down for a purpose. I'm stayin' with the Halsteads all the rest of my life. The girls—the kids mean a lot to me. ...An', Arizona, you've roamed the ranges for years— fourteen years. Aren't you tired of—wal, you know what I mean?"

"Tired? My God! man, if I could only see the Tonto once more—an' Nesta, an' that boy she named after me—I could lie down for good!"

He wheeled away to lean against the window. Joe had penetrated the armor of this cool, exasperating Southerner. Esther had seen a dark agony blur the blue fire of his eyes. Nesta! A woman who had named a child after him! Therein must lie his secret. Esther grew conscious of a nameless burning in the depths of her.

Suddenly she became aware that Joe was nudging her, and was quick to grasp his meaning. Crossing to the window she put an unsteady hand upon Ames' arm.

"I am asking you, too. Will you stay?"

He faced her, and that blight of pain had vanished.

"Stay heah on the Troublesome?" he asked, smiling down on her. It was then, when emotion gave her courage, that she really looked at him.

"You may change its name," she said, smiling up at him. "Have you any—any ties to which you'd be disloyal—if you stayed?"

"None, Miss Halstead."

"But this—this Nesta?" faltered Esther, unconsciously driven to know. "You spoke strangely."

"Nesta is my twin sister. I have not seen her for thirteen years. But when last I heahed from her— two years an' more ago—she was well, happy an' prosperous."

"Your twin sister? Nesta! I'm glad.... Is there any—other?"

"No."

"Then stay with us."

"You ask me—that way—Miss Halstead?" he queried, and bent a little to study her face.

"Yes. I've only known you an hour. But what's time? I just feel—and trust you."

"See heah, child, I shore don't deserve such— such—"

"I'm no child," interrupted Esther, and indeed she was realizing then something of the wonder and mystery of a woman.

"No, I reckon you're not. I shore wish you were aboot Ronnie's age.... What did this heah dog-gone Joe tell you aboot me?"

"Not much, though I coaxed him," replied Esther, and she divined, if ever in her life she should tell the truth, it must be now. "He said you were shy of pretty girls and ran from them. So I made myself look as

pretty as ever I could—which wasn't very, I guess—
and came out to see."

"I reckon you're wrong aboot how you made
yourself look. Well, an' what did you see?"

"You didn't run from *me*, that's certain. So I must
be quite homely. And so far as your weakness is
concerned you can risk staying."

"The son-of-a-gun! To tell you that!" ejaculated
Ames. "Reckon I haven't one laig to stand on.... But
there shore is a risk, Miss Halstead."

"You mean of the cattle-thieves?" she queried,
quickly.

"Shore I'd forgot aboot them." He turned, releasing her from the blue enthrallment that had
seemed to engulf and hold her, and he looked out
over the Troublesome and the colorful hills. "Miss
Halstead, if there's any risk it's not for you. That was
just half fun. I used to play at words, like any other
cowboy. But I reckon I meant to stay."

"You—will!"

"Shore. An' I'm the lucky one. Only I wish you
didn't have to know me as Arizona Ames."

"Oh, you are—I—I can't thank you!" Esther felt
overwhelmed by she knew not what commingling of
emotions. She became aware, too, that she was cling-
ing to his sleeve. Then her hand loosened, and she
turned to her father, nodding, smiling through her
tears.

Mid-September had come, ushering in the still,
smoky, blazing days of Indian summer.

Esther had climbed higher up the slopes of Troublesome than ever before, a feat commensurate with

the elevation of her spirit. It marked more than one change in the affairs of Halstead's ranch; in the instance, particularly, the fact that she did not fear to ride or climb about alone.

From the crest of the last bench she had surmounted she gazed regretfully at her trail leading down to the next below. Her trail seemed cruelly vivid—a ragged zigzag dark lane through a solid blooming mass of asters, lilac in hue, and of breath-arresting beauty. Esther gazed as one in a dream. She had waded up through a deep snow of wild flowers. In one hand she held a bunch of asters, specimens especially exquisite and of four different shades—purple, lilac, heliotrope and lavender; and in the other hand she grasped five stalks of Indian paintbrush, scarlet, cerise, pink, magenta, and the fifth so varied, so lovely with its dominating white, that she could not give it an adequate name.

These flowers did not flourish so marvelously on the lower slopes, though indeed their normal colors prevailed along the creek.

Esther had long aimed at the aspen grove which she had now attained. From her window at the ranch she had watched it glow daily more golden, luring her to adventure to the heights. Close at hand it was a little spot of enchanted land, a level bench upon which grew a few dozen white-barked quaking asps now in the full glory of autumnal gold. They stood several feet apart, but mingled their foliage in a canopy that quivered and quaked, as if each leaf was shuddering because many of them were releasing their hold on life, and soon all must fall to add to the golden carpet on the grass. And from out this golden carpet, here and there and everywhere, stood up stately, lovely columbines, white and blue.

Esther found a grassy seat under an aspen on the verge, and here she laid aside her flowers and hat, and the field-glass that had been slung round her shoulders. She leaned back against the tree to gaze and gaze, at the columbines nodding to her, at the whispering canopy above which almost blotted out the blue sky, at the slope of lilac snow leading down to the next bench, at the hazed slumbering valley and the ranch far below, at the opposite slopes, waving in color, rising bench by bench, up to the region of thin black standing poles, desolate against the forest background, and at the magnificent mountain domes beyond.

There was no hurry; the afternoon hour seemed suspended, sweet, silent, infinitely momentous, so beautiful that it made her heart ache. She was alone. One such hour as this on the slopes above Troublesome not only made up for past pangs and doubts and worries, but also wedded her to Colorado for all her life. She could not explain why, but she felt it poignantly. She could now even love Troublesome in the dead of winter because of what it must always promise for summer, and this flowering season.

Esther had never underrated her capacity for love, but of late she could not but be astounded at its appalling development. Her father, the boys, Gertrude, and even Fred, had come in for a magnifying of her affections, yet strange and marvelous indeed was it that this seemed little compared with the might of another love. A lithe rider, lean of jaw, dark of face, piercing of eye, had won her worship.

She had never denied the varying degrees of this irresistible thing—that had multiplied hours into weeks—but she had not until lately realized its might. Her shame, her fear, her secret selfish hope had gone with its realization. She did not see why she should live in perpetual conflict with her unknown self just because she loved a man. She had always known she was going to love someone, desperately perhaps, but now that the time had come she wanted to be happy, instead of miserable, because of it. And she did realize an exalting happiness, at least up here, absorbing the bigness and freedom of this solitude. Yet could she hold that lofty emotion, keep it with her always, to down the instincts and longings seemingly damning within to cause her misery?

The cattle were lowing across the valley. She could see the numerous dots of red and white blurred against the hazy background. They had been herded down from up the Troublesome, out of the zone of the poison larkspur. Esther took up her field-glass and swept the slopes, a little guiltily conscious of what and whom she longed to see. But there were no riders with the cattle, which accounted for the fact that a herd of elk were grazing with them. Esther watched the lordly monarch of that herd. He kept somewhat aloof and often he stopped grazing to look about and down. His magnificent antlers resembled the roots of an upturned stump. He was shaggy, black and gray. How freely, how wildly he lifted his noble head! Once a whistling ringing bugle pealed across the valley.

And from watching and listening, reveling in this

elemental wilderness, thinking and dreaming, and
thinking again, Esther arrived at the bewildering
question of how and why and when she had come
to love Arizona Ames.

The how and the why resolved themselves into
the joint deduction that she was merely a woman
creature and could not help herself.

But the when—that was the mystery which fascinated her, made her at once humble and furious,
impotent and grateful. What good would it do her to
know, since the stark and staring fact was enough?
But it was her unconscious way of eulogizing Ames,
which she could not resist.

Perhaps when he appeared before her that day—
could it be only three weeks past?—a spent and
haggard rider, yet the picturesque figure of her
dreams. Or possibly when she sat rigid and breathless in her room the next morning, her ears strained
to catch Joe Cabel's earnest words to her father, her
heart shocked with the consciousness that this rider,
Ames, was inevitable and wonderful to his old range
friend, yet to her terrible. Or perhaps, almost surely,
when she had had the temerity to look up into his
eyes—those blue daggers that pierced her—and had
asked him, appealed to him, importuned him to stay
at Troublesome.

Something incalculable and far-reaching had
happened then to her, but the naked searching of it
did not leave her sure this was the moment when
she had fallen in love with Ames. She remembered
the stab she had encountered with the name of Nesta.
That had been his sister. Jealousy! He had ruined his
life for this Nesta, so Joe had said. Esther must hear

that story some day before she could judge truly and vanquish ignoble jealousy. What a strange, hot, vicious incredible thing—this jealousy!

Or perhaps it had come insidiously, through the gradual brightening of her father, to the recovery of his cheerful spirits and his old energetic hopeful self. Realization of this truth had been a mark in Esther's life. How she had wept, alone in the dark! Then there was the unforgettable day when Brown stalked into the living-room, carrying a trout as long as his arm—the most bedraggled and rapturously astounded lad in all the world. "Ess, look ahere," he had cried, with eyes of light. "Arizona showed me how to ketch him. An' I gotta quit cussin'." The added wonder was that he had stopped.

Then Fred's taking Mecklin's place in the herding of the cattle—that had been an event. Esther recalled the very hour, on the morning her father, in few pointed words, had discharged Mecklin.

"See heah, Fred," Ames had drawled, in his cool way that might mean humor or kindness or menace, "get your horse an' gun. You're shore goin' to ride with me."

Fred had showed the first gladness in many a day. And like a duck to water, according to Ames, he had taken to the cattle game. What Halstead had never been able to drive his son to do, Ames had accomplished with a few words. How to explain it? There was something compelling about Arizona Ames. Then the glamour of his name! Esther thought she hated that, but it never failed to thrill her. Again she had played eavesdropper, to hear Joe relate to her father and Fred the story of Ames killing the infamous rancher-hustler, Rankin.

Had that been the hour of her undoing? If so, what had the West done to her? She, who never had as a child been permitted to read novels and romances, who at fourteen had taught a Sunday school class! But people never knew what hid deep in them.

She could not arrive at any definite conclusion. The catastrophe had to do with all these incidents and the moods they engendered. The overwhelming fact remained that she loved Ames more than she had dreamed of, and that had been quite enough.

Every moment in his presence she seemed to live a lie. She had to hide her feelings when she yearned to be honest. Any chance word or action might rise up like a traitor to betray her. And the worst of it was she wanted to be betrayed. She had no shame, she thought, with a most passionate shame. There were moments when she bewailed her state, and others, like these spent in the grassy slopes, that she gloried in her abasement.

But what to do? "Oh, dear! Oh, dear! Oh, dear!" sighed Esther. Up here she seemed wondrously happy. But down at the ranch there were times— and suddenly with hot cheeks she recalled an incident of the other day. She had saddled and mounted her horse, for a little ride, and was about to be off when Fred and Ames appeared on foot.

"Whoopee! Isn't she a handsome thing, Arizona?" Fred had called out, gayly.

Esther had taken the compliment gracefully when Ames had spoiled it.

"Tolerable. But that rig she's wearin' is shore ondecorous," Ames had replied.

Then without noting Esther's hot blush he had laid a strong hand over hers, that clutched the pommel. He gave the saddle a shake.

"Tenderfoot! Cain't you remember what I told you aboot cinchin' a saddle?"

"No, I can't," Esther had weakly though defiantly imitated. Then while he drew the cinch properly secure, Esther had to sit there, quivering at the slight contact of his swift hands, horrified at a sudden wild impulse to throw her arms round his neck. Surely that could not have been the illusive moment, for she must have loved him before she could have sunk to such ignominious mental aberration.

Late in the afternoon Esther wended a careful and loving way down through the asters, vowing, as she went, not to pull another single flower, but when she reached the creek she had her arms full. Her heart, too, seemed full, if not of flowers, then of their essence and beauty. More significant of this eventful walk was the fact that the noisy, quarrelsome Troublesome seemed now singing happily down the valley.

CHAPTER
16

ESTHER met Joe coming up the creek trail, some distance from the ranch house. In the afternoon he usually had some leisure hours, which he spent outdoors, mostly with the boys. Always, when Esther had been riding or walking, he would meet her. It occurred to her that of late his watchfulness had grown.

"Wal, I'd hate to have to say which was the prettiest—you or the flowers," he remarked.

"You old flatterer!" exclaimed Esther, gayly. "I'll bet you were a devil with the girls, once."

"No, I was a very mild boy."

"Catch me believing that. How many sweethearts, Joe?"

"Only one. I married her when she was eighteen, an' me not much older. We never had no children, but we was happy—till she died. I never got over thet. But I'm the better for it all."

"Oh, Joe! I'm sorry I was flippant," returned Esther, regretfully.

"Wal, you must have had a dandy climb. Them paint-brushes don't grow down low."

"It was lovely. I went higher than ever before. Found such a lovely little grove where I could see everywhere and be unseen."

"Unseen? Not from a couple of pairs of hawk eyes I know of."

"Yours for one pair. And whose else?" she rejoined, knowing full well.

"Wal, you can guess."

"Dad's?"

"Nope."

"Fred's?—Gertie's?—The boys'?"

"Nope."

"Oh, well, I'm a poor guesser, anyhow."

"Lass, them other hawk eyes belong to the locoedest, love-sickenest fellar I ever seen."

"Indeed? Poor man!" exclaimed Esther, solicitously.

"Let's set down on this big rock," said Joe, serious where Esther had expected humor.

"But it's late, Joe. And I'm all mussy and flower-stained. I'll have to change for supper," she protested, suddenly a little in fear of his gravity.

"Wal, you needn't change tonight. For there'll be only the children an' your dad at table."

"Fred said he'd be home today?" questioned Esther, quickly sensing something unusual.

"He didn't come home. You know Fred left Saturday to spend a day or so at Wood's. He's getting sweet on Biny again. Wal, young Jim rode over today an' he said Fred stayed only a little bit at Wood's. But he was seen on the road with Hensler."

"Oh, Joe, don't tell me that!" implored Esther.

"Sorry, but I reckon you might better hear all this bad news from me."

"Bad—news! More?" faltered Esther. The transition from her late dream to present reality hurt in proportion to its surprise and inevitability. Too good to last!

"More an' then some. So grit your teeth, lass. Your dad took it fine. Why, a month ago he'd have sunk under this."

"Tell me!"

"Wal, there was a cattle raid on us today. Up back of the ranch on High Ridge. Stevens got back shot—"

"Shot!" cried Esther, wildly. "And Ames?"

"No. Arizona wasn't there. Stevens was alone. He got shot up pretty bad, but he'll pull through. Jed drove off with him in the wagon an' Arizona followed on hossback. If they can fetch a doctor over from Craig or some place Stevens will be all right."

"Poor fellow! Oh, I hope and pray he's not in danger. . . . Cattle-thieves again!—Joe, that surely upset father?"

"Not so anyone would notice it," responded Joe. "The old gent tickled me. I tell you, lass, havin' Arizona around makes a he—aw—a shore lot of difference. I'm darned if I don't believe your dad sort of welcomed this raid. We all knowed them two-bit thieves would sooner or later try Arizona out. Wal, they have, an' d—dog-gone me! If it wasn't for you, lass, I'd be tickled, too."

"Never mind me," whispered Esther, trying to brace herself for what she knew was coming.

"Stevens didn't talk much," went on Joe. "But we got enough out of him to piece up the deal. Mecklin an' Barsh Hensler, with some fellars Stevens didn't know, tackled—"

"Barsh Hensler!—Oh, you say Fred was seen with him?" cried Esther, in distress.

"Yes, I'm d—darn sorry to say. But Ames said to your dad, 'Wait, Halstead; wait till I find out.'... An' I say the same to you, lass. Don't judge Fred in your heart till all the evidence is before you. Mebbe it ain't so bad as it looks.... Wal, Mecklin told Stevens they was callin' the bluff Arizona Ames made in Yampa. An' they was drivin' off this bunch of cattle, which luckily for us was smaller'n they had figgered on. Stevens showed fight, accordin' to his story. He's got a couple of bullet holes to back it up. He fell off his hoss back up the slope. But sharp-eyed Ronnie seen him an' told us. Your dad an' me packed him down an' was dressin' his wounds when Arizona came in."

"Then—what?" asked Esther, trembling.

"Wal, then, Arizona took charge. He sent Jed off in the wagon with Stevens, an' he cussed your dad, who was a-rarin' to go along. An' while he was saddlin' up his hoss he talked fast. 'Joe,' he says, 'go out an' hunt up Esther. Suppose she had been up on this heah side of the valley!' An' he swore turrible. 'Find her an' tell her straight without any frills thet it looks bad. But if Fred isn't really mixed up in it, why, it wouldn't amount to as much as two duces in a jackpot, an'—"

"Good heavens, Joe! How could he say that—and what did he mean?"

"Wal, I reckon somethin' like this. If Fred wasn't somehow implicated it'd be nothing for Ames to shoot the leader of this outfit an' scare the rest so bad they'd never show up in Yampa again. But if Fred *is* in it, why, it'll be serious. Take what Arizona said: 'Tell Esther if Fred's got drunk or otherwise been dragged into this dirty deal thet I'll clear his name, one way or another."

"My God! How could he? What else did—he say?" gasped Esther.

"That was all. He jest rode off," responded Joe, with a cool finality.

"Did you tell dad?"

"Wal, I jest did. He wasn't bothered much, though. He's come to be somethin' like a real Westerner lately. . . . An' thet reminds me, Miss Esther. Did you know your dad offered to make Arizona his pardner in this ranch?"

"No. I didn't."

"Wal, he did. An' thet g—er—thet dog-goned, white-headed cowboy refused."

"Refused!" echoed Esther.

"It ain't believable, but he did. I was there. Halstead got mad an' used some language thet'd do Joe Cabel credit. Ha! Ha! . . . Wal, Arizona admitted he thought it was a fair bargin—thet he was worth it—an' thet the two of them could make two fortunes here on the Troublesome. But he says, 'I jest cain't.'

"'Why in the hell can't you—if you see it as I do?' roared Halstead.

"Arizona got sort of pale round the gills. 'See heah, Halstead,' he says, slow an' cool—you know how he talks—'I love this heah girl of yours an' I cain't stand it much longer. I'll stay heah till I've got you out of this mess an' fixed to make it a big success—then I'll ride away. I've had a pretty sad, lonely life. An' if I hang round heah much longer the rest of my life won't be worth livin'. For I'm afraid I'd love Esther more'n I loved Nesta—my twin sister, an' I'll tell you, boss, thet was a whole lot.... I'm thirty-two years old an' I've got a gun record. Esther couldn't care for me, even if you sanctioned it, which shore you cain't. So let's have no more of this pardner talk.'"

Esther seemed to have merged into the stone upon which she was sitting. But inside her stormed whirlwind and lightning and heartbeats that pounded thunderously in her ears. The flowers fell off her lap, unnoticed. If outward feeling came to her it was with Joe's gentle touch.

"Aw! I told you too sudden!" ejaculated Joe, remorsefully. "I done it on purpose, Esther. But forgive me."

"Oh, Joe!—I'm so—silly! There's nothing—to forgive."

"Wal, there jest is. I've found out your secret an' it was a dirty trick."

"Secret?"

"Yes. But I reckon I knowed before you gave yourself away. Joe Cabel is a pretty smart fellar.... Esther, you like Arizona a little now, don't you?"

"I—I'm afraid—I do."

"Wal, don't you, *quite* a little?"

"I—maybe—perhaps I do." She was leaning against Joe's rough-garbed shoulder with drooping head.

"Now, lass, your secret is safe with me. Don't you savvy thet? Sure I could double-cross Arizona any day for you. An' I'm doin' it now. But never you, Esther."

"What secret? Oh, Joe—don't make me talk," she whispered.

"Wal, now, I won't.... But don't you love Arizona a little? Poor devil thet he is! Driven from range to range, not because he was bad but good. No home—none but men like me to see an' care. Never a sweetheart! True to thet sister for whom he rode out on his long bloody trail!... Don't you love him a little, Esther?"

Her head fell on his shoulder.

"I—I'm afraid I—"

"Wal, now, thet's jest wonderful. It sure fetches my prayer home. You see, I'm a lonely old codger an' I got as fond of you as if you'd been my own lass. Then I always had a weakness for Arizona. Esther, this West breeds men. I've knowed more than I could remember. It makes them wild an' wicked an' then jest the opposite, too. Men like your dad could never find homes here but for men like Arizona.... I reckon now you love him—more'n a little?"

"I reckon I do," confessed Esther, and hid her face.

"How much, lass?"

"Swear you'll never tell?"

"I'd swear thet on a stack of Bibles."

Esther lifted her face and opened blurred eyes. This kind and crafty Joe had been her undoing, yet through him she had found herself. She bent to gather up the fallen flowers. Then she stood before her friend unabashed, to give her answer some semblance of dignity.

"So much, Joe—that if you hadn't told me what you have—I couldn't have borne the fear for Fred— and him."

On the third sunset after that, Jed returned, driving the buckboard up to the ranch house. When he halloed, Esther went out to see her father and Joe helping Stevens to get down. He could not stand alone. His right arm was in a sling.

Then Esther espied Fred, his face almost as white as the wide bandage that passed round his head under his chin.

"Boss, we're back the wuss for wear," Jed was saying, "an' Ames is down at the barn."

For once the children were not clamoring at the return of anyone from town. They stood owl-eyed and mute.

"Halstead, me an' Jed will take care of Stevens," said Joe.

The rancher had not found his voice.

"Dad, come in the house," said Fred. "And you, too, Esther. I've a good deal to tell."

They went in, and Esther closed the door.

"Fred! You've been injured?" she cried, when she could find her voice.

"Yes. But it's nothing to what—it might have been. Only a hole through my ear!"

"Hole!" ejaculated Halstead, blankly.

Fred fell into a chair, which limp action and his shaking hands attested to spent strength.

"Bullet hole! I've been shot," he said, with a weak smile.

"Who shot you?"

"Ames."

Esther, feeling turned to stone, could not utter a sound.

"My God! Boy, what're you saying?" demanded his father, incredulously.

"It's the truth. The bloody devil!" replied Fred, hoarsely. "Oh, he was terrible!...But, dad, he didn't know me. He thought I was—just one of Bannard's men. The only accident about it was—when he missed me. His bullet tore off my hat—went through my ear. I'm marked for life. When he saw my face he recognized me and he said, 'Hellsfire!'"

"Augh!—What's this all about?" queried Halstead, thickly.

Esther, finding the seat next to the fireplace behind her, slowly sank and slipped into it. If some kind of transformation had not come over Fred Halstead she was indeed mad.

"Listen, Dad. I'll make a clean breast of the whole thing," began Fred, shaken by deep agitation. "Saturday I went over to see Biny Wood. I found Jess Thuber there. It made me sore, though I knew Biny didn't care particular about him. But it just struck me bad. Hadn't seen her for weeks—was crazy to—

and I had some fool notion of asking her to believe in me and stick to me."

"Son, that wasn't no fool notion," said Halstead, as Fred paused for breath.

"Well, when I left her I happened to fall in with Barsh Hensler, Mecklin, and Jim Coates. It was unlucky for me. They had a bottle. I knew I shouldn't drink. I fought it. If I hadn't been so hurt, so sore at Biny, I'd not weakened. Anyway, I did—and that set me on fire. I got drunk. It was on Saturday afternoon. I didn't get sober enough to know anything till they stole your cattle from Stevens. I remember riding. I remember Stevens was yelling when Mecklin shot him. . . . I had to help drive the cattle down. They took a lot of driving. It was late at night when we got them in a corral. There was a cabin. Next morning I was sober and sick enough to die. It was that old homestead off the road, ten miles beyond Wood's."

Fred covered his pale face a moment as if to hide it as well as shut out the picture in mind. "I realized then Mecklin could make me out a thief. I was ruined. I didn't know what to do. I wanted to shoot myself, but didn't have the nerve. Then I swore I'd shoot Mecklin. . . . We stayed there waiting. Mecklin went down the road to meet Bannard and the rest of the outfit. . . . But he ran into Ames—who beat him half to death and made him confess the whole rotten deal. But I didn't know that until later. . . . Bannard came with only two men. He was mad. And when he saw we'd only half a hundred head of cattle he cursed and raved. . . . It got late in the day and we went outside on the porch to go on with our gambling. Four of us. Hensler half drunk. Bannard mean. All of a sudden Ames came round the cabin, pushing Mecklin ahead of him with a gun. I said, 'My God!—it's—' and I choked on his name. I pulled my hat low over my face and sunk down. Aw, I was scared. Mecklin was all bloody and so weak he could hardly walk. Ames knocked him down with the gun. Then he looked us over and picked out Hensler. 'The game's up, Hensler. Your two-bit cattle-thievin' ends right heah. Mecklin has squealed on you.'

"'Who in hell are you?' yelled back Bannard.

"'My name is Ames.'

"'You this Arizona fellar?' asked Bannard, and he turned green.

"'No matter. I take it you're Clive Bannard?'

"But Bannard went so yellow he couldn't even tell his own name. Then Barsh Hensler, the damn fool, got up and bawled: 'Ban, it's this here Arizona Ames. Haw! Haw! Watch me bore him!' ... And the idiot grabbed his gun."

Fred writhed in his seat; his eyes shut; his tight skin blanched.

"Then it happened. I can't tell just how. But when that clumsy drunken madman pulled out his gun there came an awful crack. I saw a little hole show up right in the middle of Hensler's forehead. He looked queer. His gun banged. And he knocked the box over. I was paralyzed. But I heard the shooting ...the last shot got me—knocked me flat. 'Hellsfire!' yelled Ames and dragged me up and shoved me against the wall. If he hadn't held me up I'd dropped, for I thought he meant to kill me. He was terrible. But he'd recognized me.... Then I saw those men— Hensler dead on the box—Bannard dead, too, I thought then—one crawling away screaming in agony—another flopping off like a crippled chicken—an' Mecklin groaning on the porch. . . . Ames had been hit once, a cut in the shoulder that he made me tie up. And while I did it he said some things to me I—I'll never forget till I'm dead or even after. . . . We went out to the road, and when Jed came along with the wagon Ames had him go back to the cabin. Mecklin had sneaked away. Bannard wasn't dead, but near so. They loaded him in the wagon. We went on to Yampa, where Ames told that Hensler and Bannard had forced me to help steal my father's cattle. Then he said there'd been a little fight back at Harris' cabin. . . . That's all, Dad. It turned out Bannard didn't die, but he'll never be any good again. When he's well enough they'll take him away to jail."

"So, my lad, Arizona Ames saved your name?" thundered Halstead.

"He did—Dad—he did," replied Fred, huskily. "But I wasn't a thief—never! Please—for God's sake, don't believe that."

"I didn't. . . . Fred, is this lesson going to make a man out of you?"

Fred gulped and put a hand to his bandaged ear. "It will, Dad, unless Arizona scared all the man out of me forever."

Esther dragged herself away and hid in her room, her mind at a standstill, her emotions chaotic; and she did not venture out until dusk. Then, watching her chance from the porch, she waylaid Ames, unmindful of the fact that Joe was with him.

Back somewhere in the hazy murk of the past awful hours she had pondered a thought of how impossible it would ever be to touch this bloody-handed monster. But when she confronted him, when she spoke she knew not what, and he gazed down upon her with eyes that always had and always would have power to stop her heart, she took hold of him.

"There's only one thing I want to know," she whispered, hurriedly and low.

"An' I can just aboot guess what that is," he drawled in the old unforgettable accent. How could he speak so casually? "Shore I knew Fred when I saw him. I let on I took him for one of the gang. It was a good chance to scare some sense into his haid. Don't you ever give me away."

October brought cold nights, frosty mornings, and the falling of the aspen leaves and the fading of the flowers.

Esther had gone feverishly at the work of sewing, and helping Joe put up fruit for the winter, and other tasks of the season. The Sunday that Fred fetched saucy little Biny Wood home, and imitated the cool, easy speech of an important member of Halstead's household while announcing their engagement, was a decisive one for Esther. It broke the spell of days, and happiness trembled like a wraith on the threshold.

Perhaps a contagious spirit of good worked its will that day in other quarters. Halstead calmly announced at dinner that Ames had accepted a partnership in Troublesome Ranch.

"Whoopee!" screeched Brown, brandishing his fork. "Now I'll ketch every———trout in———"

"Brown, leave the table at once!" ordered Esther, sternly.

"Aw, Ess!" he importuned.

"You broke your word. You promised never to swear again."

"But, Ess, this here is different. It oughtn't count. Arizona is goin' to live with us. I'll bet dad wouldn't mind if you swore, too."

"*Haw! Haw! Haw!*" burst out Halstead, who had turned purple in the face. "I sure wouldn't....But, lad, obey your sister and try harder next time."

"Aw, I shore can take my medicine," drawled Brown, sturdily. "I reckon it's worth it."

Esther felt herself the last to capitulate to this scion of the range and she surrendered royally. She had known, even before Joe had informed her, that Arizona Ames could never of his own mind imagine she loved him.

For a time after the tragedy he had kept aloof, eating with Joe in the kitchen, seldom visible; and when he was, stern, silent, unapproachable. Then had come a sudden change, which, it turned out, had been caused by a letter Jed had brought from Craig. Ames seemed transformed, and Esther had vast curiosity about that letter, and that old hateful recurrent fire along her veins. Nesta! Yet Esther was happy for him. She waited days longer than she had ever thought she could wait. Then on a Sunday afternoon while her father snored in his room and the children played outside, and Joe, with a knowing wink to her, basely deserted his friend, Esther found herself alone with this Arizona Ames, late stranger on the Troublesome, who had now become imperatively necessary to their happiness. She would drive that sadness from his face, that haunting thought or memory of she knew not what, if it lay in a woman's power. But she could not face him just yet.

Presently from behind, she glided upon him and before he could move she encircled his drooping head with her arms, and pressing her hands over his eyes, she held him closely. It had taken all the courage she could muster. But when she felt him shake, all through that lithe strong form, something flashed up out of her, imperious and exultant.

"Arizona, are you a good guesser?" she asked.

"Me! Poorest guesser you ever saw," he replied, suddenly relieved. "What kind of a game is this heah?"

"It's a game of—*Pretend*."

"Ahuh. An' I got to be blind?"

"Oh, this holding my hands over your eyes is just pretense. You *are* blind."

He was silent at that, relaxing ever so little.

"Well, then," she continued, with forced animation. "In this game you are to pretend—as a matter of fact you'll not have to act *very* much—to pretend you are a shy, bashful, innocent cowboy—"

"Say, there shore never was such an animal," broke out Ames, uneasily.

"I said pretend, didn't I? . . . A very shy cowboy—who had never had a—a sweetheart. He'd had a hard, lonely life, riding here and there, among those awful range people who think nothing of battle, blood, murder, and sudden death. . . . So he'd never had time to find a sweetheart and win her."

She drew his head backward ever so gently until it rested upon her unquiet breast.

"Arizona, are you listening very closely, so you'll understand how to play this game?"

"I'm shore listenin', you witch," he replied, in growing perturbation. "Esther, is this heah a square game? Aren't you stackin' the cairds on me?"

"Oh, you'll see. It's a perfectly honest game," she replied, hurriedly. His head against her breast threatened to disrupt her audacity. But she resumed, thrilling to the consciousness of her power, turning a deaf ear to a still small voice. "Now, my part in this game of *Pretend* is very, very difficult—much more so than yours. I have to play being a bold brazen girl, ter— terribly in love with the shy cowboy. Secretly, horribly, shamefully in love with him!...Shall I go on with instructions?"

"Shore, go on, Miss Halstead, anyway, until I'm daid," he said, in a strangled voice.

"Oh, I don't believe it will quite kill you," she resumed, demurely. "Now the game is that this girl, this brazen creature, will slip behind the cowboy, like this, and hide his eyes like this...and pretty soon, according to the game, she must take one hand from one of his eyes, so that he can see it's not exactly a dream—and caress his cheek—like this—and smooth his hair—like this—and then kiss the tip of his ear...I—like that!...and then—whi—whisper..."

"*What?*" he rang out, in a terror of incredulity.

Esther wavered on the brink. Her heart was pounding in her throat. No way back, and she had to go on! But if it had not hurt her so to torture him—

what delicious fun! What surprise for him and bliss for her!

Suddenly an iron hand seized hers and began to draw her.

"Then she has to whisper," went on Esther, now scarcely coherent—"to whisper—in his ear—like this....*Arizona Ames, guess!*"

He seized her other hand and drew it down, so that presently her arms were round his neck, and he was trying to bend his head back to see her face.

"Esther, if this an' this an' this is a game it's bitter cruel," he said, huskily. "I'm no boy to play with. I'm a man that life has cheated. An' all the hungry heartache of the years has centered on you."

"Ah!" she cried, softly, and spent her torture in that. "Let me go on, Arizona, as if it *were* a game.... This unworthy girl will kiss his hair—like this—here where it's silver—and whisper—*I love you, for all you are!*...Then he will treat this heartless girl— who has lived a lie so long—this false-faced girl— as she deserves. He will tear her to pieces, break her bones—hug her to—"

Then it was not that Esther's love and voice failed her, but that what she had begged for seemed literally to happen. The dim world whirled away, and she was rudely torn from enchantment—which was Ames' devouring arms and lips—by a shrill piping screech from the doorway.

"My Gawd! Brownie, come hyar! Arizonie is huggin' sis to death!"

Ronnie's wild alarm brought a swift thud of feet.

"————!" shouted Brownie, in fiendish glee. Then with wild shouts the imps ran off.

*　　　　*　　　　*

That night, when the rest of the household slept and the October moon soared white above the Troublesome, Esther lay in Ames' arms and heard the story of Nesta.

"This heah letter of Nesta's an' your game of *Pretend*, Esther, have aboot paid me back for all," concluded Arizona. "If you'll marry me soon, we'll go pay Nesta a visit. The Tonto is best in October."

"Soon? How soon, Arizona?"

"Shore it'd have to be terrible soon," he said, fearfully, as if he were proposing sacrilege.

Esther kissed his cheek. "Wal, Arizonie, it shore cain't be too soon for this heah cowgirl," she drawled.

Then he told her about the Tonto Basin, that ragged country of his youth, from which he had ridden away on the long range-trail. How different from Troublesome Valley! Esther saw the grand zigzag golden rim with its black fringe, and the black ridges and the blue canyons between, and the amber Tonto Creek and the dark Rock Pool where poor Nesta had tried to drown herself. She saw the silver spruces of his boyhood, and the wild turkeys that clucked down the leafy trails, and the brown pine-matted aisles of the forest, where his bare feet had trod. How he had loved this country and his people—and sweet Nesta, who had been a part of him!

Zane Grey, author of over 80 books, was born in Ohio in 1872. His writing career spanned over 35 years until his death in 1939. Estimates of Zane Grey's audience exceed 250 million readers.